Souls of Air

Mons Kallentoft

Translated from the Swedish by
Neil Smith

HODDER

First published in Great Britain in 2016 by Hodder & Stoughton
An Hachette UK company

Originally published in Swedish as *Vindsjälar* by Bokförlaget Forum

First published in paperback in 2017

1

A CIP catalogue record for this title is available from the British Library

Paperback ISBN 978 1 444 77638 6
eBook ISBN 978 1 444 77640 9

Typeset in Plantin by Palimpsest Book Production Limited,
Falkirk, Stirlingshire

Printed and bound by
Clays Ltd, St Ives plc

Hodder & Stoughton .... that are natural, renewable
.... rown in sustainable forests.
.... xpected to conform to the
.... ntry of origin.

.... td

.... nt

Prologue

[The wind]

Fingers around a neck. Hands.

They press.

Hard, harder, hardest.

Air currents move across the heavens and gather between the stars, forming a cold, polished wind that races on, down towards the earth, thrusting aside the great drifts of forgotten lives residing in the dense forests. They make their way between the pines and firs, the black-and-white birches. Tug at the moss, cut the bark from the trunks, and the trees wonder: Isn't it supposed to be summer?

The wind sinks lower.

Unsettles the waters of Lake Roxen, drives in across meadows and fields, up over the glowing lights of the motorway, over leaky retail barns and mass housing projects, over railway tracks and blocks of flats, towards the lights of the city and cobbled streets where a few nocturnal drifters are making their way through the mild summer night.

A park, a red-brick building, and there the cold wind tries to find a way into a room, it makes itself small and slips in through a gap in the window, waits for a while. Inside the room is the smell of death, of life that has been lived and will soon be over.

The mouth seeking air, in spite of weariness, in spite

of the fingers pressing harder on the neck.

And the wind that was born not long ago in a starlit heaven gathers itself together. Lets itself be sucked down into the lungs of an unknown body, becoming the last breath that fills them, becoming memories, violence and caresses and the heart that stops beating and the consciousness that slips into a blackness that becomes a clear, shining whiteness.

The fingers around the neck have turned white.

But now they relax.

Only death breathes now.

There is no more fear. No uncertainty.

The wind listens to a voice that it alone can hear:

That's me lying there.

Is it over now?

There were so many words. I was tired of them. But I still want them back.

The sun crawls slowly above the horizon, waking the city, giving life to the smells of a dying summer. The stinking contents of rubbish bins, the chlorine of swimming pools, thousands of plants in bloom.

A storm waking. Fingers squeezing a neck.

Whose fingers? Whose neck?

The polished wind withdraws, and then the morning is still. A young woman moves towards the building and the park, walking slowly in the first light of day.

PART I

Respectable love

I

Tuesday, 10 August

Tove is breathing deeply. Walking down Drottninggatan. Enjoying the warm summer air filling her lungs.

The façades of the *fin de siècle* buildings look like theatre sets made out of sand in the freshly woken sunlight.

It is only a quarter past six.

She ought to be tired, but isn't.

Her body is awake, her mind too, and her muscles feel fresh, as if her whole being is hungry for the day, the sort of hunger you only feel when you know you're going to do something useful for other people.

There's no chill in the air, she's not cold even though she's only wearing a thin summer dress. The summer has been warm. And sunny. But not as crazily hot as that summer a few years back. She can't bear to think of what happened back then. She's put that behind her.

Her mum hadn't even got out of bed when Tove left home a few minutes ago to go to her summer job at the Cherub Old People's Home. She didn't want the job at first, she would rather have worked in a clothes shop or a bookstore. But in the end the Cherub was the only remaining option.

On the very first day Tove realised she had ended up in the right place, that she liked the old people, even if a few of them could be mean and demanding. The physical aspects of the job were distasteful at first, but she soon got used to them. Learned to disconnect her sense of repulsion and just wipe up the shit, and if the smell was too bad she simply held her breath or breathed through her mouth.

The people who live at the Cherub are all handicapped in some way, but are mentally alert, more or less. The shame they feel at their physical helplessness is visible in their eyes, and is far worse for them than any discomfort I might feel, she thinks. The old people need help, deserve it, and I'm going to make it as easy as possible for them to accept it, and to go on living.

It's not really any more complicated than that.

She realises that she will end up like that herself one day, in a similar bed with the same need of help, if she lives long enough. And her uncle, Stefan, is in the same state, in a nursing home in Hälsingland. Only last night she asked her mum if they were going to visit him, but her mum hadn't wanted to set a date. She never does.

Tove moves closer to the buildings along Drottninggatan, away from a bus that roars past on its way to the University Hospital.

The sun is hot on her bare legs, and she remembers herself as a young child. On a beach somewhere. Yelping and shouting and her body thirsting for the sun's rays as she emerged from the cold water.

Tove thinks about the residents.

Tyra Torstensson.

Eighty-nine years old. A bit confused, but charming, half-blind, and as good as completely deaf. Unsteady on her legs, kind and grateful, almost submissive. She was a secretary back when she worked, for a lawyer, and has suffered more sorrows than most in her life, but each time she just got back up again.

'Are you awake, Tyra?' Tove has to shout when she rouses the old woman every day after her afternoon nap.

Weine Andersson.

A farmer. Old and tired, every joint in his body worn out. But he never complains. Not even about the food. His children treat him with respect when they come and see him, which they do often.

Viveka Dahlgren.

A clergyman's wife. With fancy paintings by Krouthén in her room, and a bottle of port in her bedside cabinet. She's the widow of a former bishop, abandoned by her three children, who have all moved far, far away from Linköping. She was a volunteer at the City Mission until her body could no longer cope. Until her sense of balance started to go.

Mrs Dahlgren can be a bit arrogant, looking down on me and the others, making a fuss and demanding things that there really isn't time for, but I think she just feels lonely.

How do you end up that lonely, even though you've got children? What makes your children abandon you? Go away?

Viveka Dahlgren is ninety-two now. Almost all of her friends are dead. There's no one to hold her thin-skinned hand, and those of us who work there don't have time.

Could I abandon Mum? Tove wonders as she crosses Drottninggatan.

Maybe that's what I did when I started school at Lundsberg.

When she's home for the summer she wants to live with her mum. Doesn't get on well with her dad's young girl-friend. Anyway, he lives too far out in the countryside.

The resident she likes best of all at the Cherub is Konrad Karlsson.

He's a fighter. Well read. A worker who improved himself through his own efforts. A worker who, just as he should have been enjoying his retirement, had a severe stroke and ended up paralysed down half of his body.

But not paralysed in his soul.

She can see his lined face in front of her. Would just like to sit with him, something she very rarely has time for. Would like to talk to him, see him listen to what she has to say, how he seems to have all the time in the world for her in particular. She wants to see him nod, reflect, and then hear his good advice about whatever it she's wondering about.

Unlike her mum, he really listens. It's nice, Tove thinks, having an old person to confide in.

Konrad Karlsson.

His body may be weak, but he's still got fight left in him. He was the person who wrote that letter to the *Correspondent*, the one that caused such a huge fuss. He listed ten points, detailing the failings at the Cherub and how cost-cutting had led to poor care so that the care provider, Merapi, could make a healthy profit.

Over the past week Konrad has seemed tired, as if the heat were slowly eating him up.

Don't let the heat take him.

Stefan's home is also run by Merapi these days. The care there has got worse than it was before. All the good staff have resigned. Tove doesn't want to think about it. She herself works for Merapi, even if it doesn't feel like it. She works for herself. Even so, she's part of a failing care system, whether she likes it or not.

Tove is approaching the park now, can see the tops of the birch trees and smell the scent of summer-Linköping.

Growing, alive.

As if everything alive in the city were enjoying the heat and the sun. But every now and then she picks up the stench of decay in her nostrils, proof that the city's inhabitants can't keep the dirt at bay altogether, that life and death are both happening all the time.

There's a smell at home, in her mum's flat.

At first it was only there sometimes, but now there's a definite stink in the flat all the time. As if something has died. A cloying, sickly smell. She and her mum have tried to locate its source, but it's impossible to say where it's coming from. At first they thought it was the sink, but when they leaned over the plughole there was no smell there. Same thing with the shower. And they've tried keeping the windows closed, so the smell can't be coming from outside.

Some days it's stronger, others weaker, but it's always there.

Her brain gets used to it after a while, but her awareness that it's there is always nagging away at the back of her mind.

How does the jungle smell?

She's applied to do voluntary work at the end of the summer. In Rwanda. That, and a whole load of options at university. She's hoping that Rwanda works out, but hasn't said anything to her mum about her plans. But she knows she's curious. She'd probably go mad if she found out.

Mum. Is she awake yet?

She hasn't had a drink for almost a year. Not since she broke up with Peter. She's been alone since then, she seems calmer, as if something happened to her when she was in Vietnam, solving that case of the missing girl. Sometimes she seems almost tranquillised.

She exercises and works, and doesn't appear to be either frustrated or happy.

She just *is*, and that's not like her.

It scares me, Mum, the fact that you've decided to make do with nothing.

2

Malin Fors stretches out in bed. Reaches her arms up towards the wall, points her toes down, pretends that horses and chains are attached to her limbs.

But nothing happens. Her body just feels lethargic.

She heard Tove leave a short while ago but pretended to be asleep, didn't feel up to talking to her so early in the morning.

It's nice to have her home, even if it is just for the summer. Tove got dumped by her boyfriend Tom, who finally seemed to realise that it wasn't fitting for a smart boy from Östermalm to go out with the only scholarship student in the whole school. And what would he want her for now, anyway, now that their days at Lundsberg are over and he is no longer shut away in the middle of the forest for weeks on end?

Tove seems to have taken it well, even if she doesn't want to talk about it. Perhaps they were making use of each other, making life at school bearable together. She no longer goes on about designer shoes, or bags and clothes. She seems to have found her way back to her old self, the wise, incisive person she always was, in spite of the chaos surrounding large parts of her childhood.

I'm proud of what she's doing now.

Looking after the elderly. Without grumbling, almost with joy. A crap job in most youngsters' eyes, but not Tove's.

Malin pulls the covers over her head.

Seeking refuge from the light filtering through the venetian blind.

But the covers can't keep the light out, can't give her darkness, they just make everything flat and shallow, as if her whole world were tiny and the sky made of cotton that needs washing.

Tove.

The look in her eyes sometimes, over the breakfast table. On the sofa in the evenings.

You despise me, Malin thinks. And I can understand that.

She breathes in the stale smell under the covers, the stench of the flat, faint, like a trace that barely registers in her nose. She can't bear to think about childhood and chaos, can't bear to focus on how her whole being is consumed with anxiety at the way she neglected Tove. It's too late now anyway, and she forces herself into a sort of neutral state, where she can control her feelings instead of vice versa. Where her lungs fill with air without her consciously having to breathe. The state she's been in since she returned home from Vietnam.

But I can't lie here any longer.

In my cave. Under a sky made of cotton.

I have to get up.

To the station.

And, ideally, fit in a run first.

Run the night's dreams to ground. Run some life into me, into my body.

Tove opens the gate of the Horticultural Society Park. Walks through it, thinking once again how neat all the beds are, how the grass looks greener now that it's been left to grow slightly longer.

She looks through the trees and bushes, off towards the

large clearing in front of the stage. Thinks about how all her former classmates at the local school had a party there to celebrate leaving school, presumably smoking joints and fucking amongst the trees on the observatory hill. Drinking warm beer. Cold and refreshing in memory.

She turns and hears the gravel crunch beneath her feet. There are no children in the playground yet, but they'll soon be there, and beyond the playground the volleyball court lies deserted. The elderly residents love sitting on the Cherub's big balcony, watching the children play. Listening to the noise from the volleyball court. Weather permitting, they'll sit there for hours watching the commotion, enjoying the noise and the happy shouts.

The Cherub was built in the eighties.

Three storeys, heavy red brick with bright red, blue and yellow aluminium window- and doorframes. Tove can see the front of the building clearly beyond the birch trees and the tall hedge that runs along the edge of the path and leads up to the glass canopy framing the main entrance.

This full-time rota is ridiculously harsh, she thinks. It feels like there ought to be twice as many staff. At least it does when things don't run smoothly, which is most of the time.

The head of the care provider lives in the city. Evidently he was the one who set up the company, which has its headquarters here. She knows they're raking in obscene amounts of money. They bought a whole load of care homes from regional councils when social care began to be privatised. Got them cheap. Far too cheap, according to her mum. 'Daylight robbery', as she exclaimed once when she read an article about a doctor's surgery in Berga that was quickly sold on to its staff for twenty times what the council had got for it. The fact that the article was written by her former boyfriend, Daniel Högfeldt, didn't improve matters.

How old could he be, the head of the company? Forty-five, maybe. He looks more like fifty. At least. He visited the Cherub once, just after I'd started. What was his name?

She can't remember. But he walked around in a shiny grey suit, pretending to inspect the way everything worked. It was in connection to one of Konrad Karlsson's letters to the paper, and he had a smart PR woman with him who kept taking pictures on her iPhone. It was obvious he had no idea of how a care home functioned, and in the second-floor corridor he had put his arm around Tove's shoulders and said: 'Now you're taking good care of our old folk, aren't you?' And she realised he might just as well have said 'customers'.

The PR woman took a picture, and Tove later saw the photograph on the company's website.

Hans Morelia.

That's his name.

Oh well, never mind him.

Tove takes hold of the cool door handle, and registers the way the smell of the summer morning, of dew drying on the grass, is replaced by a smell of disinfectant and life approaching its end, simultaneously rapidly and slowly.

For Tyra and Viveka, for Konrad and Weine.

If she can manage to make the days a bit better for them, then that's a good way of spending the summer.

3

The shooting range is always quiet early in the morning.

There's no smoke rising from the crematorium over at Lilla Aska, a kilometre or so away. No body being burned yet, no faint smell of charred human flesh to unsettle the mind.

The only sounds are birdsong and the vague rumble of distant morning traffic beyond the fields and dense clumps of birch trees.

It's nice to come here early.

Creep in alone, shoot a few magazines at the fixed targets, even though I'm not a member.

How could I afford that?

Sometimes I shoot at birds, at squirrels, but I never hit them.

I don't want to hit them.

Maybe wound them a bit, frighten them, just like I want to scare the shit out of that bastard.

A fever is raging within me, I'm shooting it out of me now, on lonely mornings like this.

I squeeze the trigger. Pretend I can see a face bleeding over by the ridge.

No one has ever found me here.

I shoot.

See frightened birds fly across a blue sky.

4

How much can anyone love another person?

As much as I love Lova, Hans Morelia thinks, and closes his eyes, breathing in the fleeting scent of his nine-year-old daughter, the way she smells of a better, more alive version of himself. As if there were nothing but life in her body, and death was utterly alien to it.

Lova is pure love.

Hans Morelia is standing on the terrace of his villa in Ramshäll. The house was built in the seventies, in a modernist style inspired by Palm Springs, and inside on the white walls hang works of art chosen by their consultant in Stockholm. Black-and-white photorealist paintings of buildings in New York. Hans Morelia is tired this morning, and can't remember the artist's name – he's hopeless at names, but the paintings look nice, and they impress visitors.

He takes hold of the steel railing that surrounds the terrace and looks out across Linköping.

From up there he has a view of the whole city, and the sun makes the grass of Folkungavallen sports ground look almost blue. The enclosed swimming pool at Tinnerbäcksbadet shimmers white, but the bigger pool around it, which has a tarmac base, is dark as the abyss, as if anything could be concealed in the water. He can make out the pale façade of the Hotel Ekoxen, a black car on the road in front of it, and beyond the hotel lies the greenery of the Horticultural Society Park. The treetops form a chlorophyll-rich canopy, and through gaps in the foliage he can see the Cherub, and glimpses of its colourful window frames.

The problems there.

The old man who wrote all that rubbish in the *Correspondent*.

It could have been even worse, but they managed to limit the damage and put a lid on things, and the paper didn't seem to want to take matters further, seemed to want to stay on the right side of him, the way it did with everyone of any significance in the city. The story didn't take off in the national press either, even though some left-wing troublemaker wrote an angry article in *Aftonbladet*, and the old man appeared on television.

But the old boy won't make any more fuss. Not any more.

Cars and bicycles on St Larsgatan.

Pedestrians like ants.

He's wanted to move away from Linköping for a long time, up to Stockholm, move the entire office there. But that hasn't happened. Everything has been changing so quickly and he's had so much else to think about and plan. And Lova most definitely doesn't want to move, she's happy at Ånestad School, and gets on well with her class-mates. There's nothing he wouldn't do for her, so they'll be staying here, in this miserable, stuck-up backwater whose inhabitants get dressed up in fancy suits and dresses just to go for a Saturday walk in the city centre.

Madeleine is happy belonging to the limited social scene of the city.

Extremely happy.

His wife wants to be queen of Linköping, and she will be as long as the deal goes through. She'd sell her own grandmother for that, Hans Morelia chuckles to himself.

How did I end up here? he thinks, as he looks over towards 'the tower', the high-rise office block in Tornby where Merapi's headquarters are located. Fifty employees work there, taking care of administration, invoicing, and the coordination of the different parts of the business.

I made my move at just the right time, he thinks. I had enough contacts to be able to set up the company quickly and finance the purchase of the woefully undervalued units.

Then, once the sell-off was finished and he had a portfolio containing seventy healthcare operations, old people's homes, X-ray departments, orthopaedic clinics, surgeries, sheltered housing, and plenty more, spread across the whole country, and his company was officially valued, he had assets of two billion Swedish kronor, his income was huge, and his debts amounted to just one billion. He was, quite simply, far richer than he could ever have dreamed of.

He had been in the right place at the right time.

Then followed years of big, complicated deals. For a while he owned pretty much half of Sahlgrenska University Hospital in Gothenburg. And now that it's time to sell, he's good for one and a half billion kronor as long as the deal with the Americans goes through without any problems.

'Dad.'

Lova is calling him from the living room.

'Dad, have you seen my iPhone?'

Hans Morelia turns around.

His daughter is standing by the terrace door smiling at him. Her fine blond hair frames her face with its gently rounded cheekbones and mascaraed eyelashes, even though she's not really allowed to wear make-up.

Could any young girl be prettier or more beautiful than her?

Impossible.

Could anything bad happen to such a beautiful girl?
Impossible.

She's above all the brutality of the world.

He and Madeleine have tried to have more children, but it hasn't happened, and somehow all the love that Lova spreads around her is enough. Deep down he doesn't actually want any more children. He can't contain any more love than he already feels for Lova.

'Try the kitchen table, darling.'

'OK. Can we buy some new riding boots later on today?'

'You know I've got to work. We'll get them next week.'

She pulls an unhappy face, then smiles, adjusts her jeans and goes back indoors.

He turns towards the city again, and looks across to the hospital. Merapi runs the urology department and infection clinic there.

They're earning money. More than ever.

And they're doing so thanks to *kaizen*, a Japanese expression that he has adopted, which means making every detail a bit better, a bit more cost-effective, for instance, not putting fresh paper on treatment beds if the paper isn't dirty or crumpled from a patient.

He tries to see the patients as customers, who should receive the service they can expect, no more, no less, but who should still feel happy and safe; the service that can be afforded in a system of taxation like Sweden's, where most people don't have private health insurance; the level of service that is reasonable if the company providing the care is to maintain realistic profit margins. How much would it cost to treat every little ache?

Recently he has sometimes felt he is being stalked. He has thought he could see someone standing in the garden in the evenings, in the darkness, but he knows it must be his imagination. There's never anyone there when he goes out to check. He's just a bit paranoid, because of the deal. When the media coverage was at its height, their security company suggested he should have a bodyguard. But he thought that was ridiculous. In little Linköping! Then the package of excrement appeared through the letter box. As luck would have it he was the one who found it, and he hasn't mentioned it to Madeleine or Lova.

At first he was going to report it to the police. But in the end he didn't bother. That was the price you had to pay if you earned as much money as he did. But the lack of boundaries implicit in someone sending a package of that sort scared him.

Lova is safe here, and you can't give in to fear.

I'm not inhuman, he thinks, the way some bloggers and left-wing journalists claim. If you're a director and entrepreneur in the business of providing care, sometimes you have to be blunt and look at the numbers.

What do people think? That care is free?

Look at Spain and Greece. They've been finding out the hard way what things cost.

He's allowed to think things like that, but must never say them out loud.

He knows that.

Just as he knows that he can't cruise around in his sports car every day in Linköping. He can only drive the Maserati that's parked down in the garage occasionally. It gets up the noses of the city's touchy citizens.

Hans Morelia looks down, at his shiny brown John Lobb shoes, and he feels ashamed, knows he mustn't think like that. He knows there's a difference between his company and others, that their business is unique because the customers are people in difficult situations. Sympathy is one aspect of the business model, part of the whole ethos of the company, even.

Linköping is almost beautiful this morning. As the sunlight shines down on the kaleidoscope of roofs and the surrounding fields, on the water and forests far off on the horizon.

So what does he have here?

The Americans are there somewhere.

Nexxon.

To them, a billion or two is nothing. They have hundreds of billions, and healthcare in Sweden is a growth sector for the future, according to their analysts.

Hans Morelia wants to sell now, he's only forty-five, but the past ten years have been a hell of a journey, and his blood pressure is uncomfortably high, and refuses to go down, despite the medication. He's tall and skinny, but out of shape, and the years are showing on his thin face.

Better to sell up.

Take a break for a few years.

Try to focus on Madeleine and, even more, on Lova. Get a private tutor and drift around the world for a few years. Madeleine would love the luxury of the hotels. Lova would love seeing the world. He knows that. She could manage without Ånestad School. She's not so young any more, in a couple of years' time she'll be a teenager, and then she won't care about me at all, except for when she wants money.

I don't have any illusions, Hans Morelia thinks, closing his eyes and making Linköping disappear.

Something strikes him as odd.

When he closes his eyes everything goes completely black, even though it's a bright morning and it ought to be almost white inside his eyelids.

Instead just disconcerting blackness.

But there's nothing to worry about.

What could happen?

Kaizen, down to the very smallest detail.

He opens his eyes and turns around to go and see what Lova's doing, before getting in his car and driving to the office, to face the challenges of the day.

5

The air from the hairdryer is warm against her neck, like a fleeting, gentle caress. Malin feels her hair flutter and dry out, and in her mind's eye sees the strands flying about in the mirror as they gradually approach the point where they could get scorched.

She doesn't open her eyes.

Doesn't want to see her morning-tired face, the ever deeper wrinkles, the lines on her forehead that will soon, anytime now, become a permanent frown.

Almost forty.

But she's in better shape than ever, could run a marathon without any trouble, and she wouldn't be ashamed of her naked body if there was a full-length mirror in the flat.

She's let her hair grow, and her bob has grown out into long, even hair that brushes her shoulders. Sometimes she pins her fringe back with clips, but usually she prefers just to brush it aside; the gesture seems to have a calming effect, like fingering the beads of a rosary.

It's been a year in neutral.

A year of control.

Of denying needs, handling them.

Handling the longing for a warm, soft body whispering warm, soft words in her ear.

Peter.

Bastard.

She hasn't spoken to him since she threw him out, after finding him with his American medical student in the duty doctor's room at the hospital.

She's seen them in the distance on Linköping's pedestrianised shopping streets, and has turned on her heel and gone a different way, each time feeling like a hostage in her own life. And what does she do then?

When she can't drink?

When she can't settle down at the bar of the Hamlet and fill herself with beer and lukewarm tequila?

I suppress it. Think about other things, about nothing, and I swim and lift weights and run, run as fast as I can, as far out into nothingness as possible.

Warm air at the roots of her hair now, and this year it has sometimes felt like her brain would catch fire. But it never has. Just like her soul, it's getting used to an emotionally neutral state where nothing means anything.

Of course she feels a desire to drink, but she can control it. Her thirst doesn't run quite so deep any more.

She's been working too. Working and working. Alone at the station late into the evenings, she has tried to wake herself to life, tried to find a way back to her old, limitless self, where everything happens at the same time, where good and evil, love and death blur into each other to form a dangerous but enticing whole.

But I'm safer like this, she thinks. Less of a danger to myself.

She switches the hairdryer off. The sudden silence is wonderful and she opens her eyes and looks at her face in the mirror.

Wrinkles around her eyes.

Me.

Malin Fors.

I'm older, more experienced.

So why do I know less than ever about who I am and who I want to be?

In the living room Malin opens the window.

No one can see in, so she doesn't care that she's naked.

She lets in the newly woken air of the summer morning, and down in the park by St Lars Church she can hear birdsong, she can't tell what sort. The recently renovated walls of the church glow in the light, and the white stucco seems to want to flee from the sky beyond.

She breathes in.

Thinks of when Tove was small and lay asleep in her bed, her ribcage rising and falling, rising and falling.

Filling herself with life.

The first thing you do when a badly injured patient is admitted to Accident and Emergency is stabilise their breathing. Everything else is of less importance.

Tove must have arrived at work by now, she'll be wearing her mauve cotton tunic and getting ready to go in to see one of the old folk, maybe that Konrad she talks so much about, the one she's been discussing the proletarian writers of the 1930s with.

Business college.

She never talks about that any more.

In the kitchen Malin makes herself a cup of coffee with the new espresso machine. One of the black coffee cartridges.

Strong and hot.

Bitter.

What shall I wear?

Why not nothing at all?

Her body feels neutral, as if it simply *is*; a functional machine that only occasionally reacts with an uncontrolled impulse in the crotch or heart.

She sucks her cheeks in, takes a sip of the coffee, then another, until the cup is empty.

The old, broken wall clock from Ikea has finally been replaced by a silvery digital monster. No more pointless ticking from a second hand that isn't there, just an angry red glow.

Time to get to the station.

No hurry yet, but soon, and she can't help hoping that something's going to happen after several weeks of summer stillness.

She wonders what Tove is doing over at the Cherub, wonders what's going on there in God's waiting room.

6

In the changing room in the basement Tove pulls on her mauve cotton tunic. It reaches her knees, and beneath it she wears a washed-out T-shirt that must have been there since the council ran the home.

She puts on her white Birkenstock sandals.

Her mum bought them for her.

Tove is alone in the cramped, stuffy room. She can hear the ventilation rattling above the false ceiling. Looks at the battered blue metal lockers along the walls. Some of the people she works with must have had the same lockers for the past twenty years; on their lockers they have pictures of their children, grandchildren and summer houses, and beaches – Tenerife, perhaps.

I must be the last to arrive, Tove thinks.

Looks at her wristwatch.

Shit.

The handover with the night staff started one minute ago: hope they aren't waiting for me. The night staff tend to get grouchy if you hold them up, especially if it's because you didn't get there on time.

Tove leaves the changing room and heads for the staffroom they use for meetings. The textured wallpaper looks shabby in the sharp light, and dust particles swirl in the air. Everyone is seated around a low, white coffee table. The night staff, three women, are all hollow-eyed and tired.

Apart from them there are two more women and one man. The day shift, her closest colleagues.

At one end of the table, on a ladder-backed chair with her back to the window facing Djurgårdsgatan, sits Hilda Jansson, manager of the Cherub. She straightens her thin body and fixes her dark brown eyes on Tove.

'So you've decided to join us, Tove?'

No one else around the table says anything. Instead they drink their coffee and yawn, and Tove apologises, slips on to a chair and waits for Hilda to go on. Tove isn't worried about being told off, she knows the old people like her. And that gives you a degree of leeway. Besides, Hilda seems impressed by Tove's mum, by what she's read about her in the paper. She thawed out a bit when she realised who Tove's mum was.

Who are the others around the table?

The man is about forty years old.

Kent. An assistant nurse. Family man.

The two women are Stina and Lisbeth. Both around sixty, and real stalwarts, plump and wrinkled from smoking, and likely to end up as 'clients' here soon, Tove has often thought.

The night staff are also veterans, all three of them. It's regarded as slightly more prestigious to work nights; on a full-time rota you only have to work thirty-five hours a week, and you get several days off in a row.

But the nocturnal work makes the women look more like demons than people. Especially Siv. She's sitting closest to the window, and her face almost seems to blur into the grey façade of the block of flats opposite.

Berit looks like she's being pressed into the sofa by a huge fist that's holding her short, fat body in place, and her appearance betrays the fact that she has long since stopped believing that anything good will ever happen to her.

Next to Berit sits Maj. Her short hair is dyed red, her eyes have been dulled by alcohol, just like Mum's, and Maj's thin, almost emaciated face is furrowed by too much hard smoking.

This is what it looks like, Tove thinks.

The backbone of Swedish social care.

Hard work, aching limbs, exhaustion. But somehow coping, with a smile.

How can anyone bear a place like this for twenty years? Thirty? One summer is OK, that feels fine. But longer than that? Under these working conditions, and with such crap wages?

How does anyone do it?

By refusing to participate in Merapi's stupid cost-cutting competition between its various establishments, where they want to see who can save the most disposable resources in terms of percentage. Like some fucking sales contest.

Sure, they whinge. But far less than they could.

Tove's thoughts are interrupted when one of the cleaners comes into the room.

She's wearing a veil to complement her white coat.

'Can you come back later?' Hilda Jansson snaps. 'We're just about to start.'

The cleaner slips out and the handover meeting begins.

It's been a quiet night. All twenty residents have slept more or less as expected, and none of the ones who have been a little under the weather recently because of the heat has got any worse.

Tove now has a cup of coffee, even though Hilda glared at her angrily when she stood up and went over to the coffee machine in the corner. The taste of the bitter liquid lingers in her mouth as she looks at the solitary print by Peter Dahl on the wall above Maj's head. The picture is the colour of fire, and seems to show a dance hall. And then she looks at Maj's hands, which are trembling slightly, probably from an urge to smoke, or an urge for something else, something worse.

Weary questions are tossed out into the room, and receive even wearier replies.

Name after name after name.

Tyra, Weine, Åke, Gerda.

She smiles as she thinks of the faces belonging to the names. But then her smile stiffens as she thinks of another way of looking at it: the names merely signify human flesh that has to be preserved and looked after.

Several of the Cherub's residents have no relatives who care about them, and some never receive visitors. A couple of them are immigrants, and their families visit more often, almost daily, but it never seems to occur to the relatives to take their old folk home.

It doesn't work like that in this country.

Here we follow Swedish traditions and customs.

Wolfram.

Beatrice.

Victoria.

Several of the old people share their names with princesses and future queens, and the men's names sound like ancient relics.

Hilda could gabble the residents' names, ailments, medication, and planned doctor's appointments in her sleep.

Special diets.

Pressure sores that need dressing.

Favourite food.

Prunes. Linseed.

Injections.

Catheter bags that need changing.

Tests that need taking.

This is the residents' home. Their reality.

Hilda can seem hard as a commanding officer, but Tove knows that deep down she cares about the old people.

'We did our last around an hour and a half ago,' Berit said. 'Everything was fine then. They'll start waking up soon.'

'OK, our turn now,' Kent says. Tove knows that he paints in his free time, he's received a grant of fifteen thousand kronor from the district council, and she can't help thinking that Merapi are unlikely to give him a grant for his watercolours of the Östergötland landscape.

'Well, thank you, night owls,' Hilda says, getting up. 'Any questions about today's work?'

'We'll do them in the usual order,' Stina says.

And they all get to their feet.

The morning routine is about to start. The old folk will get to enjoy another day of life.

Malin leaves the window open in the flat, and hurries through a Linköping that is still waking up. She walks along Hamngatan, past H&M, cuts across Trädgårdstorget and up towards Skolgatan.

The investigating team is now back to full strength after the holiday months of June and July. She herself had three rainy weeks off in June. She didn't do anything special, just counted off the days until she could go back to work again.

She thinks about Elin Sand, their thirty-year-old star player, a promising detective, who seems to prefer to keep most of her life private. Malin's been wondering if she's a lesbian, but knows that it's entirely up to Elin who she chooses to sleep with.

Sometimes they exercise together down in the gym, and Malin finds herself getting annoyed that Elin can lift ten kilos more than her without any problem, and can do many more reps. And Elin seems apologetic about the fact that she's younger, stronger, but she can go to hell with her apologies. She shouldn't be in the gym at all. She ought to be focusing on becoming a better detective.

Waldemar Ekenberg is smoking more than ever, and the way he dresses has got even scruffier. These days he walks about with the same coffee and ash stains on his synthetic brown trousers for weeks on end, and he still resorts to violence occasionally.

Johan Jakobsson has been on a course in Tokyo. On information gathering, and he came home full of enthusiasm, complaining about how 'sick' it was that everything was so expensive in Japan, everything but the underground, but he's learned a lot of new things.

'You can ask me to look for anything, Malin, and I'll get it for you.'

He and his family have moved to a bigger house in Linghem after his father-in-law died and left them a decent amount of money.

Malin turns into Linnégatan, towards the Horticultural Society Park.

She walks past the building where Peter lives, looking the other way, but she refuses to take a different route: painful memories aren't going to rule her life. It's the curse of living in a small town, never being able to get away from anyone, least of all yourself. You're constantly reminded of who you were, who you are, and – in all likelihood – who you're going to remain. And that's rarely pleasant.

Sven Sjöman, head of the Violent Crime Unit, is in his last year now, and once again he's asked her to take over the reins after him. But she's still resisting. Has asked him to stop going on about it. She won't let herself be persuaded.

Sven is too old and tired for his persistence to have any

effect. Karim joined in for a while, but he's given up now. When it comes down to it, he's not really interested. It's obvious that Karim Akbar is focusing on other things, this autumn he's going to be getting married to his prosecutor girlfriend, Vivianne Södergran. Rumour has it that she's pregnant and wants him to make an honest woman of her.

Karim's book on immigration issues and integration was published in January, and was considerably more politically correct than Malin had expected. He's done well on the television chat shows, and she knows that the Social Democrats have noticed him and that he's working as a consultant for the group responsible for the party's future policies.

Zeke Martinsson. Her partner. Her mainstay at work, and occasionally outside as well. He's happy with his new life, with Karin and Tess.

Börje Svärd.

He's shaved off his moustache, and still has the same number of Alsatians, even if one of them died and had to be replaced. His colleagues joke that he's stepped up his efforts to be the late-middle-aged Casanova of Linköping.

Good for you, Börje, Malin thinks, and feels jealous, wishes that she could relax and indulge in some time-honoured no-strings-attached fun.

But where would it end?

In a mental-health ward, Accident and Emergency, a treatment centre?

Does she even have it in her any longer?

Can she feel happy?

Malin opens the gate to the Horticultural Society Park, thinking:

This city is full of people just as confused as I am.

7

No dead squirrels today either.

The wheel steady in my thin, arched hands. Fingernails stained by little flashes of gunpowder.

I'll have to file them off at home, once I've cleaned my gun.

Ammunition's expensive, but when I bought the pistol I got a fair bit as part of the deal.

I'm calmer now. Like the day itself.

But then I turn on the radio. The news. Any damn news at all, and as I hear the newsreader's voice crackle and hiss from the single working speaker I get angry again.

Red mist furious.

There isn't even any justice in the way we absorb a voice on the radio.

I clutch the wheel. Take deep breaths.

I mustn't let rage get the better of me.

Unless maybe I should.

I don't drive down Drottninggatan on the way home. I take the detour around the cemetery, past the old fire station and on towards Vasagatan.

I drive straight into what has become my life.

The pistol is in the glove compartment.

Must clean it.

Must file my nails.

It will just have to take the time it takes. The time I've got, I tell myself.

8

Tove received one day of training. On a course for her and the other summer temps.

She starts with Eivor Johansson, and will move on to Konrad Karlsson.

Eivor is a former social worker, and suffers from mild dementia; her brain is no longer capable of sending the signals to her legs telling them to move or bear her weight.

Eivor is also alone.

During the month Tove has worked at the Cherub, Eivor hasn't received any visitors, not even the woman from the Philadelphia Church who has power of attorney for her. But Eivor is always in a good mood regardless, and considers herself to be living in the best of all possible worlds. From her flat she has brought a portrait of her deceased husband, and a photograph of a seven-metre-long sailing boat to the home. She also has a lacquered mahogany bureau, and a couple of ornate candlesticks that are never lit, in spite of her pleas. Candles are forbidden at the Cherub because of the fire risk, as they are in all of Merapi's healthcare facilities.

Eivor is more tired than usual this morning.

She had trouble sleeping last night, and was given an extra Stesolid to stop her getting anxious and calling for help. Her bony back is sweaty yet surprisingly soft under her nightdress as Tove helps her sit up on the edge of the bed. The thin veins in her legs look like they're trying to get out of the body they belong to.

Once Eivor is sitting steadily Tove wheels across the over-bed table. Pours some warm water and gentle soap into a stainless steel bowl, wets a washcloth and asks Eivor to wash the sleep from her face.

Slowly, slowly, Eivor moves the cloth across her cheeks.

'And now your teeth.'

Tove holds out a toothbrush.

Eivor brushes, and her eyes seem to focus on the trees out in the park, on the greenery, as she listens to the constant stream of birdsong.

When she's finished brushing her teeth she rinses her mouth and spits, then Tove asks if she needs a bedpan, and Eivor shakes her head in silence.

'What would you like to wear? It's going to be a hot day. Very hot, for August.'

'Is it summer?'

Eivor's blue eyes sit deep among layers of wrinkles and Tove can see genuine surprise in them, and how taken back the old lady is at this news.

'It's summer,' Tove says, 'just like it was yesterday and will be tomorrow. Have you forgotten?'

Eivor doesn't answer. Instead she says, after some consideration: 'The pale blue dress,' and Tove helps her remove her nightdress, underwear, and incontinence pad, gives her a fresh washcloth, and Eivor washes between her legs.

She doesn't need an incontinence pad. But she gets one anyway, day and night, because it isn't always clear that the staff, we, I, will have time to help her to the toilet, and washing and staff are more expensive than pads.

So, on with a fresh pad.

Suppressed shame on Eivor's face.

On with her bra and fresh briefs, then the dress, and

Eivor's body is frail and transparent, yet somehow full of a peculiar energy, as if a mass of inaccessible memories were keeping it going.

Tove combs Eivor's thin grey hair, rushing because she knows she has to move on.

Leaves it hanging down rather than setting it up the way she knows Eivor prefers.

Tove adjusts the sheets.

'Do you want to sit in your chair or on the bed until breakfast comes?'

'I'll lie on the bed,' and before Tove hurries out she makes sure that the top end of the bed is raised at the correct angle and that the over-bed table is pushed across so that breakfast can be served quickly and efficiently.

She turns the television on.

Breakfast news. Some rock group playing a terrible ballad.

'A bit of company,' Tove says, and Eivor nods, her face a complete blank.

The worn veneered door of Konrad Karlsson's room.

Room number seven.

Tove knocks, once, twice, three times, but there's no answer, and she feels a pang of anxiety.

Not like Konrad.

He's always awake when she arrives. And she's there every day. The days she works, anyway.

If possible, they go to the same people every day, they've divided the work that way so the old people don't have to cope with too many different faces, but also so that the workload is shared fairly, taking into consideration the different care requirements of the residents.

There's always more than enough lifting to do, no matter how the work is allocated.

Tove has read shocking articles about old folk who have

had forty different home helpers in a month. There's no respect in that. No security. It would take less than that to make you ill.

She knocks again. Feels a faint breeze blow in from the window at the end of the corridor and move past her, a sudden coolness in the heat.

It must be ten degrees warmer now than it was an hour ago, and the building's ventilation is no good at dealing with heat.

'Konrad?' she says loudly to the door. 'Are you awake? Can I come in?'

No answer.

He's asleep.

You're asleep, aren't you?

And she pushes the door inward and is confronted by a sight that makes her clap her hands to her mouth, then scream, a scream that moves out of her, into the familiar yet alien room.

Grass can crunch under your feet.

Did you know that, Tove? Standing over there by the door screaming.

Calm down, now.

A life has ended. What has happened has already happened, what you're seeing is nothing to be frightened of, and I know you can handle far worse and still retain your hope and friendly outlook.

I got to know you. To be your friend for a short while. To listen, and be listened to.

I talked about many things, but never the grass.

During properly hot summers a certain type of grass gets so dry that it crunches when you walk on it. As a boy I used to run barefoot across the meadow back home in Tjällmo, and the grass would crunch beneath my feet and I would be sweating and wishing that there was some sort of breeze.

I swam in dark forest lakes. Sneaked there on my own, and when I walked out into the warm water the air felt cool against my skin.

That was after the war winters. Cold, dark, white winters when I would sit in Mother's lap at home on the farm watching Father push through the snow to give the cows hay in the barn.

The image of Father surrounded by clouds of snow.

My first memories of him. I have more, but not many. Am I going to see him at last now?

He can't have felt anything. It must have happened quickly, and I heard Mother's scream through the forest.

Of course she screamed.

Her words like a gust of wind straight into my soul.

Or was I the one who found him?

It's so long ago now.

I can't feel anything on my skin now.

Am I going to see you as well, my beloved Sara? Are we going to be together, with our Josefina? She went too early, just like you.

I've missed you both so much, but haven't allowed myself to feel that loss.

It was time for me to stop feeling bodily pain. And now I can feel with my soul. I dare to.

So don't be frightened, you who are looking at what was once me.

Calm down, Tove.

9

Calm down, Tove, calm down.

Catch your breath, still your heart, don't fall, breathe.

She hears her own voice, unless it's Konrad Karlsson's voice, like a mantra within her, and she wants to stop screaming.

'No, no, NO!'

Is that what she's screaming? Or is she just thinking it?

Tove takes a deep breath, forcing the air into her lungs, and she hears the sound of her own voice, but it's getting quieter, and she realises that she's stopped screaming.

She breathes.

Tries to look, tries to persuade her legs to bear her.

What am I seeing?

She does what she always does, tries to be logical, measuring and weighing emotions and details.

Konrad's room.

The worn Chesterfield armchair. The reproductions of Öyvind Fahlström's paintings. The Moroccan carpet. The Finnish table with the heavy wooden top. The laptop computer, closed, on the bedside table; the mobile phone.

Konrad's things. Carefully chosen. Things he had told her about.

And the bed, and can I hear the others now? Footsteps heading in this direction?

But no one comes, and I am alone.

Shouldn't be alone here. Not now.

The bed.

I have to go over to it. Konrad Karlsson's blue face. His lifeless body in a white nightshirt. His head is hanging in a noose formed out of the cable of the alarm button, and the cable has slipped up his neck towards his ears. He isn't breathing.

She's reached the bed now. Wants to lift Konrad down from the noose, but something inside her is yelling: Don't touch him! Yet she still has to touch him. Stroke his blue cheeks, close his eyelids over his bloodshot eyes, give him some sort of peace. Give this moment some sort of dignity.

Why, Konrad?

You were so happy yesterday when we were talking about Neal Cassady. You said he was the sort of man you always wanted to be, but that you had ended up being his opposite. And then you said with a smile: 'But you could be a Neal Cassady,' and I replied: 'I don't know what I want.'

But you must have been tired of this?

Of struggling.

Of being tormented.

Of having a body that was paralysed down one side.

'Konrad, Konrad, Konrad,' she whispers, feeling her eyes fill with tears. She rubs her eyes, and the walls of the room crowd in on her and her legs give way, but she doesn't fall, just sits down on the bed next to Konrad, and they are alone here, in the loneliest room of her life.

'Come on, then!' she shouts. 'For God's sake, where is everyone?'

And Tove stands up, walks around the bed and sinks on to the armchair. Outside the window a swirl of wind is tugging some leaves from the top of a birch tree, and the leaves fly up into the sky, high, high up until they disappear from view.

A cry reaches up from the volleyball courts: 'Fuck! Fucking bastard hell!'

Tove feels arms around her shoulders.

They're shaking her, firmly, carefully.

'Tove.'

She recognises the voice. It belongs to Hilda. She sounds upset, but she's clearly trying to stay calm and controlled, and now Tove opens her eyes and finds herself looking straight into the woman's horror-stricken eyes.

'It's OK, Tove,' she says. 'This sort of thing happens occasionally. Not often. But occasionally.'

Konrad is lying on the bed, with the grey cable of the alarm button around his neck, his face the same colour as the desolate polar ice at night.

'Nothing's OK!' Tove says. 'How can you say that?'

And Hilda looks like she's trying to find some platitude, as if she's about to say: 'Konrad's in a better place now.' But then she seems to change her mind and says nothing, and turns to look at Konrad.

'I've told them the alarms shouldn't have cables,' she says. 'Lisbeth has called the police. They'll be here soon. And the duty doctor as well. The police and their medical officer will take care of everything.'

'The police?'

Tove sees her mum's face before her. Her steady detective's gaze. Yes, something like this would be a police matter, an old person committing suicide.

Tove looks at Konrad Karlsson. Life has left him, he himself has left his flesh, and in the dead man's face there is no fear, no emotion at all. She stands up.

'The police,' Hilda says. 'We ought to get out of the room for the time being.'

But Tove doesn't want to leave Konrad on his own.

Someone ought to be with him, even though he is no longer there.

'He's gone, Tove,' Hilda says, but his stubble has grown overnight and is still growing now. Tove shaved him yesterday, wants to shave him again, and his catheter bag needs changing, it's time for new sheets, and what did he say about Neal Cassady?

Words, gone for ever.

'FUCK!' she hears from the volleyball courts.

'No,' Tove says softly. 'I don't suppose he's here.'

'Wherever he is, he isn't here.'

Mum, Tove thinks. Maybe Mum will come. She wonders where Lisbeth, Kent, and Stina are, and as if Hilda can read her mind she says: 'The others have got work to do, the routines need to be kept up. We mustn't upset the old folk.'

'What about me? What do I do?'

'Go to the staffroom. Wait there, and someone will come along for you to talk to.'

Someone to talk to?

Tove remembers all the psychologists she's seen, and how they couldn't do a damn thing to help her.

'I don't need to talk to anyone. I've been through worse. I'll go and help the others.'

But have I been through anything worse? Tove thinks.

Konrad was my friend.

What really happened here?

10

Tove stops in the corridor, she can hear Lisbeth talking to a resident in one of the rooms.

For the first time since she started work at the Cherub she notices that the corridors are painted a very pale pink, and the day feels even warmer now, far too hot. She stands still, and behind her she hears Hilda leave Konrad Karlsson's room, and Tove wonders: Who's going to watch over him?

She can feel her mobile in her pocket, heavy, and she takes it out, thinking: Must phone Mum, must phone her.

'Tove. Tove? Are you there? Try to calm down.'

Malin has just emerged from an uneventful morning meeting, and now she is walking towards the open-plan office in the police station, attempting to understand what her upset daughter is trying to tell her.

Malin can hear her fear through the phone, and whispers: 'Just calm down,' and Tove calms down, tells her what has happened, and concludes with the words: 'I'm standing next to his bed, Mum. Can I take him down from the noose, it looks like it hurts?' and Malin wishes she were with her daughter, knows how fond she was of Konrad. She wants to help Tove release his head from the noose, hold her, tell her that everything will be all right, because it always is.

'You mustn't touch him,' Malin says. 'Don't touch him. We need to take a look first.'

She wonders if anyone has contacted the police, but before she has time to ask, one of the uniforms passes her a note:

Suicide at the Cherub old people's home. Can you take it?

She nods, and hears Tove's voice on the other end of the line: 'What do you need to take a look at?'

'We need to confirm the cause of death in cases like this. You know that.'

Tove sniffs, and Malin hears her breathing get quicker. A hand appears on her shoulder, it must be Zeke, and Malin turns around.

Three minutes, Malin gestures with her free hand just as she reaches her very tidy desk.

What happened to all the mess?

'I'm on my way, Tove. I'm on my way. Don't touch anything.'

'OK. Come right away. Promise.'

Silence on the phone.

Tove has ended the call. And Malin feels like ringing her back, but stops herself and turns toward Zeke: 'I've got to go.'

'I'll come with you,' Zeke says, and judging by the look on his face he knows what this is about. Malin wonders briefly if Elin Sand ought to go with her instead, but there's no sign of her.

Elin could learn something, Malin thinks. But on the other hand: Can I handle having her with me?

Her phone rings again.

Tove.

Malin ignores Zeke and begins to walk towards reception.

'He didn't have a reason, Mum, not really. He was happy yesterday.'

'Happy can be sad, Tove,' and as Malin walks out through the door she repeats to herself: 'Happy can be sad.' Silence on the line once more, and she realises that Tove has hung up again.

Zeke appears by her side.

'That's where Tove works, isn't it? The Cherub?'

Malin nods. And they walk towards the car, parked at the far end of the car park in the shade of the old birch trees, a long way from the old barracks in which the station is located.

'It was Tove who found him,' she says.

'Sod's bloody law.'

Ten minutes later Malin and Zeke walk in through the front door of the care home. They take the lift up to the third floor, to room number seven, or flat seven, as the receptionist says.

The receptionist doesn't seem to know what's happened, Malin thinks, and when they step out of the lift Tove is standing just a few metres away. She forms a dark silhouette as she stands there backlit by the window at the end of the corridor.

What have you seen?

Far too much.

Malin has been on similar calls twice before.

Once to the old geriatric hospital in Valla. Closed down now. A woman had hung herself from a radiator using a pair of stockings. She had somehow thrown herself out of her wheelchair with enough weight and height to strangle herself.

The second time was a young man who had broken his back in a motorcycle accident and was left paralysed. He hanged himself in Ward 10 of the University Hospital, using the cable of the alarm button, just as Konrad Karlsson is supposed to have done.

But on those occasions Tove wasn't involved.

Malin runs over to her daughter and hugs her tightly, and Tove hugs her back, whispering: 'It was so horrible. Why would he have wanted to commit suicide? He wasn't sad. He wasn't.'

And Malin can feel Tove shaking, and she squeezes harder, wants to make the shaking stop.

From the corner of her eye she sees a woman introduce herself to Zeke, hears: 'Hilda Jansson, manager,' and Zeke and the woman disappear through a white plywood door.

Mother and daughter hug silently for a long time, and gradually Tove stops shaking. Then they let go slightly and hold on to each other gently. This moment needs to take time, demands time. Even so, Malin can't help feeling impatient, wants to go into the room, feels that this is the first thing she has wanted for a very long time. But she stays where she is, holding on: I'm not going to leave you this time. In the end Tove pulls free and says: 'Go in now, I can tell you want to. And I've got work to do,' and before Malin has time to object, Tove has vanished down the stairs to the second floor.

Malin hesitates for a moment. Then goes into the room.

So what can I see? she wonders.

You can see me, Malin Fors.

Konrad Karlsson.

My body is free now. No more paralysis, no more pain.

I was just a little boy when my father was buried. In the cemetery in Borensberg, on a summer's day as beautiful as this one. Mother kept hold of me. She was clenching her teeth, didn't allow herself to cry. For her the truth was not allowed to exist. I remember that I didn't cry either, that I didn't dare.

My children will bury me now. Maybe they'd like to have done that a long time ago.

I'm moving about in my domain. Searching, looking for my loved ones.

Capricious winds pick up and die away in the pale greenery. Children are making a noise in the playground, the volleyball players are taking a break, and on the terrace two floors below us a few of the other old folk are sitting in the sun. They've been pushed out there in their wheelchairs, or have walked there themselves, slowly, using various types of walker.

I liked your daughter, Malin.

She's got a good heart.

Protect Tove, make sure no harm comes to her.

Make sure what happened to me doesn't happen to her.

The old man is frozen in an eternally wrong position.

His thin, pale arms stick out from his nightshirt, seem almost to have been placed on the yellow-and-white striped sheet by someone else. His hands are gnarled yet still slender. Electrician's hands. Sensitive to the world while he was alive.

Malin looks at the catheter bag hanging full from a hook on the side of the bed facing the window. The height of the bed is adjustable.

Suicide.

Nothing to suggest otherwise.

He could, with a lot of practice and determination, have managed to tie the knot, raise the bed, pull the noose over his head, and then slowly slip down into darkness.

She's seen stranger things.

The only thing that doesn't make sense is what she's heard about Konrad himself.

According to the manager, Hilda Jansson, he hadn't been depressed. On the contrary, he was a fighter, and took pride in his efforts to get care for the elderly improved. And Tove made a point of saying how bright he seemed as recently as yesterday.

But eleven years in this place.

In this room, stuck in a bed or wheelchair, dependent on other people's help.

She turns towards Hilda Jansson.

'When were the night staff in here last?'

'They're supposed to do their last round at half past five, so some time then.'

'And he was alive then?'

'As far as I know.'

'As far as you know?'

'Yes. Sometimes you skip patients you know sleep soundly. And Konrad hated being woken up.'

'So he could have been dead at half past five. And when does the previous round take place?'

'Just before one.'

'Thank you,' Malin says. 'Useful to know. We're going to need more precise details from the night staff.'

'Maybe you could call them this afternoon, if it isn't urgent? They'll be asleep now.'

'We'll call this afternoon,' Zeke says.

They've asked Karin Johannison, their forensics expert and medical officer, to come. Malin made the call, she knows that Zeke doesn't like calling her about work unless he absolutely has to.

Even if there's very little doubt in this case, Karin still needs to examine the room and the body, and conduct a post-mortem.

On Konrad Karlsson's bedside table are a laptop computer and a mobile phone. A battered paperback of Kerouac's *On the Road*. There are copies of *Aftonbladet* and *Svenska Dagbladet*, both dated Monday, 9 August, and in the wastepaper bin are a Dime bar wrapper and three lottery scratch cards on top of several blue napkins.

'Did he have any relatives?' Zeke asks.

Hilda Jansson nods.

'His wife's dead, but he's got two children. A son and a daughter, Yngve and Margaretha. They're not here often, but his granddaughter Gabriella comes fairly regularly. She's evidently the daughter of another daughter who died a long time ago.'

'Have they been informed?'

'No, not yet. I wanted to wait until you arrived. In theory they're supposed to be told first, but there's no manual for cases like this, it happens far too rarely, thank goodness. Can I call them now?'

'Absolutely,' Zeke says. 'But be sure to point out that they can't see him yet. Karin needs to do her work first.'

'Karin?'

'Our forensics expert,' Malin says.

'What should I say, then?' Hilda Jansson wonders. 'What am I allowed to say?'

'Tell them the truth,' Malin says. 'Say it looks like he committed suicide, but that the police are investigating for the sake of formality.'

Then she looks at Zeke. Knows he's waiting for Karin to arrive. He's bound to feel like hugging her, kissing her when she arrives, but they're managing their relationship well. Almost exaggeratedly professional, and Malin can't help feeling relieved. A police station, still less a crime scene, isn't the right place for whispering sweet nothings of any description.

But what did I just do with Tove?

On duty.

She needed someone, I needed someone.

'I'll go and do that then,' Hilda Jansson says. 'And I'll keep an eye on your daughter.'

'Thanks,' Malin says, and then she and Zeke are alone in the room.

'Karin ought to be here soon,' Zeke says, and his voice is hoarse and neutral. 'We should probably wait until then before we do anything. In here or outside?'

'We'll wait in here,' Malin says, and looks at Konrad Karlsson again. He looks both at peace and tormented, as if he has got what he wanted, but in the wrong way.

12

The gun is clean now.

I've thrown the newspaper and kitchen roll I used in the bin, don't want it hanging about indoors.

I've cleaned the tube brush as well. Greased the pistol, then put both it and the ammunition in the little hiding place under the sink.

I've scrubbed and filed the powder stains from my nails.

Looking out of the window at the clear sky, I did wonder if I should go for a swim down at the Tinnerbäck pool today. But I'm going to stay at home, and now the water of the shower is coursing over me.

The tepid drops hit my head, shoulders, and chest, and run down over my body. I can stand here like this for ages. Often for an hour or so. Enclosed by water and the mouldy shower curtain.

There's nothing better than loneliness for someone wanting to justify hatred.

Hang on, though.

Did I really just think that?

The water is tepid.

I can take from him, the man who's stolen from all of us.

I can steal his soul.

13

Hans Morelia parks in front of the Cherub. The nurse, the one who runs the place, Hilda something, called him.

'I thought you'd want to know,' she said over the phone.

This couldn't have happened at a worse time, Hans Morelia thinks as he gets out of his black BMW 760. We don't want more scandals, articles, and letters about the poor conditions in any of our establishments. We need peace and quiet now, on all fronts, nothing that could unnerve the Americans' willingness to cough up the money.

He hesitated at first and wondered about sending his PR manager, Rebecka Koss, but decided to come himself. In reception he walks towards the lifts: now where's the nurses' office again?

First floor.

The short, dumpy receptionist says without his having to ask: 'You'll find Hilda on the first floor.'

Soon he's standing in a cramped, windowless office, being told what's happened. Hilda Jansson tells him that the police are in the room now, they're waiting for the medical officer, who needs to confirm formally that they're dealing with a suicide.

'Good, good.'

'I thought you should probably know first. We don't want any more articles. That sort of thing makes some of the old folk anxious.'

'The Swedish press don't often bother to write about suicides.'

Hilda Jansson looks up at him.

'He was a tough old boy,' she says. 'Intelligent and articulate, and what he wrote needed to be said, even if it was challenging.'

Hans Morelia can remember some of the letters word for word. What they all had in common was that they attacked him personally, accusing the company of causing suffering with its desperation to cut costs, and its 'crazy, unethical and utterly mercenary ambitions to increase the profits of the company in advance of an eventual sell off.'

Did the old man know he was playing with fire?

And this Hilda Jansson, an employee of Merapi, has the stomach to call the old man's scribbles *necessary*?

Hans Morelia says: 'Strange that someone who's receiving such good care as you provide here at the Cherub should want to commit suicide.'

Hilda Jansson snorts. Gives him a dark look.

'You won't get anywhere flattering me like that. I'm sure you understand that I only called you for the good of the residents.'

Shortly after that Hans Morelia walks into room seven without knocking on the door first. Inside two police officers are standing with their backs to the window, quietly, as if they are waiting for someone.

No cordon.

Good.

The police officers turn towards him.

Stare at him.

'And who might you be?' the female officer says in a cold voice, and he explains who he is and why he's there.

'You're in charge of the whole thing, then,' the male

officer says. There's a coolness in his voice as well, and Hans Morelia realises that they know who he is, they've read about his business dealings in the papers, and they despise him.

He looks at the body on the bed. Pulls a grimace, then wonders if it looked genuine.

A grimace in the face of death.

Silence.

No more letters, no more fuss.

And the female police officer says: 'We'll have to ask you to wait outside, our forensics expert will be here shortly, and we need the room to remain as untouched as possible.'

'Will you want to talk to me?'

'Have you got anything you want to tell us?'

'I'm here more often than you might think. I take a degree of pride in visiting the factory floor. Our care facilities.'

And now she gives him a mocking smile.

'Well, you can toddle off away from this particular floor. I'm sure we'll be able to find you if we need to.'

The healthcare magnate has left the room and Malin feels like giving him the finger behind his back. A childish gesture, she knows that, but it can't be helped: people who are parasites on other people, particularly those who are ill, rouse her anger, almost her hatred.

Blue or red. You can't trust any of them. The whole fucking lot of them seem to think it's OK to make a profit from welfare.

And the weakest end up paying the price.

Just look at Stefan. He never gets to go out any more, and they've stopped putting butter on his rusks, so now he's stopped eating them. Do the residents here get butter on their rusks?

She saw some of the employees just now. Rushing from

room to room. They seem to care about the old people, they work hard in spite of the scant resources and everything that has been written about the Cherub.

If Stefan lived here, at least she would have confidence in the staff.

A man like Morelia has no compassion.

I really am properly angry with him.

Because he's pissing on those of us who pay tax.

Greedily hollowing out the morality of the tax system.

Even worse, hollowing out so much more than that.

He's unbalancing society.

If he earns so much from being inconsiderate, why should I be considerate? In a world without morals, there's no need for empathy.

Men like Hans Morelia reduce every interaction between people to business opportunities.

And in the long run he's ruining things for our children, for Tove, but even more for her children.

If she has any.

My grandchildren.

Who the hell would want to live in Hans Morelia's world? You'd need to be as rich as him just so you could afford to buy whatever healthcare you need.

I'm being naïve, she thinks. Stupid. Anachronistic. Old-fashioned.

But fuck him, and fuck the world he's creating for himself. For us.

Malin sticks her middle finger out to tell him to fuck off, but she doesn't raise her hand.

14

Hilda Jansson is sitting in the nurses' office with the phone in her hand. She looks at the clutter around her, wonders when she's ever going to have time to tidy it up. It's actually hard to reach the medicine cabinet because of all the paperwork.

She's tried to get hold of both of Konrad Karlsson's children, but hasn't managed to reach either of them.

She's only seen them a few times over the years, and has worked out that there were clearly issues of some sort, but never wanted to stick her nose in by asking.

You simply didn't ask Konrad Karlsson about things like that.

Gabriella, his granddaughter. Kind, and shy.

Green eyes.

Sad, lonely eyes. And Hilda feels no inclination to make that call, even though she knows she must.

It was a mistake to ask Hans Morelia to come. What good could he do? She misjudged him last time he was here, thought he genuinely cared about conditions for the residents. But when he burst in a short while ago in his fancy suit, she realised that had been nothing but a sham, that he really didn't care at all.

She wonders if she might be being a little too hard on him. Surely you couldn't be successful in the healthcare industry without having a degree of compassion?

What strange paths compassion takes, she thinks.

The phone feels horribly heavy in her hand. Her fingers don't want to dial Gabriella Karlsson's number. She doesn't know how she's going to ask her to come to the home, doesn't know how to tell her how her beloved grandfather died.

That it should have to end like that . . .

Hilda holds the receiver to her ear. Dials the number. Slowly. One digit after the other.

Gabriella Karlsson is slumped on a chair in her flat on Vasagatan, close to the Abisko roundabout. She is staring straight ahead of her, at the colourful painting of Shiva she bought in India.

What am I going to do now?

She feels like crying, ought to feel some sort of grief, but there's something unreal about the moment.

Grandfather. I only saw him yesterday evening, she thinks, and he was in a pretty good mood. He seemed pleased with the newspapers, the chocolate, and the scratch cards I took with me. Usually he just thanked me politely and then launched into a conversation about whatever book he happened to be reading.

She presses something new and alien and black down into her stomach, she can't let it into her throat, because it might suffocate her. Her mobile slips out of her hand as all the strength seems to go out of her muscles, and she even finds herself having to concentrate just to keep breathing.

She looks at her fingers against the thin fabric of her blue dress.

Hilda wants me to go to the home. I was only there yesterday.

He's gone.

The only member of my family that I had any contact with.

She has a photograph album in the bureau in the living room. Grandfather's life in pictures, with Grandma, Mum, and then her, with Dad, in the little house in Jägarvallen.

No pictures of her uncle or aunt.

Granddad with a cable tied around his neck.

Get up.

Go to work.

Work, work, eat lunch, work, go home, same thing tomorrow.

He had an electrician's worn-out shoulders, from working with his hands high above his head.

Bang.

Then a blood vessel bursts in your brain just a few years into retirement.

I was twenty years old at the time, about to go to Lund to study, but I stayed here for your sake. Because I'd promised Mum I would, I said I'd look after you, that was the last promise I made to her before she lost consciousness, before the bacteria finally consumed her lungs.

You looked after me then.

And I was happy to stay when you needed me.

Wanted to do it.

Granddad, you always said: 'If we don't take care of each other, who else is going to?'

Karin Johannison has arrived at room number seven inside the Cherub old people's home.

She can't see anything odd, anything strange about the scene. She's photographed the old man, taken fingerprints from all the strategic surfaces in the room, and now she walks up to him and brushes the cable around his neck, but it's impossible to get anything from the narrow, shiny surface.

She's thinking that this is one way for everything to end.

Every young person's nightmare. But in a home.

Suicide.

No signs of a struggle. Of any resistance.

Carried out some time after midnight, probably between two and three, to judge by the extent of the rigor mortis.

Time to get him down. There's a relative who wants to see him. On her way here soon.

Best to let the staff make him look a bit better.

They won't be able to do anything about the blue colour of his face.

Karin picks up the remote control for the bed. If I'm going to do this on my own, I need to raise the bed, pull the noose over his head, then let the bed down again. She presses the button to raise the top end of the bed. Nothing happens. The bed's motor merely stutters, and she gives up, looks at the old man, and thinks that he's fairly thin, can't weigh much. She takes hold of him around his back, and with her free hand tries to loosen the noose, but it turns out to be difficult, and she wonders: Could he really have tied the noose with his single working hand?

Was that really possible?

She lets go of him, and manages to untie the noose using the fingers of both hands. The knot comes undone before she has time to put her hand behind his back again, and Konrad Karlsson falls onto the bed with a thud. At that moment a grey sparrow settles on the windowsill, peers inquisitively into the room for a few seconds, then flies off.

Done here.

Once his relative has seen the body, it will be taken by ambulance to the pathology unit and I'll do the post-mortem.

She studies the marks around his neck, thinking that they aren't particularly deep.

Blue, yellow, and red.

They seem to have been made by the cord. But something

else could have made them, a pair of hands, for instance. Impossible to say.

Air forced out.

A final breath.

She wishes she could go out into the corridor, to Zeke. And just hold him tight.

Malin hears what Karin says in the corridor. Feels the beads of sweat make her dress stick to her back.

She brushes her fringe aside. They're almost done here, and she hasn't seen Tove again. A psychologist is supposed to be on the way, someone for the staff to talk to.

It's going to be the hottest day of the year so far. No doubt about that.

August fulfilling the promise of July.

Karin is standing next to Zeke, and they're touching now, aren't they, their hands brushing against each other?

Malin hears Karin say with almost complete certainty that they're dealing with a suicide. She's taken the body down, covered up the marks on his neck, and fixed his jaw, so the relatives can take their leave of him in peace.

'I tried to raise the bed to get him down, but it seems to be broken.'

'Really?' Zeke says.

'Could he have got himself up there?' Malin walks over to them.

'It's not impossible,' Karin replies. 'Depends how strong his good side was. It can't have been easy, but we shouldn't underestimate human willpower.'

'Time of death?'

Malin looks along the corridor, and sees Tove go into a room together with a male member of staff wearing a similar tunic, and Malin can see assurance in Tove's movements, as though she knows exactly how to behave.

'I'd guess somewhere between two and three o'clock this morning.'

'OK,' Malin says, thinking how odd the business of the bed is, but perhaps it broke just as Karin was about to raise it. Neither Hilda Jansson nor Tove said anything about a broken bed.

Tove comes out of the room again.

Malin calls her over.

'Was Konrad's bed broken yesterday?'

'No,' Tove says, and hurries on.

The lift door opens in front of them, and out steps a beautiful copper-haired woman, around thirty years old. Her eyes are red from crying, and Malin realises who she is.

Malin stops her and asks: 'Have you spoken to Hilda Jansson? She's explained what's happened?'

The woman looks into Malin's eyes. Seems to understand instinctively who she is.

'I know Granddad's dead. I want to go in and see him. But she didn't really tell me how he died. What are the police doing here?'

'Let's go and sit down over there,' Malin says, gesturing towards a sofa over by the window.

Gabriella Karlsson looks like she's about to protest, then goes with her.

'That can't be right,' Gabriella Karlsson says, shrinking deeper into the sofa next to Malin. 'He wasn't remotely depressed. He loved life. It might be hard to believe, but he had a rich life. Richer than most of the drones out there in the city. I mean, Granddad appreciated all that life has to offer more than most people . . .'

Gabriella Karlsson leans slowly towards Malin.

The air goes out of her lungs, taking the end of her sentence with it.

'Maybe he just put on a brave face to you?' Malin says, aware of how wrong the words sound.

'He never pretended to be anything he wasn't. He was the most honest person you can imagine.'

Malin sits in silence, doesn't want to say any more, and anyway, what could she say?

'He wasn't physically strong.'

Gabriella straightens up again, and Malin suddenly misses her weight, the proximity of another human being, regardless of the circumstances.

'You were here yesterday?' Malin asks.

'Yes. I left at about eleven o'clock last night.'

'And he was the same as usual?'

'Yes. I squeezed his hand just before I left. It was warm. He always had warm hands.'

Malin murmurs to herself. Hears a noise from one of the rooms.

'I want to tell you something,' Gabriella says. 'My mum died when I was a teenager. Quickly, just a couple of days after contracting a bacterial infection. Granddad looked after me then. Mum and Dad were divorced and Dad had moved to Saudi Arabia for work. Granddad was the one who found the flat in Vasastan for me.'

Malin puts her hand on Gabriella Karlsson's shoulder, then quickly removes it again.

'What am I going to do now?' Gabriella says. 'What's going to happen?'

'There has to be a post-mortem.'

'Why?'

Malin looks into Gabriella's eyes. No need to answer her question.

'Can I take his computer? His phone? Other things?'

Malin hesitates. She shouldn't let her. But this is a suicide, so they won't need anything. She nods.

'Just don't delete anything from them.'

Gabriella Karlsson closes her eyes. She takes a few deep breaths before looking at Malin again.

'What am I going to do? I've been coming here several times a week. What would you do?'

'Do you work?' Malin asks.

At first Gabriella looks surprised, then she replies: 'Yes, I'm studying for a PhD in history at the university.'

'Then I'll give you a piece of advice,' Malin says, handing Gabriella her card. 'Throw yourself into your work. Don't think too much, or it'll drive you mad.'

You see me now, Gabriella, and I see you.

I see how confused and sad you are. I see you stroke my cheek with your hand, but I can't feel it.

Your hand, your thin, white fingers, remind me of Mother's. She used to stroke my cheek like that in the flat in Borensberg, where we ended up after the farm was sold and the bank had taken its share. I would lie in bed in the living room, trying to sleep, and Mother's palm would stroke my cheek. She was alone.

There was nothing but loneliness in Borensberg.

And the ice that settled thin as a breath on the Boren River, the swirling, cold snow that burned my face as I walked further and further out, when the others chased me onto the ice, shouting: 'Poor brat, little bastard, your dad was an adulterer and you're a son of a bitch.'

Further and further out.

They never caught me.

But life caught me, Gabriella. I did wrong things, and I did some right ones. I tried to do right by you.

Now you can be free.

I know you're wondering what really happened last night.

Life was finished with me, that much is beyond any shadow of a doubt.

15

Hans Morelia rubs his eyes, thinking about Lova. How his love for her is so strong that it forces out everything else. How her friends and schoolmates become shapeless brats for whom he can't muster up any feelings at all.

Lova.

He sometimes looks at her and thinks, is a miracle like her really possible?

She shall have the most expensive riding boots that can be bought.

He thinks about the figure in the garden. The one he saw. Or was he just imagining that?

From up in his office the buildings of the city look like pale Monopoly houses. Linköping looks so unassuming from high above.

Money is about height. About substance. Cleanliness. Views. Evidently that old man, Konrad Karlsson, had money.

Hans Morelia is leaning back in his desk chair in his corner office on the twelfth floor of Merapi's headquarters, which is also the headquarters of the other businesses in the company: Take Care. Golden Days. Good Time.

The Tuscan calfskin of the seat is soft against his back, and through the glass doors he can see the febrile activity in the open-plan office, people doing their jobs carefully and efficiently, people counting and invoicing, analysing and purchasing, people trying to make money.

He's always been generous with share options.

A lot of the people sitting out there in the office will become millionaires if they manage to close the deal with Nexxon. Overnight they will become some of Linköping's wealthiest citizens. Just as others did when IFS, Industrial and Financial Systems, was listed on the stock market twenty years ago. The receptionist there was able to buy one of the fanciest villas in Ramshäll.

From his office Hans Morelia can see the spire of the cathedral, and the oblong wooden box of the library. He can see the river and Cloetta Centre where the LHC ice hockey team play their matches. He has a box there, but rarely uses it. His employees make use of the seats according to a rota.

He had lunch down in the canteen today. Mixing with his employees, wanting to make them feel that he's one of them, just as he does when he visits the Cherub or any of the many other care facilities he owns.

It's three o'clock now, and he wonders about making a quick visit to the gym.

But then the phone on Hans Morelia's desk starts to ring.

Malin Fors lifts the bar towards the ceiling. When she went down to the gym she was surprised to find Elin Sand there already, in a training vest that's far too small for her, busy adding weights to the bench press.

'We can spot each other,' Elin said, giving her a smile that Malin thought was an invitation to competition, and now she is lying with her back against the bench, with too much weight on the bar, and looking up at Elin's face from below.

Sixty kilos, three times twelve, and Malin screams out loud, screams: 'COME ON NOW FOR FUCK'S SAKE!'

She finds strength in breathing out, breathing in and

screaming, and her vision goes white and black at the same time, perhaps the way it did for Konrad Karlsson.

And Elin Sand's smile from underneath.

Push.

Shit.

'Come on!' Elin Sand yells. 'One more!'

I'm not going to give you the satisfaction of helping me, Malin thinks, and shuts her eyes, pushes the bar upwards and feels the veins in her temples expand to bursting point.

Done.

Ha!

The bar settles into its cradle with a hard metallic clang. Elin doesn't have time to help.

Malin notices the stagnant air. The stench of sweat that seems to seep from the vomit-green walls. She sits up on the bench, rests her elbows on her knees, and breathes out. Feels her muscles slowly recover.

Then she stands up, raises her chin towards Elin, and says: 'Your turn.'

Elin pushes the bar towards the ceiling with ease.

Once, twice, three times . . .

Something about Elin's apparently effortless movement makes Malin think of Stefan. Incapable of moving a single muscle in his body.

She's been to visit him three times in the past year.

Stefan is getting thinner and thinner, and on each visit he was unshaven, dressed in dirty clothes, and increasingly distant.

She's accepted that he's never going to understand who she is. Has reconciled herself to that.

. . . seven, eight, nine . . .

Trying to give love without getting any real response. Without expecting any. Sending love into him and hoping it finds its way, to a place that only he can access.

. . . ten, eleven, twelve . . .

Elin Sand seems quite untroubled by the weight. She puts the bar down and gets to her feet without comment.

Fucking machine, Malin thinks, and says: 'Haven't you got anything better to do than hang about down here?'

Elin frowns, seems to be about to say something, but holds back.

'Do you want me to spot you?' she asks instead.

'I'm done with the bench,' Malin says.

She lies down on a yoga mat and starts to do sit-ups, and from the corner of her eye she sees Elin Sand move through the gym.

She does two hundred sit-ups.

Rests.

Does more sit-ups and lets her thoughts roam free.

I can't accept the fact that Stefan is being poorly cared for, she thinks.

She's called the director of the regional council in Hälsingland to point out the failings. But nothing has happened.

Hans Morelia.

She couldn't help herself when he showed up at the care home earlier today. She just couldn't. And the fury that bubbled up inside her when his well-manicured figure breezed in felt good. As if something inside her were waking up. Something that was actually her.

Fifty more.

Up, down.

She feels her stomach muscles work.

She's been thinking that they ought to find a new home for Stefan, move him somewhere that's still run by the state. Or by a company that's less obsessed with profit than Merapi.

'I'm going now,' Elin Sand calls.

Why should I care? Malin thinks.

A few more.

Done.

She stands up, feels the pain in her stomach.

Tove's right, we need to go and see Stefan.

They promised things would improve last time, and we can go tomorrow. Tove's not working, is she? I can take some time owing, there's nothing much happening at the station during the summer lull.

Then Malin's phone rings, she hears it buzz on the little table over by the dumb-bells.

Is that you, Tove, wanting to talk about what happened this morning?

Elin Sand stands in front of the mirror in the changing room of the gym. She has to bob down to see her face.

How crabby can a person be? she thinks, and tries to smile at the thought of Malin Fors. But the smile isn't genuine. Because she knows that if she can't gain Malin's respect, she'll never get any from the others either.

That's how it works here.

Elin takes a red lipstick out of her bag. But changes her mind before applying it.

Hans Morelia is holding the phone close to his ear. He recognises the voice at the other end. It's sharp and dark and belongs to the journalist from the *Correspondent*, Daniel Högfeldt.

He interviewed Högfeldt when they were looking for a new head of PR, but Högfeldt chose to take a job at Stiff Technologies instead. The last thing Hans Morelia read about him in the paper was that Högfeldt had left Stiff and gone back to being a reporter for the *Correspondent*.

Daniel Högfeldt has somehow found out about what's

happened at the Cherub. He's been asking about it, and now he says: 'Is it a common occurrence for patients to kill themselves in your care facilities?'

Straight to the point.

Clumsy, coarse.

'No. As far as I'm aware, this is only the second time it's happened,' Hans Morelia says.

'What about the first time? Where and when did that happen?'

'I'm prevented from disclosing that because of patient confidentiality.'

Daniel Högfeldt seems happy with that answer, and Hans Morelia wonders why he's talking to the journalist at all: how come his call was put through? But he follows his PR advisor's policy of honesty and openness. Secrecy only leads to a load of rumours that are difficult to control.

'Do you think the suicide could have anything to do with deterioration in care as a result of your cost cutting?'

'The quality of care within Merapi's businesses hasn't deteriorated, if anything it's got better. We've conducted research that—'

'I'm aware of that research. Into patient satisfaction. But the thing about research is that you can get exactly the result you want if you're the person who commissions it. You just have to ask the right questions and omit others. You know that just as well as I do. That's certainly the case with the private research company you used.'

Hans Morelia doesn't react to the allegation.

Who the hell does he think he is, this Daniel Högfeldt?

'Shouldn't you be watching your patients more closely, to ensure that something like this can't happen?'

'We can't watch over all our patients and clients twenty-four hours a day. The majority of them are basically healthy people who want to be left in peace.'

'But surely you should have seen the signs?'

'I can't discuss any individual case.'

'You don't think the reduction in staffing levels and the resulting increase in stress has anything to do with this?'

'I can't comment on that.'

'No personal thoughts?'

'OK, what are you trying to get at here? An old man has committed suicide, which is extremely tragic. Not least for his relatives. Surely you normally take that into account when you write about suicides?'

'Usually we do,' Daniel Högfeldt says, 'unless the circumstances are exceptional.'

Hans Morelia squirms on his chair. He stares at the painting on the wall, a large watercolour of young women who look like wild animals.

Shifts his gaze slightly.

And looks at all the future millionaires on the other side of the glass.

Malin listens to the voice on the phone, brittle but still full of vitality, and remembers the sculpted face from the care home, the red hair, the sorrow in those green eyes.

The gym stinks of sweat, but the smell is still better than the stench at home on Ågatan.

'I just wanted to say that I think it's really odd that Granddad could have got himself into that noose, even with the help of the bed,' Gabriella Karlsson says. 'He couldn't really have done it on his own. His shoulders were worn out, one side of his body was paralysed, and once he was lying down he had great trouble even raising himself into a sitting position.'

Malin feels like saying that willpower can release unexpected energy, that panic and exhaustion can do the same, but she holds back, because there may be something in

Gabriella Karlsson's observation. Could someone have helped Konrad Karlsson? And Malin realises that the question is hanging in the air, unspoken.

'Do you know if his bed was broken yesterday?'

'No, why?'

'Just wondering,' Malin says.

The green walls of the gym are making her feel sick. She wants to go for a run along the banks of the river, she hasn't finished tormenting her body yet, she wants to feel her heart almost burst in the hot, stagnant air, feel her body become mute with exhaustion and dehydration.

'Had your grandfather's mood changed recently?'

'No.'

'I'm sure your grandfather is where he wanted to be now,' Malin goes on. 'Perhaps he just couldn't face it any more.'

'Do you really believe that?'

Maybe it's true, Malin thinks.

Where are you? At home in your flat?

I know nothing about you beyond the fact that you're grieving.

Gabriella.

Who are you? You were one of the last people to see him alive.

'He was an electrician, after all,' Malin says. 'And they tend to be very nimble-fingered, masters at managing cables.'

Silence at the other end of the line.

'OK. Well, I just wanted to let you know,' Gabriella Karlsson says.

16

Beneath the big white parasols in Stora torget the tables are full of people drinking rosé wine and beer, savouring the late summer heat.

The hottest day of the year has turned into its most pleasant evening.

It's nine o'clock, and Malin and Tove have just finished their hamburgers on the outdoor terrace of the Central Hotel. Tove is drinking her second beer rather too quickly.

But Malin can still see that she's trying to drink considerately. She sees the condensation slowly trickle down the outside of the glass, sees the shimmering liquid and quickly grasps her own glass of cranberry juice and drains it.

Tove puts her beer back down on the table.

Malin says: 'Yes, I'd like a drink, but don't worry – I can handle it.'

A few tables away sit three men in their mid-forties, with package-holiday suntans. One of them is extremely handsome and Tove can see him looking at her mum, trying to catch her eye, but her mum's ignoring him, if she's even noticed. Then the man looks at Tove instead, his eyes roaming along the hem of her skirt, and she wants to make him look away, doesn't want him looking there.

She'd rather tell her mum to look in the man's direction, take a bit of a chance, but the last time she tried that, when she persuaded her mum to go and surprise Peter in his room up at the hospital, it really didn't turn out well.

A musician has started playing inside Mörner's Inn, and the music entices people in from the pavement. The sign of the Central Hotel glows green in the growing darkness, and the wooden decking of the terrace smells of cigarette butts and spilled beer and food rotting in the gaps. But there's also a scent of dew, of a summer's night, and even the sweet, distant smell of the river in the air.

'Do you feel like talking about what happened at work today?' Malin asks, looking at her daughter.

'No. Hilda thought I should talk to the psychologist who showed up, but I didn't. It's not a problem, Mum.'

She's OK, Malin thinks.

She's a thousand times stronger than me, and Malin thinks about the phone call she received in the gym, thinks about what Gabriella Karlsson said, and how it echoes what she herself has been wondering. Karin's post-mortem will give them the answer, and – if someone did help Konrad Karlsson with the noose – do they even want to know that? If someone helped him to die?

It's understandable that he didn't want to live any more, and in that case he had a right to end his life.

At a time of his own choosing.

Why should anyone have to travel to a clinic in Switzerland to get help to die?

The problem is that he doesn't appear to have wanted to die.

Tove says as much again now: 'I still can't get my head around the fact that he killed himself.' She takes a cautious sip of the beer, and Malin can tell that she's drinking less that she would really like to.

You're a bit too thirsty.

You're still upset.

Malin feels like telling her not to drink at all. And for a brief moment she wonders if Tove's thirst stems from her own, if her weakness, her desires, have been passed on to Tove? And shame almost makes Malin beckon the waiter over and order all the drink in the whole fucking world.

She wants to nudge Tove in the right direction. But knows that would only achieve the opposite result. Knows that she has zero credibility on the subject, so instead she asks another question. A work question.

'Did you ever talk to Konrad's granddaughter, Gabriella?'

'Not much. Mostly just hello. She was very quiet.'

'But you knew him pretty well, didn't you? You were friends, weren't you?'

Tove nods.

'It's OK to feel sad.'

'I don't want to talk about it.'

'Just don't try to soften the pain with this.'

Malin points at the beer. And quickly realises her mistake.

'That's rich, coming from you, Mum.'

'Did he ever talk about himself?'

'He talked about his wife. She died of cancer. He tried to encourage me to make the most of life.'

'Did he talk about his children?'

'He didn't like talking about them.'

Malin would like to ask why, but can see that Tove is upset. Grief is in her eyes, and Malin feels like hugging her but can't bring herself to do it.

'We mostly talked about books. Most recently Kerouac. He liked the book, the freedom it expressed, even though he could barely move.'

Malin sees Tove snap, as her eyes fill with tears, and she leans forward and holds her.

'It's OK, Mum. But he was a bit like Granddad. I mean, I haven't . . .'

'I'm sorry your grandfather's an idiot. You know that.'

'He was such a good listener. Wise.'

Tove pulls away. Wipes her tears with one hand.

'I thought we could drive up and see Stefan tomorrow,' Malin says, and Tove brightens up.

'You're off tomorrow, aren't you?' Malin says.

Tove nods.

And Malin can see thoughts swirling through Tove's head, presumably she had other plans, but she smiles and says: 'Yes, let's go and see him.'

Then Tove takes a deep gulp of beer, absorbing the drink as if it were a natural part of her.

Hans Morelia is standing on his terrace, looking out at his garden. Over towards the dense confusion of trees and shrubs. Lova is asleep, Madeleine watching television.

He's drunk half a bottle of Bourgogne, and perhaps that's why he thinks he can see someone over there. Among the trees.

'Is there someone there?' he calls. Then he calls again. No answer, no movement among the trees.

I'm imagining things, he thinks, and goes into the house. He pours himself another glass of wine.

Malin and Tove are walking home.

They pass the bars and dives along the upper part of Ågatan, almost have to push their way through the throng of people outside. Even though it's only Tuesday evening, everyone wants to be out, make the most of such a fine summer's night.

They go past the sports bar that was the scene of a drive-by shooting just a few months ago. Two rival gangs of Syrians are still fighting for control of the street.

There.

A familiar face.

No.

And Malin ducks, turns her head away, but it's too late. He's already seen her, and now she hears his voice.

'Malin . . . Malin!'

'Daniel.'

It must be two years since she last saw him, but he's the same as ever, his chiselled jawline leading to a soft chin, below a mouth with a perfectly full upper lip.

She's already heard that Daniel is no longer together with Helen Aneman, the radio presenter, an old friend of hers with whom she has completely lost touch.

Is he single now?

Pull yourself together, Malin. But the thought cheers her up. So I've still got it in me.

'How are things? It's been a while.'

He leans forward and gives her a hug.

She stiffens and feels like pushing him away, definitely doesn't want to return the hug, and she hears Tove snigger.

'Relax, Mum.'

And then Malin wants to keep hold of him, feel his warmth, but she still pulls free, leaving Daniel with a hurt expression.

The pink light of the sign outside the bar.

The touts trying to entice customers into the kebab restaurant, Hakepi.

The warm air rolling down the hill from the cathedral, its green tower lit up against the sky, the gold cross at the top.

I used to love having him inside me.

And Malin digs her fingernails into the palms of her hands.

'Fine,' she says. 'How about you?'

'Good, I'm back at the *Correspondent*.'

Tove's stopped sniggering now, and Daniel Högfeldt holds out his hand and they shake hands. It occurs to Malin that they never met back then, when she and Daniel were fucking each other's brains out. Because that was all we did, wasn't it?

His brown eyes.

I'd forgotten your brown eyes. Your soft, warm hands.

And Malin says: 'It's good to see you. But we've got to be up early tomorrow.'

'I'm off to see a few colleagues in Stora torget. A standard hacks' piss-up.'

They part as quickly as they met, disappearing from each other once again. Then Malin hears Daniel's voice: 'Is there anything else you can tell me about the old man at the Cherub?'

That is what he shouts, isn't it?

Ever the journalist.

But what does he know about Konrad Karlsson, and why is he interested in a suicide? Does he want to get at Morelia, Merapi? Can he smell scandal?

Tove doesn't seem to have heard the question. She's still walking. Malin stops, feels like saying something caustic to Daniel, tell him to stick it up his journalist's arse and fuck off.

But he's gone, swallowed up by Stora torget. And with him goes his question, if it ever existed.

Daniel Högfeldt stops outside the Central Hotel. Looks for his friends on the outdoor terraces.

She looks older, he thinks. But not tired or worn out, healthier, actually, as if she were no longer drinking. At the same time she seemed distant, though. Not really there.

He wonders if he should call her.

Have I even got her number any more? I can always get hold of her at the station.

Malin.

Again.

After the madness with Helen.

Why am I drawn to crazy women? he thinks, as his eyes search among the tables.

There they are. He waves to his friends.

She's still hot, Daniel Högfeldt thinks, permitting himself that thought.

She can't hurt me any more.

The stench is hanging heavy inside the flat when Malin and Tove get home. They forgot to leave the windows open.

'Shit,' Malin hisses, and Tove holds her nose.

'Where the hell's it coming from?' Malin says as she opens the kitchen window.

When they've opened all the windows in the flat, they lean out of the living-room window, looking at the grey-white façade of St Lars Church.

Breathing in the clean, fresh air.

'I'll give Anticimex a call, they can come while we're out tomorrow. We've got to put a stop to this.'

'Yes, we really have,' Tove says.

17

I walk past you. All of you sitting on the pavement terraces drinking beer. I've had a few myself, but I can't sit with you, nor do I want to.

None of you notice me, and why should you? Nothing special about me, nothing worth bothering about or noticing. I am the same colour as the hotel, as the pavements, as the night sky. I sound like the mumble your voices merge into.

You can sit there together and try to reduce me to nothing. You might even succeed, but when you least suspect it I'll pop up again. And when that happens, you really should steer clear. Your smiles will freeze, your mumbling will turn to screams.

The pistol is in its hiding place. Glistening with oil, and not long ago I was standing in a garden, looking in through big windows.

At happiness.

Wealth.

All the things I will never have.

But perhaps I could take the most valuable thing someone else has?

18

Malin had to wake Tove up an hour ago. The three beers Tove drank last night meant that she was tired when her alarm went off, but not hungover. Now she's asleep, with the passenger seat folded back. Malin takes her eyes off the road and looks at her daughter, her perfect skin, the thin veins on her exposed neck.

She avoided asking Tove about the autumn last night. About what her plans were. She wants to let Tove raise the subject herself. Not that Malin is worried about Tove, apart from those beers – she recognised that sort of thirst all too well.

She doesn't want to think about how happily and naturally Tove gulped down the forbidden liquid, because if you don't think about something, it isn't happening. Tove's just sad about Konrad Karlsson. There's nothing wrong with a beer or two after something like that. Just not too many.

Everything is tranquil around them.

The forest – birches, pines, firs – edging the road is beautiful, almost inviting at this time of year.

No problem getting the day off. Sven said: 'Sure, things are quiet here, after all.'

It takes five hours to drive up to Sjöplogen, to Stefan, and Malin hopes they've got everything sorted out now, and that Stefan will be in a better state than last time. Things could hardly have got any worse.

He won't recognise Tove or her this time either. But perhaps he'll give her one of his smiles, might give a little sigh of pleasure like he sometimes does.

Malin keeps trying, she wants to feel attached to him as the brother he is, the person he is, but it's hard when there's no intellectual response. Or at least none that she recognises.

But I want to, she thinks.

I know it's right, I want to find pure compassion, and the wheel vibrates in her hands. She looks away from the road towards Tove again, still sleeping. Her soft cheek is speckled with the light coming through the side window, the shadows of the foliage.

Almost there.

Hope he's OK.

Hope so.

They park in front of the beautiful old building. The plaster is worn and the grass in the garden could do with cutting, the trees with pruning. They don't see any patients out in the garden, even though the sun is high in the clear sky and the temperature is a very pleasant twenty degrees.

It's cooler this much further north.

They go inside the home, pressing the button to open the door automatically, trying not to worry about the fact that there's no sign of any staff, that no one has noticed their arrival.

Malin and Tove are trying hard to stay positive, even though they manage to get up to the second floor, where Stefan's room is, without being noticed, and try to feel happy as they open the door. But when they walk in and the stench of excrement hits them, far worse than the stench in the flat, when they see the figure lying in bed, curled up against the wall, they are initially disgusted, then angry. Stefan blinks as he scratches at his backside with his fingers. His fingernails are torn and there's a filthy incontinence pad, heavy with piss, lying at the head of the bed.

'Bastards,' Malin whispers. 'We'll sort this out, Stefan, don't you worry.' She strokes his thinning blond hair, and he doesn't react, just scratches and blinks. It's like being in a room full of nothing but shame, a crime scene.

This is wrong.

Fundamentally wrong.

I'm ashamed of being human.

'BASTARDS!' Malin shouts, and Tove takes hold of her arm.

'Calm down, that won't help anyone. He'll get frightened, won't you, Stefan?'

The door opens behind them and a young man and an even younger girl in white coats peer in, and Malin yells at them: 'What the hell's going on here? Why is he lying in his own shit? Have you got any idea what's going on here?'

'Who are you?' the young man asks calmly.

'His relatives. Get out of here.'

The pair slip out as quickly as they arrived, and Tove doesn't try to calm her down any more, and says simply: 'I need stuff to wash him with. And fresh clothes and sheets. He needs to have a shower. I wonder where the storeroom is. And the bathroom. I can shower him while you make the bed and sort out some clean clothes. But first I'll try to get rid of the worst of it, so we don't get shit on our clothes. Can you pass me one of those plastic aprons over by the basin?'

Malin hands Tove an apron, watches her put it on.

The stench.

If humiliation has a smell, this is it.

A slightly older man with a goatee beard puts his head inside the room, he's the new manager, and when he sees what's happened, and that Malin is there, the woman who tore a strip off him last time she was visiting, he quickly retreats.

But Malin leaps towards the door and yanks it open, and outside stands the man, the boss, the manager. The man who lets things like this happen.

I'm going to kill you, she feels like saying, but she just shakes her head, and Kurt – was that his name? – looks scared. She takes several deep breaths through her mouth.

'How can something like this happen?' she finally says.

And Kurt says: 'Perhaps it's time to see things more realistically. Some patients pull their pads off, that's all.'

Malin wants to hit him, could hit him, and she might go to pieces at any moment. She clenches her teeth. Imagines a tumbler of shimmering, amber, oak-aged tequila. Inside her she drains the glass in an unfamiliar bar, a bar she has never been in.

Tove has found Stefan's washbowl in the wardrobe. There's soap and washcloths by the basin, and Stefan is quiet and still now, seems to be enjoying the warm water on his skin. His weak chin is relaxed and he's no longer scratching.

She rolls the sheets away. Drops the dirty laundry on the floor. Carries on washing Stefan.

Through the door Tove can hear her mother's raised voice, cold and controlled, but she can no longer hear any excuses, just slippery acceptance: 'Yes, of course it's unacceptable. But I'm afraid this sort of thing does happen . . . Cutting the staff budget means that we don't have time . . .'

Don't have time to do what? Tove thinks. Treat people like you, Stefan, decently?

And she knows how hard it is to find the time, how tired and stressed everyone is.

'It might be some consolation,' the man named Kurt goes on, 'that Stefan probably isn't aware of this unfortunate incident. He lives in a world of his own.'

A world of his own? He's got feelings. A sense of smell. Get it? Tove thinks.

He's just as much of a person as you.

Stefan offers no resistance when she sits him in his wheelchair naked and covers him with a clean yellow blanket she found in the wardrobe.

She pushes the wheelchair towards the door, opens it, and there stand her mum and Kurt the manager, silent, wary, as if their discussion had suddenly come to an end, to the surprise of them both.

'Where's the shower?' Tove asks.

'Hang on a moment,' Kurt smiles. 'You don't have to do that. I'll get—'

'Are you stupid, or something?' Tove hisses. 'Do you think I'm going to let any of you come anywhere near Stefan right now?'

The garden of the care home is flooded with light. Stefan is asleep. The anxiety he showed when they pushed him out of the back of the building and down the ramp has gone now, vanished as the sunlight hit his cheeks and the smell of excrement and chemicals was replaced by slowly maturing apples.

The bench they are sitting on is hard beneath Malin's buttocks, and the branches of the apple tree above their heads loll heavily towards the ground.

They're alone in the garden, and Malin wonders what to think about the manager's explanations and fresh promises, assurances that Stefan hadn't been lying like that for long. But he obviously had been, the shit had dried in, he could have been lying there since yesterday.

'We've got to get him out of here,' Tove says.

'I know,' Malin says. 'But where to?'

'We'll take him home. I can look after him.'

'You know that won't work.'

'So what do we do, then? Drive him to the nearest hospital?'

'Not a bad idea,' Malin whispers, and she looks at her brother, the thin body inside the clean clothes, his withered legs beneath the cotton fabric. He's sleeping soundly now, and his chin is resting on his chest in an unnatural position that somehow manages to look strangely comfortable.

'We're going to have to leave him here, Tove. I'll find out if he can be moved. But we can't take him with us. And we can't just take him to hospital.'

'Never,' Tove whispers. 'I'm not leaving here without him.'

19

The windows are close to the ceiling, and there are clouds in the sky beyond them, moving fast, and Karin thinks that it must be very windy up there, a thousand metres up. Turbulence shaking planes on their way from somewhere, towards unknown destinations. She used to like travelling, but now, after everything that has happened, she'd rather stay at home. Be with Tess, Zeke. Try to be a family.

She's often wished that the pathology lab was above ground, but somehow that wouldn't feel right.

You can just about tell that it's summer out there, but inside the lab the world consists of loneliness, surgical spirit and bodies that life has left behind.

It's almost five o'clock. Konrad Karlsson arrived yesterday, but this is the first chance she's had to conduct the post-mortem, she's been teaching on a university summer course all day. The man's two adult children have been to see the body.

Karin is still waiting for the results of the blood samples she took down at the care home. It takes longer during the summer because of holidays, but the results ought to come through any time now.

Konrad Karlsson's dissected body is lying on the post-mortem table in the middle of the room, covered by a white plastic sheet.

There's something that's not right.

The marks on the man's neck are indistinct, even for an old man who'd had a stroke and was bound to have poor circulation. They may have been made after death. Perhaps they should be larger, if they were inflicted while blood was still flowing through his veins. A noose, hands. Something else. Impossible to tell.

But on closer examination his eyes showed signs of strangulation. Tiny, almost microscopic drops of blood on the lining of the eyelids, which she was only able to see with a magnifying glass, and strong, direct light.

When she removed his nightshirt she saw bruises under his arms on both sides, as if someone had struggled to lift him up.

But they weren't that pronounced either.

He could have been dead when they occurred.

Conclusion: Konrad Karlsson could have been helped into the noose after death.

Which points to two different scenarios.

Someone murdered him and then tried to make it look like suicide. Or he wanted to make his own suicide look more dramatic than it was, and asked someone to help him. In that case the blood tests might well indicate an overdose of some sort.

Murder.

It doesn't scare her, no more than the body in front of her does. She's taught herself to be detached. She even has to do that with Tess sometimes. About the secret. And how it ought best to be handled when the child is older.

It's time to call Malin now. Or someone else in the crime unit.

The body is otherwise undamaged inside, no noticeable bleeding around any of the tissues. His organs looked like a typical old person's, and in his stomach she found the remains of a cheese sandwich and a Dime bar.

His brain is undamaged, apart from the dead tissue where the stroke hit him.

He was unlucky with the stroke.

The damage to his brain was in the parts that govern motor function, and to a certain extent the taste centre. But his intellectual capacity would have been unimpaired.

Lucky?

Konrad Karlsson's shoulder joints were badly worn, particularly on his healthy side, which must have caused him great pain.

The phone rings over on the desk.

Must be the lab.

They always call the landline when they know she's down here working and waiting for results. They know the mobile signal is hopeless.

'Karin here.'

'This is Veronica. We've got the preliminary results for you. His blood contained high quantities of the sleeping medication Xanor. Enough to knock out a bull, a fatally high dose.'

'Xanor, you said?'

'Yes.'

One of the most common sleep-inducing drugs used in the health service.

Thoughts are whirling through her head.

Someone could have tricked him into taking it, or he could have taken the lethal dose himself. And then been lifted up into the noose.

I can't make any sense of this, she thinks, and hears Veronica's voice on the other end of the line.

'Are you there, Karin?'

'Yes.'

'A dose like that would have knocked him out pretty quickly.'

'Thanks,' Karin says. 'Let me know if you find anything else.'

She hangs up, goes back to the table and stands next to Konrad Karlsson.

Can Xanor be administered intravenously?

She quickly checks on the computer.

Yes.

Need to look for puncture wounds, more closely than I already have.

Karin pulls the sheet back. She examines his skin, centimetre by centimetre, pretending that she's inspecting a lawn or a rug, that she isn't working on a human body. But there's no sign of any hole left by a needle, other than the one in his jugular vein that she made when she took the samples.

She covers him with the sheet again.

So you must have taken tablets. Or taken them dissolved in liquid.

You weren't alone. Someone must have made it look like you hanged yourself. That much I do know. Karin can feel thoughts and facts chasing each other around inside her head.

There's nothing more logical than death, nothing more illogical.

Maybe the murderer wanted to make absolutely certain that you would die, didn't know if the dose of Xanor was fatal? Or perhaps didn't expect us to be able to find it in his blood?

Malin, she thinks. You'll be able to make more sense of this than me.

There's too much that doesn't make sense.

The fact that you seemed to enjoy life, Konrad.

The absence of a suicide note. Unless it's on your laptop?

The fact that someone must have hung you up in the noose after your death.

The overdose.

Something happened here. This isn't an ordinary suicide, and in all likelihood it wasn't even suicide.

Too messy to be a case of euthanasia.

Someone meant to harm this man.

You were murdered, Konrad Karlsson.

You were murdered.

Murdered.

I was murdered.

So who was I? What was the life that has now come to an end actually like?

A very long time ago I caught the bus from Borensberg in to Linköping, to vocational college. There was no question of me going to high school, not even with my grades. I was allowed to become an intellectual manual labourer, started work as an electrician to pay off the last of the debts from the farm, the debts Mother was so ashamed of.

She said: 'You've got to.'

So I did.

It was just her and me.

I was sixteen when I ran my first cable, connected my first box, screwed up my first armature. And it filled me with emptiness. The hateful emptiness of work that keeps us alive.

In death I want to see the people who were taken from me.

My father.

A daughter, my wife.

But they're still hiding.

Come out, come out, I feel like whispering. I'm with you now.

20

Malin waves her hand above Stefan's face. She's trying to fan him, because the room feels strangely warm.

They've put him to bed, after speaking to the manager and several of the staff, and everyone has reassured them: 'It won't happen again.'

'Has it happened before?'

'Oh, no. Definitely not.'

Now Malin and Tove are standing by Stefan's bed. He's awake, and his blue eyes are staring at the window, possibly through it, at the evening sky with its lingering veils of cloud. There's an emptiness in his eyes, but hopefully also a calmness. Tove puts her hand on his shoulder, and Malin finds herself thinking: Can you feel that hand? Do you even know that you have a shoulder? Do you know that we're actually here?

'Goodbye,' Malin says. 'I'm going to sort this out, they're going to look after you from now on.'

'We can't leave, Mum.'

'We've got to.'

Tove looks at her.

'How can you be so bloody emotionless? It's like nothing gets through to you any more.'

Malin turns her back on her daughter and walks towards the door.

'Say goodbye, Tove. It's time to go, we've got to drive home.'

'I'm staying here.'

Malin opens the door, shuts it behind her. Stands and waits in the corridor.

Five minutes. Ten.

Then Tove comes out. Her face contorted into an angry grimace.

'I hate it when you force me to be like you.'

They're halfway back to Linköping, and darkness is slowly falling as Malin and Tove stand in the car park of a Statoil petrol station. Tove is still angry, and isn't talking.

'Are you still thinking about Konrad Karlsson?' Malin asks.

Tove shakes her head.

'I'm trying not to. Right now I'm thinking about Stefan.'

Malin doesn't answer, just takes another bite of her hotdog, thinking how impossible it is to take care of anyone else, how it throws up an unwillingness to renounce anything in her own life. Anything at all.

I've left Stefan there.

In spite of what happened.

I'm no better than Morelia, Malin thinks. Then her phone rings.

Karin.

'Malin here.'

Is Karin still at work? Shouldn't she be at home with Zeke and Tess? But then Malin can usually hear Tess or the television in the background.

Malin listens as Karin tells her what she's discovered, and curses herself for not paying more attention to what she now realises was a crime scene. She hears Karin outline what she thinks happened to Konrad Karlsson, that he was probably murdered and that there's definitely a crime of some sort behind his death.

She throws the last of the hotdog away.

Sees Tove shuffling impatiently.

Feels the forbidden excitement that wells up whenever she's confronted with a crime, and then uncontrollable anger. Who the hell would kill a defenceless old man? And why?

She can't help feeling surprised, even though she did already have her suspicions.

Her mind is racing now.

Catching up with yours, Karin.

'Are you still there?' she hears Karin ask.

'Yes.'

'I've informed Sven,' Karin says. 'We agreed that I should call you.'

'OK.'

'We also agreed to lie low until tomorrow, until you get back. I've made sure that room seven is sealed off, but unfortunately it's already been cleaned up. We'll get going tomorrow, and we'll have to inform the family. It feels a bit unnecessary to upset them until we know more.'

Assuming they weren't involved, Malin thinks.

'Give Tess a hug from me,' Malin says, and ends the call.

Malin puts her phone away and turns towards Tove, who snaps: 'What is it now?'

'Looks like you were right. Your friend Konrad didn't commit suicide. He was probably murdered. Or was at least helped to kill himself.'

Tove's pupils dilate, black holes of surprise.

You're scared now as well, Malin thinks.

'I knew it,' Tove says. 'He'd never have committed suicide. And you can forget the idea that he asked someone to help him. He must have been murdered.'

'You think so?'

'I know so. Why would he ask for help with something he didn't want to do?'

Malin goes on to explain what Karin's just told her, initiating her daughter into the mysteries of death. They talk, and Tove swears that her lips are sealed. The complicity of mother and daughter drowns out the sounds of the petrol station.

Malin's phone buzzes as she's walking across the deserted Trädgårdstorget, long after midnight.

Meeting 7.30 tomorrow morning.

Sven's message has been sent to the entire investigative team.

This part of Linköping is quiet, but she can hear the noise of people drinking over at Stora torget and Ågatan.

The newsagent's on the corner is advertising betting on the horses: 'Your best chance of winning!'

Malin thinks of all the people who spend their lives hoping that chance will grant them a big win.

It's an absurd dream, but for many people it's the only one available.

Tove is lying asleep on the sofa.

She had seemed more reassured than upset by the news that Konrad Karlsson had been murdered. As if some kind of order had been restored.

There's a sort of no-man's-land between life and death, Malin thinks as she crosses Drottninggatan. A place where no rules apply, where anything can happen.

Assisted suicide, or murder?

It doesn't make any difference.

Until they establish what happened they have to regard this as murder, given that it's a distinct possibility, but they also have to remain open to the alternative.

No-man's-land.

But death is still death. No one can avoid it, and, even if it is final, it never ends.

A last breath. A few litres of air. Full of oxygen, then drained of oxygen.

Death is scentless, yet it still smells, and she walks through the Horticultural Society Park and the night smells of death, of dampness, life.

The door to the Cherub old people's home is unlocked, and there is no one at the reception desk. She creeps up the stairs.

Carries on towards room seven. Past the tape.

A hospital bed against a wall.

Otherwise the room is completely empty, clinically clean, and she looks out at the park, at the motionless, black trees, the starry sky above them.

Soon a new client will fall into Merapi's embrace.

To be treated like you, Stefan? Like you, Konrad? But at least you had a voice, Malin thinks, and makes a note to read the letters he sent to the press.

She goes over to the bed – the same bed? – and tries to raise the top end. It rises with a low hum, and she lets go of the button.

The bed has been repaired.

She feels an irresistible urge to lie down, and moments later is lying flat on the bed, imagining that she can't move.

What must it be like to lie like this for eleven years?

You'd have to cultivate an incredible calmness just to put up with it. Summon up hitherto unknown powers of resilience.

It occurs to her that she might well be the most restless person in the world, and she wants to sympathise with Konrad Karlsson, with Stefan, find some sort of sympathy beyond her anger, but there's nothing there.

She lies there on the bed, trying to imagine.

What's happening to me? Malin thinks.

Who am I becoming?

Who have I become?

Malin gets up and walks over to the window.

Outside the darkness lies dense among the trees, and across the paths and lawns.

Then she focuses her gaze.

Is there a man standing down there among the trees? Looking this way? What's he doing there?

The murderer, waiting for an opportunity to take another life?

She turns and runs out of the room, down the stairs and out into the car park. She feels her heart pound as she goes around the building and rushes into the park, towards the trees where the figure was standing.

But he's gone now.

Was he ever there?

That night Malin dreams of white bats shrieking as they hang from the rafters of a derelict house.

They screech, flap their wings, bare their teeth, but seem unwilling to let go of the wooden beams they're clinging to.

As if they're waiting for something that never happens.

And in the room beyond the bats she can see Konrad Karlsson's face, at different stages of his life.

Outside lies the city, surrounded by flat countryside and forest, and a lake where burning waves suffocate all life.

Tove dreams of all the friends she's left behind.

People from school in Linköping, her former boyfriend,

Markus, and Josefin, and then Tom at Lundsberg, who dumped her, and whom she probably wanted to be dumped by. In her dream that feeling is unambiguous, the feeling of not wanting to belong to Tom's world, of never being able to fit into it, of being stuck between worlds with no firm foothold in either one.

She dreams of posh girls and ordinary girls, and in the dream her remaining friends have no names. She enjoys the loneliness, because she has chosen it and it belongs to no one but her.

And she dreams of Konrad Karlsson.

Of his blue face, his head in the noose.

Of sitting on his bed, absorbing his wisdom, enjoying more time in his stimulating company.

And every so often an agitated alarm would blare out.

A lamp blinking out into the atmosphere, and into a lonely, silent room.

Karim Akbar is exhausted, so he lets himself orgasm, ignoring the fact that Vivianne is nowhere close to coming yet. The bedroom in their villa in Lambohov is messy, but neither of them ever has the energy to tidy up.

He rolls off Vivianne, but she doesn't look disappointed, more relieved that he's finished – when did they start making love out of habit? When she got pregnant?

When his book became a success?

When he started to get more and more lecture bookings?

Or when the Trades Union Congress called to invite him to an interview for a managerial position?

Stockholm.

Why not? He's tired of Linköping, and Vivianne wouldn't have any trouble getting a job with the Public Prosecution Service there, not with her contacts. After her maternity leave.

He's had enough of his job.

Of all the problems.

Of the staff.

Of Malin.

She seems to have repressed all her emotions, and now works like an automaton. But she still has her old intuition, and she's not drinking. In which case, everything is fine.

Sven.

He called a short while ago, to say that they were probably dealing with a murder.

A pus-filled boil.

Perhaps the murder of the old man is a boil bursting? Perhaps there'll be a huge fuss, seeing as the care home is run by Merapi? Perhaps that was the point?

He thinks about his father, who committed suicide. Karim found him in the bathroom where he had hanged himself. Weak and cowardly. He thinks that he's going to be a good father this time. Much better than he was with his son.

So the old man in Merapi's care home didn't kill himself.

Lots of media tomorrow. No question about that.

Can I bear to hold a press conference? Do I have to?

He lets his body rest heavily on the mattress, feels Vivianne's hand on his arm, feeling for his hand, then moves it between her legs.

OK. For your sake.

Johan Jakobsson is sitting in the dark in his basement, in front of his computer. The screen flickers blue, and he feels how dry his face is after a blustery day out on the lake.

His family is asleep.

The new house.

He's got an office in the basement now, he can work in peace without disturbing anyone upstairs.

But they're sleeping now, his wife and children. He woke up and couldn't get back to sleep. Might as well get some work done.

Tokyo almost finished him. It was all but impossible to make sense of the city. Life was reduced to an endless series of misunderstandings the moment he set foot outside the hotel or lecture halls.

What can I find out about Konrad Karlsson?

Anything?

There's always something to find out about everyone.

And he taps his way through the night.

Börje Svärd is lying alone in bed in his house in Tornhagen.

The bed feels big, which is nice, there's plenty of room for him, and no one is demanding his attention, no one wants anything from him.

The dogs out in the garden are quiet. The older one is taking care of the new one, barely more than a puppy. Other single people would keep the dogs indoors. Maybe even on the bed, heaven forbid.

Börje keeps them in a pen.

They'd make a hell of a racket if anyone were to come into the garden.

What sort of world, what sort of city, is this? he wonders. Where a disabled pensioner can be murdered in his bed?

It must be about money. One way or another. About greed, anger, joy and despair, all the things that come with money.

After Anna died, a life insurance policy that she had taken out before she got MS paid out. It wasn't a lot of money, but their two children got to know about it and wanted a share.

Their own children, buzzing around like flies.

He gave the entire amount, three hundred thousand kronor,

to a muscular sclerosis charity. If the money prevented just one single person from suffering like Anna did, it was worth it.

The murder victim.

Waldemar called earlier, he'd spoken to Elin Sand, who in turn had spoken to Sven.

Konrad Karlsson had evidently spent a very long time living in care.

Anna. You were younger, and ill for longer, but at least you were able to live at home. In the home you created as a reflection of your beautiful soul.

I shall never meet a soul like yours again, but the woman I'm meeting tomorrow has a body that will do.

I can pretend she's you, Anna. I hope you don't mind that?

You know how lonely I am.

Waldemar Ekenberg is asleep.

His wife isn't working tonight, and she's having trouble sleeping. Not because of Waldemar's snoring, but because she can never get used to the chaos her irregular shifts cause to her body clock.

She's lying beside him, but not touching.

He snores and snores.

Coughs.

He smokes too much. Filling his lungs with toxic fumes.

His attempts to give up have been embarrassingly pathetic, and she knows he enjoys smoking, feeling the thick, aromatic air in his lungs.

After all, she smokes as well. So she knows.

He's got calmer as the years have passed, and even if she suspects that he can be a bit crazy at work, he's meek as a lamb at home.

Almost.

He received a call this evening. Didn't want to talk about it.

As usual.

But they don't need words. Silence is good enough.

Elin Sand is looking at pictures on her computer. She sitting on the sofa in the living room, and she can hear sporadic cars using the Abisko roundabout below.

The volleyball team.

She misses those days. She sometimes wakes up in the middle of the night and gets up to look at pictures of their matches, their camaraderie.

She has something of that at work, as well as with her friends.

But it's never quite the same.

She longs to have someone next to her, the woman she met a few months ago, the woman she recognised in the aisles at Ikea, the woman who came up to her and said: 'Hi, do you remember me?'

'I'm hardly likely to forget,' she had replied, and that broke the ice, and made everything somehow obvious. She loves the softness she can feel in herself now, the way she's in touch with her feelings. Malin Fors could do with a bit of that.

Sometimes she takes her own crap out on me, Elin thinks. Most recently in the gym, when it became abundantly clear that Malin didn't want her anywhere near her.

I suppose I'm just going to have to put up with that. There's only one way to stop it, and that's by getting a better job.

That would show her, and the rest of them.

21

It all has to go somewhere.

The anger I feel.

Sometimes I follow the girl. I don't know why. I've sat in the car in the car park outside that tall building. Seen his drones come and go. Their eyes firmly fixed on the money.

I'm lying in bed now, looking up at the ceiling. There are spiders' webs in the corners, but I can't see any spiders.

Could I take aim at another human being, and pull the trigger? Abduct someone?

The girl.

Living grief is the worst of all. Anger. Feeling shut in.

I'll wake up tomorrow, and maybe tomorrow will be the day when everything happens. The day when I finally find the right way to go about it. Finally find the courage.

There's no order to anything. Dirt, bills, thoughts. I can't bear anyone else telling me what to do, but I still can't make any decisions myself.

I've got the pistol.

I know how to do it.

The girl.

She's the solution.

22

Sven Sjöman is standing in the hall of his house in Ånestad, putting on the tie his wife gave him for his birthday. He doesn't often wear a tie, but today it feels right. They're going to be having a morning meeting to set up the investigation into Konrad Karlsson's murder.

What happened?

They'll have to find out if the old boy had any money. If he'd upset anyone. If he had any enemies.

The idea that a sick old man might have had enemies might sound ridiculous, Sven thinks, but he's experienced far stranger things in the course of his career.

Seventy-nine years old.

He suffered a stroke when he wasn't much older than I am now. I only just managed to survive prostate cancer. That's how it felt, anyway.

I shall retire next year, and I want Malin to succeed me.

So what state are you in now? You seem to have calmed down, you're back in control of your feelings, your impulses.

You're playing at being in control.

You think you can suppress everything instead of dealing with it.

You're deceiving yourself.

I know.

Nothing can ever be swept under the carpet, everything ends up out in the open at some point, and can cause all sorts of trouble.

The tie feels tight around his neck, it's a warm morning.

He's going to miss mornings like this, full of conflicted anticipation about the day ahead.

The whole of the violent crime unit is gathered in the conference room in the police station, seated around the table.

Waldemar Ekenberg is leaning back in his chair, dressed in a short-sleeved nylon shirt. Johan Jakobsson looks hollow-eyed, he's probably spent half the night working, Malin thinks, digging out anything he could find about Konrad Karlsson.

Karim isn't there, but Börje Svärd is, he looks like he's lost some weight, probably keeping himself in shape during the swimming season, and his associated escapades with the ladies.

Zeke is sitting next to her.

And, at the end of the table, Elin Sand, wearing a white cotton dress that's a little too figure-hugging.

Those cheekbones.

Perfectly formed, Malin thinks.

She wishes she could treat Elin better as part of the team, but she hasn't felt capable of that, even if they'd probably enjoy each other's company, what with them both being fitness fanatics.

As a detective she's still a bit like a puppy. Unless I just can't help seeing her as competition?

So what?

Sven Sjöman is wearing a tie, and it seems like he's got a bit more energy now that he's made up his mind that this will be his last year. Even so, he's still more sluggish than he ought to be at times.

He writes Konrad Karlsson's name on the whiteboard, and outside the windows, in the garden of the preschool, the children are running about, playing in the sun, secret games that no grown-up could understand.

There are fewer children during the holidays, but the preschool is still open, and Malin watches the wind ruffle a little blond boy's hair.

'So what do we know?' Sven says, then goes on to outline what they've got.

The time: that Konrad Karlsson probably died some time between two and three o'clock in the morning.

That he somehow received an overdose of the sleep medication, Xanor, although exactly how is as yet unclear.

'Was he given that often?' Zeke asks.

'We need to speak to his doctor at the Cherub,' Börje says.

'Or the manager, Hilda Jansson,' Malin adds. 'She's bound to know.'

Sven explains about the marks Karin found on Karlsson's neck and under his arms, suggesting that he was already dead before he was put in the noose.

'She forgot to cordon off the room,' Waldemar says. 'Bloody sloppy.'

The room falls silent, and everyone turns to look at Zeke, who remains impassive.

'Everyone makes mistakes,' Sven says. 'Just look at the Palme investigation.'

The detectives laugh, then, once they've quietened down, Sven points out the lack of a suicide note, and goes on to say that Konrad Karlsson was, reportedly, a happy man: 'This whole thing stinks. We treat it as murder. Why would anyone who helped him to commit suicide make it more complicated for themselves? The pills on their own would have been enough.'

'I'm not so sure,' Johan says.

The group falls silent, waiting for Johan to go on.

'Konrad Karlsson had written several letters to the papers, about what he believed to be poor care. He was certainly a thorn in the side of Merapi, the company that runs the home, to put it mildly. And now Merapi is about to be sold to an American venture capital company, Nexxon. There's an article about the deal on the *Dagens Industri* website.'

'What do you mean?' Malin says. 'That Merapi might have something to do with this? That they wanted to shut him up and stop him writing more letters that could jeopardise the sale of the company? It seems a bit far-fetched to suggest that such a large-scale deal could be affected by something like that, Johan. Even if he didn't exactly mince his words.'

Malin looks at Johan.

Aware that he's thinking more than that, and hoping to provoke him into saying more.

She thought the same thing herself earlier that morning.

Johan goes on: 'What if Konrad Karlsson staged his suicide in a way that would get as much attention as possible? Took enough sleeping pills to drift off, having given his accomplice instructions to make it look like a brutal hanging. In order to focus media attention on the circumstances inside the company's care homes. Stick a spoke in the wheel.'

'One final sacrifice,' Malin says, noticing the sceptical look on Sven's face.

'Do you really believe that?' he asks, and Malin notices the way the other detectives smell: smoke, sweat, soap, toothpaste, aftershave.

'We need to keep an open mind,' Johan says. 'That's all I mean,' and Malin realises that there's far too much scope here for wild speculation.

'We'll hold back from talking to anyone at Merapi,' Sven

says. 'We haven't got a good enough reason yet. But it might turn out to be necessary later on.'

'Did he have any money?' Waldemar asks, to no one in particular. 'Did his kids stand to inherit much?'

Johan says: 'I haven't got that far yet.'

'We'll have to file information requests with his bank and the Tax Office,' Sven says.

It feels like the conversation is drifting, and Malin wants to tell Sven to get a grip on things, to create some sort of structure.

'We need to start by trying to find out what happened in the care home that night,' she said. 'Establish a timeline.'

Sven picks up the theme: 'Maybe there are surveillance cameras in the area? Inside the Cherub, or the entrance, at least? We need to talk to people living nearby who might have seen something, but primarily the night staff. Even if they said they didn't notice anything unusual when we spoke to them on Tuesday. And the day shift. One of them could have been involved.'

Sven pauses, looks at Malin.

Who looks away.

The day shift. Tove.

Sven goes on quickly: 'And we talk to any residents who can actually be questioned. As well as Konrad Karlsson's family. Children and grandchildren.'

'Have they been informed of the latest developments?' Waldemar asks.

'No,' Sven says. 'We'll do that when we speak to them.'

'Did he have a computer?' Johan asks. 'He should have done.'

Malin remembers the computer from her first visit. His mobile. And that Gabriella had wanted to take them with her, and that she had let her. She curses that decision now.

'Yes, he did. And a mobile. His granddaughter, Gabriella,

has them. We'll have to get them back,' Malin says. 'There might even be a suicide note on the computer, although that seems highly unlikely.'

Johan nods.

And Börje leans across the grey surface of the table and says: 'What's the situation with mercy killings these days? There've been a couple of cases of people helping old people in homes to die, as acts of mercy.'

Börje raises his hands to indicate quotation marks around the last word.

Silence in the room once more.

And Malin finds herself thinking of his wife, Anna.

Realises that Börje must have given a great deal of thought to the whole concept of mercy.

'I'll get that checked out,' Sven says. 'In case some nutter's just got out after serving their sentence.'

'Could other old folk be in danger, then?' Börje asks. 'Do you think we could even be dealing with a proper lunatic here?'

'The uniforms can call around to other homes and see if anyone has noticed anything suspicious.'

Elin Sand has been sitting silently throughout the meeting, but now she says: 'Maybe this is a case of assisted suicide after all. Whoever helped him die could have just got scared and panicked. Who wouldn't? He or she probably isn't a professional, and the noose was a clumsy attempt to make it look like an ordinary suicide. Make it look like Konrad Karlsson did it himself. Whoever helped him would have cared about him a very great deal, so they'd now be both very upset, and very frightened.'

None of the other detectives says anything.

Don't really want to consider what she's just said.

But Elin Sand could be right.

'You've just said what I was going to suggest,' Malin

says. 'Well, if we keep an open mind, the answers will come. Sven, do you want to share out the work? Who's going to interview whom? Johan, you keep digging. Anywhere you can.'

What am I doing? Malin wonders.

She looks at Sven, who smiles before carrying on. He meets her gaze, as if to say: See? You're already leading the team. Whether you like it or not.

Elin Sand is sitting at the end of the table, looking unhappy.

'Let's get going,' Malin says.

23

The crooked apple trees look like Snow White's dwarfs, Malin thinks. They're a good match for the tiny cottage in whose garden they stand.

The faded rust-red wooden house lies a few kilometres outside Klockrike, and the broad expanse of the Östgöta Plain stretches out in all directions; golden fields of rape sway back and forth beneath a sky that is getting bluer and bluer.

A rusty black Mercedes, an old model, is parked next to the house. This must be a terrible place in the winter, when the cold bites at your soul and icy storms rage unchecked.

Yngve Karlsson.

So this is where you live. As Malin and Zeke get out of the car they see a man working in a vegetable garden behind some ragged gooseberry bushes.

He's tall and lanky, his clothes hang from his body, and he seems relaxed, even if Malin can't help sensing that he'd like nothing more than to turn and run off across the plain.

He's clearing one of the beds, jerkily tossing the weeds behind him, and is evidently content to let her and Zeke go to him rather than the other way around. He takes a quick glance at them and seems to conclude that they're OK.

They walk through the garden towards the vegetable

patch, and Yngve Karlsson straightens up and holds his hand out towards them.

'You're police, aren't you? I heard about Dad on the local news a little while ago. They're saying you think he was murdered.'

Shit, Malin thinks. How the hell has it got out so quickly? Someone at the station must have leaked the news, and then the reporter didn't bother to find out if the victim's family already knew.

There's no visible emotion on Yngve Karlsson's thin face as he mentions his father's fate, and the look in his soft blue eyes is one of resignation.

Malin shakes his hand, then her mobile starts to ring.

She recognises the number.

Gabriella Karlsson.

Malin excuses herself, gestures to Zeke, then clicks to take the call as she moves away through the garden.

A voice at the other end, thick with crying.

'So he was murdered? Who could have wanted to do that? I just read it on the *Correspondent*'s website. Why wasn't I told before them? Surely I had a right to know first?'

What can I say? Malin thinks.

'It's true that we suspect that your grandfather was murdered,' she says.

'But how?'

The voice sounds more composed now, and Malin is surprised to find herself wondering if Gabriella Karlsson merely wants to hear how much they know.

So the *Correspondent* hadn't revealed how Konrad Karlsson had been murdered.

'We're in the middle of the investigation, so I can't go into—'

'Surely you can tell me?'

'I'm afraid not,' and Malin can hear desperation now, grief, but is it genuine? Is Gabriella Karlsson faking it?

No.

She seems to have been the only person who really cared about Konrad Karlsson.

Malin looks over at Zeke and Yngve Karlsson. It looks like they're talking about gardening, as Yngve lights a cigarette with trembling hands.

'Gabriella, we're going to want to talk to you again. Perhaps I can explain a bit more then.'

'When?'

'Some time today. I'll let you know. By the way, have you got your grandfather's laptop with you? And his mobile?'

'Yes.'

'We're going to need to look at them.'

'I'm going to the Tinnerbäck pool. You can come there. I'll take his things with me.'

Gabriella Karlsson is breathing deeply, seems to have calmed down, accepting that she is merely one small part of a process that needs to run its course.

I'll never get used to the sound of dentist's drills, Elin Sand thinks.

Margaretha Karlsson receives her and Waldemar Ekenberg in her treatment room at Dentalia, a private dental clinic on the third floor of a fancy art nouveau building on Hospitalstorget. She's sitting on a stool at her desk in a white coat, and Elin Sand can tell from her translucent blue eyes that Margaretha Karlsson drinks too much. She's skinny, but she has an alcoholic's red, swollen face, and she looks considerably older than her fifty-five years.

The sound of the drills in the other rooms penetrates the walls, and Elin and Waldemar are standing in the doorway, haven't been invited to sit down on the two spare stools.

Elin is annoyed with Waldemar.

In the car just now he called her 'Poppet'. And when she told him to shut up, he just grinned at her.

Margaretha Karlsson looked shaken when they told her that her father had probably been murdered. But she quickly composed herself, and now doesn't seem particularly surprised as she says: 'He wasn't short of enemies. I don't suppose the company that runs the home was especially fond of the things he wrote.'

'Did he ever mention any kind of threat from them?' Elin Sand asks, looking at the treatment chair and feeling a shiver of unease run down her spine.

Margaretha Karlsson shakes her head.

'Nothing at all?' Waldemar Ekenberg asks.

'I had no contact with my father. He was an extremely difficult person. You might have got the impression that he was a wonderful man, but he was very judgemental towards me and my brother.'

'In what way?'

Now that Margaretha Karlsson has started to talk, Elin Sand wants to push her to say more.

'Nothing we did with our lives was good enough for him. I became a dentist. I've got a family. But that wasn't good enough. Messing about with other people's teeth? When you've got a good head on your shoulders? That's the sort of thing he used to come out with, and you soon get fed up of being put down like that. In the end I just had enough.'

'When did you last see him?'

'About two years ago. I went to visit him on his birthday.'

'And you haven't spoken to him since then?'

Margaretha Karlsson shakes her head.

'No.'

'What were you doing on the night between Monday and Tuesday?'

Margaretha Karlsson laughs.

'You can't seriously think that I murdered my own father?'

Neither Waldemar nor Elin answers.

'OK. I was at home asleep. You can check with my husband. I'll give you his work number.'

'Thanks,' Elin Sand says.

'I suppose there's a lot to do now,' Waldemar Ekenberg says. 'Sorting out his estate and everything.'

'Gabriella's in charge of that, thank God. That was all arranged a long time ago. She was the only one he trusted, and the only one he actually liked.'

'What about you and your brother? Do you get on?'

'We're very different. He's a bit of a loner. So no, we don't have much to do with each other.'

Another drill starts up in one of the adjoining rooms, and Elin Sand feels oddly exposed.

'Do you own this clinic?' she asks. 'Or is it part of a larger business?'

'I own my treatment room, so to speak. A company within a larger company. Merapi wanted to buy the whole clinic, but the amount they offered was a joke.'

Margaretha Karlsson looks at Elin Sand.

Seems to want to say: Time for you to leave now.

'Thanks. I don't think we've got any more questions for the time being,' Elin says.

On the way down in the lift Waldemar puts his hand on her arm and says: 'You did well there, Poppet.'

Elin feels like smashing his yellow teeth in and ramming them down his throat, but she clenches her jaw and says nothing, just focuses on the movement of the lift instead.

Yngve Karlsson has made coffee in the shabby kitchen of the cottage, and says: 'I like living out here. Managing on my own.' He pauses before going on: 'I'm on holiday at the moment. Otherwise I work for Mekaniska in Motala.'

Malin tries to make herself comfortable on the stiff, ladder-backed chair, and looks around at the pale blue 1950s cupboards, and the coffee is hot and fresh, just what she needs to give her a bit of energy.

'Did your father have any enemies? Is there anything we ought to know about him?'

Yngve Karlsson shakes his head.

Slowly at first. Then more firmly.

'I don't think he had any enemies. Who would that be?'

'The people he wrote letters about?' Zeke suggests.

'Is that what you're thinking? Seems a bit far-fetched.'

Yngve Karlsson's tone is aggressive as he makes that last remark.

'Maybe not,' Malin says. 'There's a lot of money at stake.'

'Speaking of money,' Yngve Karlsson says. 'My father had money. Several million in the bank. He was very good with shares. I think he was still trading right up to the end. Through his computer. He enjoyed it. That much I do know.'

Yngve Karlsson is almost spitting the words out now.

'So he was a rich man?'

Malin can barely conceal her surprise, and feels momentarily at a loss for words.

'I've never been very interested in money, but my father was. I think that was one of the reasons why we didn't get on, why he had no respect for me. He kept a firm bloody hold on his money.'

You're very definite about that, Malin thinks. Angry, almost. About your lack of interest in money. But you're still going to get some, and Malin looks around at the faded wallpaper and sagging beams in the ceiling. This house needs renovating if you're going to stop it from falling down. And those betting slips over on the kitchen worktop are pretty unambiguous.

'There'll be a lot to inherit, then,' Zeke says.

'Bound to be. We'll see once his estate has been sorted out. That could take years, though. And who knows what might happen in the meantime?'

Yngve Karlsson's voice is dripping with bitterness.

'When did you last see your father?' Malin asks.

'Like I said, we didn't get on. It's a long time ago now. I visited him at the Cherub five years ago. But he asked me to leave after just ten minutes. Said he needed to sleep. You need to understand that he was quite an odd character, and could be very hard towards me and Margaretha.'

Yngve Karlsson's voice is calmer now.

As if he had come close to losing control, but had pulled himself together again.

'What about your other sister, Gabriella's mother? She died of an infection, didn't she?'

'So you know about that too?'

Zeke murmurs affirmatively.

'He was nicer towards her. I don't know why,' Yngve Karlsson says.

'Nicer in what way?' Malin asks.

'Friendly. Towards me and Margaretha he was mostly just unpleasant.'

Yngve Karlsson closes his eyes and takes a deep breath. He seems to want to say more about his dead sister, but changes his mind and says instead: 'I know he and Gabriella got on well. He liked the fact that she was interested in history.'

'I'm afraid we have to ask this,' Malin says, pushing her fringe aside. 'What were you doing on the night between Monday and Tuesday?'

Yngve Karlsson shakes his head.

'I was here, at home. Like I always am. I prefer to be on my own. I get nervous just seeing anyone coming towards the house.'

So I saw, Malin thinks.

'Can anyone confirm that you were at home?' Zeke asks.

'No,' Yngve Karlsson says. 'You'll just have to take my word for it. And out here on the plain that still means something.'

On the way out Malin notices a gun cupboard in the living room.

Is that a pistol in there?

She considers going over to check, but decides against it.

'Do you hunt?' she asks.

Yngve Karlsson smiles.

'A long time ago. I've only got my shotgun left now. I use it to shoot squirrels sometimes. And if you live as isolated as this, you never know who might show up.'

Judgemental? Hard?

I helped build Saab's second assembly hall for the Flying Barrel, and the old boys worked me hard. The boss gave me every tiny little job that needed doing outdoors during that freezing winter.

I met your mother at the outdoor dance floor at Linköping Folkets Park, and Josefina was born just a few years later. Your mother, Sara, was very young, and we lived in a one-room apartment on Konsistoriegatan.

And then you came along. Yngve, Margaretha.

And now you think I was a hard man.

I just wanted you to do something with your lives. The way I was never allowed to.

Three children.

All of you young when your mother died.

She fell sick in February, died in the cruellest of Aprils. Young people aren't supposed to die of pancreatic cancer, but she did.

She used to shout out for you at nights in the hospital. I never told you that.

I can't leave them, she used to scream.

Then she died in my arms, and we buried her together. Do you remember that?

We were left alone.

My mother, your grandmother, kept her distance. She'd met a new man, and they moved to Jönköping.

I used to read my books after you'd all gone to bed. Sitting up in the living room of the little house I'd bought out in Jägarvallen.

I may have been a bit hard sometimes.

The women from the council didn't trust a single father, the scrawny electrician whose shoulders slumped more and more with each passing day. I had to maintain discipline. But you used to sit with me, on my lap, on the sofa, in front of the black-and-white television.

Yngve. Margaretha.

I had trouble coming to terms with your lack of ambition. I understand that now.

You had every opportunity, even though your mother left you so early.

I put my faith in your sister. She was going somewhere.

I'm trying to find Josefina here.

Is she a breath now, the beautiful daughter who left me?

Is your mother here? Her pain and anguish.

Maybe I should have asked your forgiveness. I never did. I wanted your gratitude instead, but I never got it.

I was certainly bitter about a lot of things. I didn't want to admit it, and no one else wanted to see it. A sick person can get away with being demanding, but it's best to keep your bitterness to yourself.

You wanted my money.

I won a decent amount on the racing at Mantorp a few years before I fell ill. And I made a profit from the sale of the house in Jägarvallen.

I managed to grow the money, wanted to prove to myself that all those hotshots in Stockholm weren't so special. I bought and sold shares, options.

When I fell ill, it was already too late.

For you, and for me. But mostly for us.

It was always easy with Gabriella. She did as I wanted. As I hoped.

Now I can't help wondering: How much did you really like me, Gabriella?

24

The cancer hours.

The time between twelve and two, when the summer sun makes your skin bubble, waking deadly cancer genes to life.

It's just gone one o'clock, and Malin feels hunger take hold of her stomach, squeezing it until she feels nauseous.

Her back is wet with sweat. The sun is relentless between the clouds, and all around them children are throwing themselves into the water, either the chlorine-stinking fifty-metre pool, or the black depths of the freshwater pool.

Malin wishes she could slip into a bathing suit and escape the heat, swim herself into oblivion, feel her muscles drain of energy, until she reaches the state of nothingness that only physical exertion can achieve.

But not here.

Now she's concentrating on Gabriella Karlsson, who's lying stretched out on a strangely colourless towel on the grass.

Malin is crouching down beside her, while Zeke has slipped into the shade of an oak tree. By the kiosk, at the top of the tiered seating area, there's a long queue of children on their summer holidays, eager for ice cream and hotdogs. She says hello, then goes on: 'Would you say you had a special relationship, you and your grandfather?'

Gabriella sits up. Adjusts her turquoise bathing costume.

'I didn't have anyone else.'

'And he supported you in your research?'

'He was the one who got me interested in history. When I was thirteen or fourteen, we used to go off in his car at weekends. We drove around Östergötland, and he taught me about everything that's happened here over the centuries. He used to spend hours talking about the Linköping Bloodbath and the battle of Stångebro. He brought it all to life.'

You sound like you were a bit too soft on him, Malin thinks. Or am I just being cynical? Maybe you're a truly good person, Gabriella Karlsson. The sort who takes care of people who need looking after.

Noisy cries from the water.

Hunger.

'Believe it or not, I loved it. I had plenty of imagination, and not many friends. All those stories of his. A lot of people would have found it really boring.'

In some ways you remind me of Tove, Malin thinks. You're really very similar.

A bookworm, certainly.

The sort who likes stories.

Get to the point, Malin.

But she embarks on another digression.

'You visited your grandfather the evening before he died, and didn't leave until eleven o'clock or so?'

Malin can see Zeke talking on his mobile over in the shade. Karin, probably. What are they talking about? Tess? What they're going to have for dinner?

'Did you usually stay that late?'

'Fairly often. Grandfather was always at his best in the evenings. He was often awake late into the night.'

'Did he take sleeping tablets?'

'Him? Never. He didn't like the way they made him feel drowsy. Always said his brain had enough to deal with.'

'Did anything particular happen that evening?'

'No.'

'Nothing?'

'No. I arrived, we talked about this and that. I'd taken a newspaper and some lottery scratch cards with me, the way I sometimes did. I left when the night staff were doing their last round of the evening. The usual ones, with Berit in charge. He liked her.'

'Nothing else?'

'I took him a Dime bar. His sense of taste changed after he had the stroke. He only liked sweet things after that.'

'You didn't go back later?'

Gabriella Karlsson flinches. She's clearly horrified at the inference behind Malin's question. She seems to want to reply instantly, but stops herself.

After a pause of some ten seconds, she says: 'No, I didn't. Definitely not.'

'You didn't help your grandfather with anything?'

'No.'

'You don't know anyone else who might have done? Helped him?'

Words that remain unspoken. What truths can they entice into the light? Malin thinks. What answers are concealed in the non-answers?

Listen to the voices of the investigation, Malin, listen to the silent voices, as Sven always used to tell her at the start of her career.

'He must have been murdered. He didn't want to die.'

Gabriella Karlsson puts her black sunglasses on and turns her face towards the sun, but, after just a few seconds, she turns back towards Malin again and takes them off.

Tears in her eyes.

From the sun? Grief?

'You've found out that he had money?'

'Several million, from what we've heard.'

'Something like that. I don't know exactly how much.'

Malin can see that Zeke has finished his call. He's sunk down onto the grass, and in the shade his face almost fades into the dark trunk of the oak.

'A few years ago, at one of the few Christmases we spent together, I heard my aunt and uncle talk about Granddad's money. They thought it was wrong that he wasn't doing anything with it. Because of course he had no real need of it in the home.'

'So what did he do with the money?'

'Nothing, as far as I know. He bought a flat for me. But apart from that I don't know. He never talked about it.'

'Will you inherit it now?' Zeke asks.

Gabriella shrugs.

'I suppose I'll get a bit of money. Seeing as Mum's dead.'

'Should be quite a lot,' Malin says.

'I'm not bothered about money. Anything I do get will go to charity. Granddad would have liked that.'

'Couldn't he have done that himself?' Malin asks.

'That was just a way of saying what he was like. We never talked about money.'

'What did you think about what you heard your aunt and uncle saying?'

'That they were vultures.'

'Are they?'

'Margaretha's interested in money and status, that much is obvious. She likes to think of herself as belonging to the smart set in Linköping.'

'And does she?'

Gabriella smiles.

'No. She hasn't got enough money for that. She's only a dentist, nothing special.'

'Do you think she or your uncle could have anything to do with your grandfather's death?'

'No, I don't, actually. But money can make people a bit crazy. That's pretty common knowledge.'

'Anything else you think we should know?'

'I think my uncle's got gambling debts. He gambles a lot, I know that. He used to go to the races at Mantorp with Granddad when he was little. He's mad about betting on the horses.'

Malin sighs.

Those betting slips out at Yngve Karlsson's house. But he didn't mention anything.

There were far too many things he and Margaretha Karlsson hadn't mentioned.

And neither of them seems remotely sad about their father's death.

As if he'd never existed.

Just like me. Dad might just as well be dead down there on the Canary Islands. It wouldn't make any difference.

'Is Yngve in trouble with debt collectors?' Malin goes on. 'Could he have borrowed money from the wrong people?'

'I don't know. I think he got beaten up once, but I'm not sure.'

Something else to ask him, Malin thinks.

'What about your grandfather: do you know if he received any threats after he wrote those letters to the paper about the home?'

Gabriella Karlsson leans back and rests her elbows on the towel.

'He never said anything.'

'Were you involved in those at all? Did you help him write them?'

'No. That was all him. He wrote them himself. But I

think it's good that he did. Pointing out the shortcomings in the care system. He wasn't frightened of anything or anyone.'

'What did you do after you left the Cherub?'

'I went home. Read a book. Then went to bed.'

'What book?'

'*The Third Man*. Graham Greene.'

'Were you alone?'

'Yes,' Gabriella Karlsson says. 'I'm always alone.'

Gabriella Karlsson watches the police officers walk away, alien creatures among the bathers.

It's as if none of this is happening to her, as if none of it affects her at all.

Death.

Evil.

She knows about that sort of thing in history. But in the here and now it seems to slip away from her. Could she have suppressed something? Something big, important? The mind can do that, suppressing things to help you cope.

Granddad.

You're no longer here.

She takes off her sunglasses. Looks up at the sun. Feels tears begin to flow.

Money. Alibis. Dependencies, confidences, desires; words that remain unspoken, silences that could mean anything at all.

Malin feels even hungrier as she and Zeke leave the swimming baths.

Gabriella had her grandfather's laptop and mobile with her, just as she'd promised. She made a point of saying she hadn't even looked at them, and thought their contents were just as private as a diary.

Malin turns around.

Sees Gabriella Karlsson lying on her back, staring up at the sun without sunglasses. Her skin is unnaturally white: a person who usually shuns the light, and who has realised the potential of loneliness.

'Let's get some food,' Zeke says.

Malin nods.

'Then we can go and give Johan the computer and mobile.'

25

I went down to the Tinnerbäck baths today.

Didn't go to the shooting range this morning, far too tired.

I'm lying in the sun. On the concrete seating, and I'm wearing dark sunglasses so no one can see what I'm looking at.

I like the sun.

The way it somehow banishes the darkness inside you, if only for a short while.

The pair who've just left the baths must have been police officers. They moved and looked the way only plain-clothed cops do.

They didn't look in my direction, but why would they? I've got nothing to do with them. Unless someone's filed a complaint. Seen me watching. But who would recognise me? I've lived my whole life in Linköping, but I still feel as insubstantial as air here.

Will I ever be noticed?

The pistol will make sure I get noticed. But I've never been angry enough.

I go to the ice-cream kiosk. Stand in the queue behind a group of girls. And there she is. His daughter. The girl.

She turns around. Beautiful. In a green bikini.

I smile.

She smiles back.
Then she turns back again.
And I look at her bare, wet neck.

26

Börje Svärd has gone inside room number seven.

It's gloomy, the sun has made its way across the afternoon sky and is no longer shining any light on the confined world of the room.

The bed that must have been standing against the wall has gone. Along with the rest of the furniture.

The tap in the washbasin was dripping when he came into the room, but he gave it a sharp twist and now there's nothing but silence.

No children playing in the park today. No one playing volleyball.

He saw the old folk on the terrace just now. They were drinking afternoon coffee in their wheelchairs. The ones who could lift a cup to their lips, anyway, and there had been a sense of calm in the scene, a worthiness. A few brief minutes of peace in lives that must be difficult to endure.

Euthanasia.

Assisted suicide.

It does happen. Agreed upon among individuals when it's time for the world to end.

He thinks of Anna, and how she begged and pleaded with him to help her die. During the last year she would ask him several times each day, when everything was suffering and spasms, pain and breathlessness, panic and being shut inside her own body.

'Help me. I can't bear it any longer.'

She was clear, lucid, when she managed to summon up all her strength to get the words out.

He wanted to help her, but couldn't, daren't.

He didn't want to be alone.

Couldn't kill his love, not even for the sake of love.

But I sat with you at the end, Anna. I know how your last breath sounded.

Did anyone help Konrad Karlsson?

No.

They've talked to the cleaners now. And the night staff. The two who managed to come into work early.

Siv Kramer. Maj Gröndahl.

Berit Andersson was still at home, asleep. Or just wasn't answering the phone. He and Elin Sand will have to go and see her.

Neither Siv nor Maj had noticed anything unusual, nothing odd had happened, according to them. The log said that Berit had been in to see Konrad Karlsson at about one o'clock, and everything had been normal then. Then they had agreed to let Konrad Karlsson sleep undisturbed until the day shift took over. They knew what the others had been doing the whole time, all three of them. Right through the night. Maybe they just didn't have time to look in on him?

There's no record of the bed having been broken, so perhaps it broke when Karin went to raise it.

It must be so quiet at night here, Börje thinks.

Apart from the occasional alarm buzzer and worried cry, and the sound of people partying down in the Horticultural Society Park from time to time.

It's possible to get in unnoticed at night. The Cherub's front door is unlocked twenty-four hours a day, even though the reception desk isn't staffed at night.

But wouldn't the night staff have seen an intruder?

Konrad Karlsson wasn't usually given anything to help him sleep.

The senior doctor has confirmed that. Apparently all the staff are authorised to give residents a sleeping pill when necessary, which means that anyone who requests it has access to the drug.

But that doesn't necessarily mean anything.

Nothing at all.

Sleeping pills are easy to get hold of. You can order them online, and there are doctors who are prepared to prescribe anything in exchange for money.

He looked into it once, and it would have been easy to get hold of an overdose for Anna.

But you had to breathe your last breath as nature decreed.

I hate myself for being so weak, Börje Svärd thinks.

Elin Sand looks at the woman in front of her in the cramped nurses' office.

Her worn features.

Her energy, resilience.

'We should have kept the door locked,' she says, leaning back on her battered office chair. 'The post of night receptionist was only withdrawn a month or so back, and I have to admit that it never even occurred to me that the doors were open all night. And this is Linköping. Not exactly a nest of gangsters, unlike, say, Landskrona. And the doors to the residents' rooms don't have locks. They need a lot of care, and sometimes get very confused, so it would be impossible if they could lock themselves in.'

You've got no idea of the things that go on in your hometown, Elin thinks.

'Are there any security cameras in here?'

'Not at the Cherub. Why would there be?'

'What about nearby?'

'None, as far as I'm aware. Doesn't the council have some in the Horticultural Society Park?'

Elin Sand doesn't know.

They'll have to check with the local council, find out the locations of any cameras.

'Nothing strange had happened recently? Nothing at all?'

Hilda Jansson thinks for a moment, then says: 'I know that the officers who are here are being as careful as they can be, but the residents are still getting anxious. Couldn't they wear civilian clothing?'

'I'll arrange that,' Elin Sand says. Thinks: We should have thought of that.

'You've already spoken to everyone who can answer questions.'

'Sorry. Sometimes we can be rather insensitive. Anything else?'

Hilda Jansson shakes her head.

'No, nothing. It's not unusual for patients to die in hot weather, but this year we've been OK.'

'Have you got through much Xanor recently?'

'I checked before you came,' Hilda Jansson says. 'No more than usual.'

Hilda Jansson gets up from her chair and wipes a few beads of sweat from her brow.

'You'll have to excuse me,' she says. 'I've got to help bring the residents in from the terrace. It'll soon be dinner time.'

Elin backs out of the office. Thinks that Hilda Jansson doesn't seem to appreciate the implications of what's happened.

'Be gentle when you talk to Berit,' Hilda goes on. 'She's a real stalwart. The old folks love her, and she loves them.'

* * *

The little rented two-room apartment on the ground floor in Johannelund is pedantically tidy, with designer, lacquered-wood furniture and hand-woven rugs. Small crystal figurines stand on crocheted doilies.

It would be very pleasant if it weren't for the smell of ingrained cigarette smoke.

They're sitting around the kitchen table. Elin, Börje, and Berit Andersson.

The coffee in the black porcelain mugs is lukewarm, and the woman on the other side of the table has evidently only just woken up. Her fifty-eight years are clearly visible in her face.

'I heard on the radio,' Berit Andersson says. 'Before you arrived. That he might have been murdered. I can't get my head around it. I was having enough trouble believing that he'd killed himself.'

Berit Andersson reaches for a packet of cigarettes with one hand, takes one out, and looks questioningly at the detectives.

'No problem,' Elin says.

Berit lights the cigarette. Takes a deep drag on it and rubs her back.

Elin looks at the row of framed photographs on the windowsill. A small boy as he grows up to be a man. A man with very long hair.

'That's Ronny,' Berit Andersson says. 'My son. We were left on our own when he was very young. His dad buggered off when Ronny was three.'

'That's rough,' Elin says, then feels foolish.

'It was him and me against the world.'

I know that feeling, Elin thinks.

'Did you see anything unusual on Monday evening, or later that night?' Börje asks. 'Did anything out of the ordinary happen?'

Berit Andersson shakes her head.

'It was a quiet evening. I'm the one who usually looks after Konrad, or looked after him, and it was a perfectly ordinary evening for him. His granddaughter Gabriella left at eleven o'clock. She's very nice, have I said that? I got him ready for the night, put his nightshirt on and helped him with the bedpan, then I didn't look in on him again until one o'clock.'

'Was he asleep then?'

'No, he was wide awake. But he usually managed to get to sleep later on.'

'Did he take anything that night? Tea, tablets, a sandwich?'

'A cheese sandwich.'

'And you left him alone for the rest of the night?' Börje asks.

'Yes, he didn't call for us.'

'And there's nothing in particular that you can tell us about Konrad?'

Berit Andersson thinks for a while.

'No. I don't know what I could say. He wrote those letters to the paper, of course, and there was a big fuss about that. But that wasn't really all that odd.'

Elin wonders how the sleeping medication got into Konrad Karlsson's system.

An injection? But Karin didn't see any puncture wound during the post-mortem.

It must have been in something he drank. And whoever he got it from, it must have been someone he knew. Because otherwise surely he would have wondered what the person was doing there.

'So he didn't have anything to drink?'

'He always had a glass of water by his bed.'

'Was it empty in the morning?' Elin Sand asks.

'You'll have to ask the day staff about that. It was Tove who found him, wasn't it? She seems like a nice girl. She'll probably remember.'

Karin's report from the scene.

The glass must have been included. Karin's very thorough.

Second-hand smoke fills Elin's lungs, and she coughs. And hopes her dress isn't going to stink for the rest of the day.

When they stand up to leave Berit Andersson says, quite calmly and without any warning: 'It's a bloody disgrace, what Morelia and his mob are doing to us. Tormenting us and the old folk into an early grave. All for a bit of profit.'

She says it without moving a muscle, and Elin can't help longing to feel the sun outside, the heat from a distant, brighter galaxy.

27

All the lights in the open-plan office at the station have been switched off, yet it still feels oddly illuminated. The evening sky outside the windows feels like it's being lit up from below.

Johan Jakobsson's elbow aches.

He's taken some painkillers, but his mouse-arm is still troubling him, as if the wretched joint has decided to stay inflamed for good.

A few reporters and cameramen have gathered outside the station. But they'll be waiting in vain. Karim Akbar has deviated from his usual habit of calling a press conference. Maybe he's fed up with all the fuss, wants to keep things low key. Not fuel a load of pointless speculation at this stage.

Johan called home a couple of hours ago. Told his wife he was going to have to work late.

Elin has told him that Karin had definitely taken the water glass from room seven to the laboratory on Tuesday. The glass had been empty. She'd also taken samples from it, and there was no trace of Xanor, so Konrad Karlsson must have taken the drug some other way.

She'd also been through the wastepaper basket in the room.

Just ordinary rubbish, but she took the contents away with her anyway. She also took the wrapper of the Dime bar and lottery scratch cards from the table, and logged them in the archive seeing as there could be fingerprints on the paper.

They're still running the prints Karin found in the room against the database, as well as matching them with the staff and Konrad Karlsson's relatives: the uniforms had been to take their prints.

So even if Karin should have sealed the room until the cause of death was beyond question, there's not much they could have missed.

Johan feels his elbow.

He knows that everyone in the team needs time to think, to work through all the facts and suspicions. To rest, sleep, look for answers to their questions, and try to find some way to move on with the case.

He still hasn't looked through Konrad Karlsson's computer and emails. His mobile is also lying there untouched, but they've requested a register of calls from the operator.

But Johan has found out the details of Konrad Karlsson's finances. He's got shares worth three million kronor deposited with a branch of Avanza.

Definitely worth trying to get your hands on, Johan thinks.

People have killed for far less.

He's looked into Morelia and his company as well. It's hugely profitable: in the last financial year alone the business made a profit of sixty-two million kronor. The conglomerate's old people's homes are particularly profitable, with profit margins of over 20 per cent.

What were the points raised in Konrad Karlsson's letters to the paper? The ones Merapi appeared not to have addressed?

Johan Jakobsson clicks to bring them up online.

1. Exhausted staff. Creative timetabling with an obligatory 'siesta' for the staff, which means that their working day is de facto extended to twelve hours.
2. Chronic understaffing. Residents sometimes don't get out of bed until the afternoon, if at all. They get pressure sores as a consequence.

Shameful.

I hope I've got enough money to pay for my own care when I get old.

Which is another mystery about Konrad Karlsson: he had money, but chose to stay at the Cherub. And challenge Merapi.

3. Dangerous scrimping on resources. One resident's bladder burst when his catheter bag wasn't changed. Staff are instructed not to change bags until they are completely full. Small margins mean that an hour's neglect can be lethal. The resident, a man in his eighties, died as a result of the operation that was required.

That was the case that really had kicked up a fuss, Johan recalls. National interest. And Hans Morelia, under duress, made a public apology and dismissed the senior doctor at the Cherub, a Serbian woman called Blanka Begović. According to Merapi, that had never been official company policy, but a journalist from *Expressen* managed to get hold of a copy of the medical notes.

4. Residents are left to lie in their own excrement for hours.

Four examples followed.

Johan clicks to close the window. Shakes his head.

Should anyone be allowed to make a profit of sixty-two

million at the expense of the suffering of the weak? Is that the kind of society I want my children to live in?

Eat or be eaten.

From the outside Morelia seems to be entirely without blemish. Not even any trouble with the Tax Office.

Deep inside a dark digital room Johan managed to find a post-mortem report, dated six months ago. Another old man hanged himself in one of the company's homes in Hälsingland. But the report's conclusion agreed with that of the police in that case: the man had committed suicide. For once, the report included a copy of his suicide note, in which the man had written that life wasn't worth living when he was regarded as nothing but an expense, a package to be preserved, but entirely without value.

The case never reached the media.

But other stories about Merapi and Morelia had followed Konrad Karlsson's letters to the paper.

Old people and other residents who had been left outside on balconies in near-freezing conditions. Missed meals. Patients tied to their beds. Wet incontinence pads that weren't changed because they hadn't been on for six hours. Old people who hadn't been out in the sun all summer.

Hans Morelia refused to give any more interviews about the scandals after that first one, refused to answer his critics, merely said – through the company's PR spokesperson, Rebecka Koss – that the criticisms were basically unfounded and that the matter was under investigation.

He seemed more inclined to give statements to *Dagens Industri* and *Svenska Dagbladet* about American venture capitalists' interest in the business, and about high profit margins and efficiency savings. He dismissed the scandals and claimed that they were merely isolated cases in which inexperienced staff had made unforgiveable mistakes and had been dismissed, to be replaced by 'the very best available when it comes to working on the shop-floor within the care sector'.

Apologies and promises of improvements.

At the end of the article, *Svenska Dagbladet*'s reporter offered his own reflections:

'Hans Morelia can choose to belittle the scandals that have beset the company and its occasional ethical lapses. The question is: can Nexxon afford to do the same? The company's healthcare portfolio is under pressure in several markets, and they don't need any further ethical problems.

'But perhaps Merapi's figures speak for themselves. The structure of the company is interesting, with a number of brands that could be exploited in the export market, so the deal looks likely to go ahead.'

Johan closes his eyes. Maybe someone at Merapi decided to put a stop to Konrad Karlsson's criticisms? No matter what it took. Perhaps Hans Morelia did it himself. He seems to be a man who doesn't mind getting his hands dirty.

Johan has also looked into Margaretha Karlsson's dental practice.

She made a loss of four hundred thousand in the last tax year.

High travel costs.

Use of personal capital.

Large loans, far too large for anyone on her and her husband's income.

She's clearly in financial difficulties. Three reports of missed payments in the past two months alone.

Johan flexes his arm. Feels his elbow creak. Tiredness and the flickering of the screen are making him see double.

A child could kill his or her father for a bit of money.

If the father had been unkind, harsh.

There's a boundary, but everyone sets their own limits.

Apparently her brother has gambling debts, but there's no sign of them online. But what is visible is that he's been receiving unemployment benefit for the past five months. Didn't he tell Malin that he worked for Mekaniska, over in Motala? That he was on holiday?

Yes, that's what he said. A lie, then.

Johan is hungry, and remembers the fifth point:

5. *Inedible, centrally prepared and pre-cooked meals.*

Tove and Malin have made spaghetti bolognese together and are sitting on the sofa in front of the television.

It's a proper meat sauce with chicken liver, the sort Tove likes, and she's trying not to think about Konrad Karlsson. But no matter what she does, she keeps seeing him all the time, both when she's awake and in her dreams.

Is this what grief feels like?

That someone is present even though he or she is gone for good? That the person is still there, as a black lump in your stomach, as loss, the memory of words, moments?

I barely knew him, Tove thinks. If I'm honest.

Why do I feel like this?

Today I shivered every time I walked past his room, and felt like bursting into tears.

There's been a very odd atmosphere at work, she thinks. As if they all suspected each other of something, but she doesn't want to talk to her mum about it.

They're all doing their job.

As best they can.

Hans Morelia was there again today, once her mum's colleagues had left after questioning all the staff again, her included.

The bloke called Börje had talked to her very gently, aware of whose daughter she was.

'No, I didn't see anything. No, no, no,' in answer to all his questions.

Mum beside me here on the sofa.

She doesn't seem tired, doesn't seem alert either. She hasn't called the council in Ljusdal to see if Stefan can be found a place in a different home. She's just sitting there quietly with the remote in her hand. She's not zapping through the channels, seems content to watch this documentary about an Australian bird of prey that can't fly, and is almost as big as an ostrich.

The bird has ice-cold, black eyes. It lives in the forest, and is said to have killed children with its long, machete-like beak.

Cassowary.

That's its name.

Apparently there's one at Skansen in Stockholm.

Tove gets up.

'I'm going to bed.'

Her mum looks up at her.

'Do you want to talk?' she asks.

'What about?' Tove says, and walks out of the room.

Malin leans her head back, tired, tired, tired. She wants to go after Tove. Give her a hug, tell her that Konrad Karlsson is at peace now.

But Tove's smarter than that. Knows better than to find any solace in platitudes.

Her grief is real. I can see it in her eyes.

Malin feels like shaking herself, wants this case to affect her more deeply, and she takes out her phone and calls the care home in Sjöplogen.

After ten rings a weary male voice answers.

'This is Malin Fors. Stefan Malmå's sister,' she says. 'I just want to make sure he's not lying in his own shit.'

'Who did you say you were?'

'My brother Stefan, is he lying in his own excrement?'

The man as the other end seems to think for a moment, then he says: 'And what sort of a tone do you call that?'

Malin wants to explode, but knows that her message has got through.

'I love my brother,' she says calmly. 'Even if he doesn't know who I am. So look after him. Otherwise I . . .'

Click.

The line goes dead and Malin leans back in the sofa again, switches the television off, and then she hears Tove's voice from the doorway.

'That wasn't very clever.'

'Oh, it was. It was actually very clever.'

Hans Morelia gets out of his BMW and looks up at the house and the light streaming out of the big windows facing the terrace.

It's almost midnight, and the sky above him is crowded with stars.

Lova must be asleep by now. He'll look in on her when he gets inside.

Work.

Hard work, all day. Ordinary people would never be able to understand how much work someone in his position has to put in.

The pressure, the stress, the sacrifices, the way he has to think strategically about everything, no matter how big or small.

But it will soon be over.

Soon he will be able to travel the world with Lova and Madeleine.

Then he hears rustling in the bushes, footsteps on the tarmac. Is that a car spluttering into life?

No, just footsteps.

And a sound, like someone taking the safety catch off a pistol in a thriller on television.

The noises aren't where they should be, and he turns around quickly, but behind him there's nothing but darkness and the illuminated city, a glimpse of the neighbours' neat gardens.

Paranoia, he thinks. That's all it is.

He goes down to the gate and opens it with the remote. Goes out into the street, looks in both directions, but it's empty, not a soul in sight. A squirrel runs across the tarmac from some bushes in a neighbouring garden.

Scampering.

And its scampering has a calming effect on Hans Morelia.

Calm, just like Lova must be as she sleeps.

28

Did you see me?

I can see you now. Hugging your daughter behind those big glass windows. Trying to act upset because she's up so late.

I smiled at her at the swimming pool. Saw her bikini, her neck, and I followed her as she walked home.

Wanted to take her. But I held back.

You're embracing her. I can see that you love her. That you know how dangerous it is to love anyone as much as you love her. You can go mad with worry, and if anything happened to her, if she died, you'd go mad with grief.

But you dare.

You think you're invincible.

Have I got the cold pistol in my hand, am I aiming at you, the pair of you?

Or am I lying in my bed now, the pistol safely tucked away in its hiding place, until tomorrow, when I shall pull the trigger, aim at the battered targets on the rifle range, at small animals, anything that has the temerity to get in my way?

I shall explode.

I want to.

But I don't know how, not yet.

Don't leave the girl on her own.

29

The sound of an alarm.

A mobile phone ringing?

It must be the phone, Malin thinks, but who the hell would call so early? It can't be any later than half past five or so, can it?

She grabs her mobile from the bedside table. Glances at the time before she answers.

06.17.

Something must have happened.

She hears a rasping male voice on the other end.

'Is that Malin Fors?'

'Yes.'

'This is Johan Strandkvist. Solicitor. I don't know if you remember me? We met in conjunction with your mother's passing. I was in charge of the probate of her estate.'

Malin remembers him. He was the person who first told her of Stefan's existence.

The solicitor.

Alcoholic.

Like me . . .

But a good solicitor, nonetheless. Didn't mince his words.

'How is your brother?'

'He's OK,' Malin says, and the lie makes her start to feel queasy. 'Why are you calling?'

'I'm not actually allowed to tell you what I'm about to say,' Johan Strandkvist says, and Malin can hear him slurring his words. 'My oath of confidentiality. Do you still want to hear it?'

He sounds desperate, almost frightened.

'Of course. I want to hear it.'

'Your pensioner, the one who was murdered at the Cherub, he was my client.'

Malin gets out of bed, realises how tired and giddy she feels, and sits back down. Through the gaps in the venetian blind she can see that it's going to be another sunny day.

'Are you there?'

Johan Strandkvist sounds even more scared now.

'What do you want to tell me?' Malin asks. 'And as far as confidentiality goes, you can trust me. I'll make sure you don't get into any trouble.'

Then Strandkvist whispers: 'I was charged with arranging a donation. Konrad Karlsson wanted to give all his money to charity. To various organisations.'

'All of it?'

'Yes. That was my understanding.'

'And who knew about this?' Malin asks. She's sitting on the edge of the bed now. 'His children? His granddaughter, Gabriella?'

'I don't think the granddaughter knew anything. But he wanted me to inform Yngve and Margaretha.'

'And you told them?'

'Yes. Last week. Here in my office.'

'Had the donation been completed before Konrad Karlsson was murdered?'

'No. All the papers were due to be signed on Monday next week.'

'So the money won't be going to charity now?'

'No,' Johan Strandkvist confirms bluntly. 'Now we're just dealing with an ordinary inheritance. No matter what Konrad Karlsson's wishes may have been.'

PART 2

The heart of final moments

[The wind]

What smells is the wind carrying with it across the city?
The smell of death.
Of fear, despair, hatred.
Who can catch this black wind?
You, Malin Fors.
Avarice smells like a summer meadow whose flowers
hide a corpse.
A respectable person. Good for the most part, bad on
a few occasions.
A greedy person, but one with the capacity to love.
Old people are dying in the summer heat now.
The cold wind sweeps through sickrooms, care homes,
taking groups of old people with it.
They always die three at a time, or so it's said.
Probably because no one wants to go alone.
God's waiting room smells of death now.
The generation who built this country is moving on.
What was their toil worth?
Nothing.
Look at the way you treat us.
The shame that should be yours is cloying and sickly sweet.
It smells of death among those who think they are alive.
Those who profit from others' suffering shall be punished.

30

The meeting of the investigating team vibrates with energy this Friday morning. Outside in the preschool garden the children are playing in the sun.

The room smells of coffee and deodorant that will soon succumb to the summer heat. Sven Sjöman has written the various lines of inquiry on the whiteboard.

1. Inheritance, family
2. Merapi, protecting business interests
3. Mercy killing

He pulls his stomach in.

'As Malin has just said, the family angle has opened up considerably as a result of Strandkvist's revelation. Konrad Karlsson's children have lied to us in numerous ways now, and clearly they both need money. The daughter's business is going badly, and Börje has managed to find out about the son's gambling debts. Yngve Karlsson also lied about his work situation.'

Sven gestures towards Börje, who clears his throat before speaking.

'I tried to call Yngve Karlsson just before this meeting, to ask him to come to the station as soon as possible. He didn't answer, so I called Mekaniska in Motala, seeing as that's where he said he worked. They were somewhat taken aback, and confirmed what Johan had already found out.

Karlsson was sacked as a result of cutbacks about five months ago.'

That works as a motive, Malin thinks, rubbing one eye.

'OK, we talk to his children again,' Sven says. 'Malin, Zeke, you do that.'

Malin nods.

'Try to build up a full picture. Go out to see Yngve, then pay Margaretha a visit at the clinic. Put them under pressure.'

'And the granddaughter?' Waldemar asks. 'What do we know about her? Her finances? Anything else?'

Malin thinks about Gabriella. Present yet distant at the same time.

Silence around the table.

'Johan, can you look into that?'

'OK.'

After a brief pause Sven goes on: 'Our second line of inquiry is that Merapi or someone who works there is involved. It's a fairly vague idea, and we don't have any specific evidence to work with. But we know that the business is in the process of being sold, and can't afford any more scandals. We also know that a lot of employees at the parent company will get rich if the sale goes through. So it's worth looking into more closely. How are we getting on?'

'I suggest we interview Hans Morelia now. It's time, we've got enough cause to now,' Elin Sand says. 'And we can ask him for a list of people who'll get a share of the profits when the company is sold. Talk to all of them, and ask for alibis.'

'Isn't that a bit of a long shot?' Waldemar asks.

Elin Sand turns her head.

'How do you mean?'

'You're letting your imagination run away with you.'

Waldemar is leaning back in his chair and looking at

his young colleague with a supercilious expression on his face.

'Imagination or not,' Sven says, 'I have to admit that I was sceptical at first, but we can't ignore it as a possibility any more. Waldemar, you, Elin, and Börje can be getting on with that. There'll be a lot of people to question. But it might throw up something useful.'

Waldemar groans.

Malin sees Elin Sand smile, but her expression reveals that she's not happy. The word 'imagination' seems to have made her angry, and she looks a bit like she does in the gym when her competitive spirit has been aroused.

'That presumed suicide I found at one of Merapi's care homes in Hälsingland, what do we think about that?' Johan says. 'I can look into the case in more detail. There could have been something odd about that one as well?'

'Do that,' Sven says. 'Who knows?'

'Check the staff,' Malin says. 'Maybe they move around between different facilities – someone who used to work in Hälsingland could be down here now.'

'What about the night staff at the Cherub? Have we ruled them out?' Zeke asks. 'I mean, they were there all night, and Berit Andersson was the last person to see Konrad Karlsson alive.'

'They all seem to have a good idea of what the other two were doing,' Sven says.

'But how could they?' Johan wonders. 'They must spend a lot of time inside the residents' rooms?'

'Not that much at night,' Elin says.

'And what motive would the staff have?' Sven goes on.

'Mercy,' Börje says.

'I was about to come to that.'

'According to Hilda Jansson, there was no Xanor missing from the Cherub's medicine store.'

'What about Karin?' Malin asks. 'Has she found out anything else?'

'No,' Sven says. 'She's had the analysis of those finger-prints she took. They're all from people you'd expect to find there. The staff, his own, and his granddaughter's. Now that Karin has confirmed that he must have taken the drug in something he drank, that suggests he knew and trusted whoever gave him the drink.'

'One of his children?' Waldemar suggests. 'Gabriella?'

'Or one of the staff?' Johan says.

'What had he drunk?' Elin Sand asks.

'Milk, coffee, and tea. Probably some water as well,' Sven says. Then he sighs before going on: 'So as you can see, we're not really much the wiser. All we've got are more questions. We can probably all agree that none of this seems to be particularly logical. It reeks of desperation and fear. But most murderers are desperate and confused at the time of the murder. What seems sensible at that moment can turn out to be very stupid indeed.'

'Wouldn't Konrad Karlsson have tasted the drug, what-ever it was in?' Zeke asks.

Malin shakes her head.

'His sense of taste was damaged after his stroke.'

'So he had traces of milk, coffee, and tea in his stomach,' Sven says. 'The most common drinks. And apart from the Dime bar and cheese sandwich, the remains of chicken and mashed potato. All of them standard-issue food and drink at the Cherub and other old people's homes.'

The meeting room falls silent and Malin notices that the playground outside is deserted now, and she can't see any children inside the preschool.

They must be in there, even if she can't see them through the windows.

'Surveillance cameras,' she says.

'There are a couple on Djurgårdsgatan and in the Horticultural Society Park,' Sven says. 'The recordings are on their way, but it might take a while. And our door-to-door inquiries in the area haven't given us anything useful.'

'As expected,' Waldemar coughs.

'Just like our conversations with the Cherub's residents,' Elin Sand says.

'Maybe we should try again with the people you talked to?' Waldemar says.

Elin Sand snaps.

'For God's sake, stop having a go at me!' she says, and looks around the room as if seeking support from the others.

'Give it a rest, Waldemar,' Sven says, and Waldemar laughs.

'Just having a bit of a joke. She doesn't seem to have a sense of humour. Rookies usually don't.'

Elin Sand sighs.

'The last line of inquiry,' Sven continues. 'The idea of a mercy killing. I filed a request with the probation service yesterday to see if anyone interesting has been released from custody recently – we should get the answer today. And as far as the staff at the home are concerned, I've requested details of any criminal convictions. Checking with other care homes didn't come up with anything. No one's noticed anyone acting suspiciously. And with that I think we can conclude this meeting.'

'Good,' Malin says, itching to go and put pressure on Yngve and Margaretha Karlsson.

31

Is it possible to hide in an open landscape?

Yngve Karlsson saw the detectives' car coming again. He'd been expecting them, knew they'd be back when they realised he'd lied to them.

The Östgöta Plain is wide open here, and he's lying at the edge of a field of rape, almost embedded in the vegetation, and can smell its buttery scent, hear the midges and flies buzzing through the air.

He knows every inch of ground here. Every undulation. There's no way they're going to find him, and he doesn't want to talk to them. Doesn't want to explain anything.

Wants to be left in peace. Hide. He thanks the Lord for the new, genetically modified rapeseed that produces two crops each year, otherwise this field would be nothing but stubble now. Instead of this protective yellow sea.

He always has his rifle with him. In case anyone shows up looking for the money he owes.

Hunting squirrels. Not that there are any here.

A white car pulls up. He watches the female detective get out first, followed by the man with the shaved head.

They knock on the door of his little house. He sees them point at his car, then walk around the garden, gaze out across the fields, but they can't see him. This is his territory, and he takes aim at them now, at the female detective, and holds his finger gently against the trigger.

Just because he can.

Malin can feel it. They're being watched.

He's here somewhere, and she sees that Zeke can feel it too.

Zeke calls out across the field: 'Yngve! Yngve Karlsson. Are you there?'

No answer.

'We need to talk to you, Yngve,' and Malin feels like ducking, fear is radiating through her body and her intuition is telling her to get out of there.

But she steels herself, gazes out across the swaying fields. The world is yellow and blue here, its colours bright, and the sun is burning her cheeks and bare arms.

'He's not here,' Zeke says.

'Yes he is,' Malin says. 'Somewhere. He just doesn't want to talk to us.'

I could shoot them, Yngve Karlsson thinks.

Just like I felt like shooting the people who sacked me. I'd been loyal to them for almost twenty-five years.

But that would put an end to everything. Maybe it's all going to work itself out now? Soon, anyway? Once the money's been sorted out. Because the old man can't have had time to sign those forms authorising the donation?

Yngve Karlsson follows the female detective through his sights. She gets in the passenger seat and over the wind he hears the doors slam shut. The echo of their cry is still lingering: 'We need to talk to you.'

But I don't need to talk to you.

Sooner or later it will be unavoidable, but not now.

Yngve Karlsson lowers the rifle, puts it down on the

ground, and all the energy, all the excess of power the weapon gave him, drains away.

The others are coming.

He knows they are.

And he must keep his gun with him, or flee.

Then he sees a hare dart out from the rape, some thirty metres away, and he reaches for the rifle, thinks about shooting it, but doesn't bother.

Stångebro tennis hall sits next to the old ice hockey stadium. The ventilation is poor, and Elin Sand can smell stale sweat, missed balls, and unfulfilled dreams of a lucrative professional career. The walls are lined with asbestos cement, and poisonous air seems to gather beneath the arched roof.

'He's at the tennis hall. You'll find him there.'

His secretary's reserved voice when they called half an hour ago.

The ball goes back and forth over the net. Hans Morelia's opponent is none other than the county governor, Sune Nordmark, former Social Democrat Minister for Agriculture. Elin can tell how competitive the two men are, straining and swearing and cursing even though the match is clearly pointless.

Serve.

Bang.

Bang.

Back and forth.

When she and Börje arrived Hans Morelia called out: 'We'll just finish this game.' But they're now in the middle of the third game since then, and Elin Sand can feel Börje getting irritated.

The next time the ball comes close to the sideline where they're standing she makes her move, leaps onto the court and reaches for the ball. She catches it neatly in the palm of her hand.

She lands on the plastic surface with a thump.

'What are you doing?' Hans Morelia yells, and Börje Svärd replies calmly: 'We need to talk to you. Now, not later.'

And he turns to the county governor: 'You can go. The match is over.'

It's hot. Gas oven hot, Börje thinks. The blazing sun has turned the tennis hall into a sauna.

He gets a text message as he watches Hans Morelia change into a dry shirt over by the umpire's chair. Waldemar is out at Merapi's headquarters, and surprisingly enough, their head of PR, Rebecka Koss, has given him a list of the people who are likely to become millionaires.

Hans Morelia walks over to them, his forehead dripping with sweat. He makes no attempt to wipe it, and holds his hand out to Elin Sand, saying: 'Good afternoon. What can I do for you? I've told Becka to give you anything you need, so I'm not really sure what you might want to talk to me about?'

'A number of things,' Elin Sand says. She takes a step towards Hans Morelia as if to prove her strength, and emphasise the fact that she's a head taller than him.

'That was quite a catch,' he grins. 'Professional athlete? You've got to stay in shape, haven't you, even if none of us has much free time?'

'We're not here to talk about my sporting career,' Elin says, and Börje detects a note of hesitancy and feels like intervening to help his less experienced colleague, but she goes on: 'I was in the national volleyball team.'

Morelia looks impressed, and seems to relax and become more focused at the same time.

'What do you want to know?'

'As you've no doubt heard by now, Konrad Karlsson was murdered,' Börje says. 'Is there anything we ought to know about any of your employees, anything that might be relevant to our investigation?'

Hans Morelia pauses. Seems to be piecing together a train of thought. Then he says: 'Everyone who stands to make money from the sale of the business is overjoyed, of course. Money has that effect. But I can't see why anyone would want to murder an old man?'

'To keep him quiet. Put an end to all the talk of scandals,' Börje says. 'After all, we all know what was written in the media.'

Hans Morelia raises his eyebrows in feigned surprise.

'Is that what you're thinking? But that wouldn't be a good reason to murder him, would it? That would only attract more attention.'

'But it wouldn't be about the standard of care provided, just the level of security,' Elin says. 'And you and I both know that's of secondary interest in the current situation. Care is the central issue, and the experts are saying that the Americans might pull out of the deal if anything else is uncovered. You can't pretend they're really going to be bothered about the murder, seeing as that can hardly be linked to problems in the core business.'

Hans Morelia looks at Elin, then Börje.

'The old boy was rich. There's your motive.'

'How do you know that?' Börje asks.

'It went up on the *Correspondent*'s website as breaking news an hour or so ago. It's not as if we spy on our patients.'

'How about that case in Hälsingland?' Elin Sand says. 'The suicide in one of your homes there? A man who hanged himself.'

Hans Morelia looks genuinely taken aback.

'So you know about that. That sort of thing happens from time to time. Old folk get tired of life and take matters into their own hands. We can't tie them down, after all. Suicides happen, both in our facilities and elsewhere. But of course you know that.'

'Are you worried about it getting out?' Elin Sand asks. 'Surely patients shouldn't want to commit suicide in your homes? After all, you're responsible for their mental well-being.'

'*Touché*,' Hans Morelia says with a smile. 'In which case, why would any of us – or a hit man, if we're being particularly imaginative – try to make it look like a suicide? If that, as you're suggesting, would be worse for business? There's no logic to your argument.'

Börje Svärd bites his lower lip and makes an effort to appear friendly.

'Have you let many of your employees have shares?'

Hans Morelia smiles.

'Yes. I'm a generous person. Even if no one wants to believe it.'

'Nice work,' Börje says, and can see a degree of trust in Hans Morelia's eyes. Vulnerability, perhaps even fear.

And he sees Elin Sand focus before she says: 'Money doesn't only make people happy. It can make them violent and irrational too. Have you got an alibi for the night of the murder?'

Hans Morelia laughs.

'I was at home with my family. Ask my wife.'

He turns and walks away from them under the tennis hall's harsh strip-lighting.

Says in a loud voice: 'In my world you're finished if you're as confused as you seem to be. How can you possibly imagine that a deal this big could collapse just because one old man claims to be badly treated and then kills himself?'

At the exit he stops and looks over his shoulder: 'I'm happy to talk to you again if need be. Or you can get everything you want from Rebecka Koss.'

Don't belittle me, Hans Morelia. Don't belittle people like me. You're nothing without us.

Malin Fors is about to talk to my daughter in her ridiculously expensive villa in Tannerfors.

Margaretha has cancelled her appointments today. I can see your pain now, your grief at what never was, at the state of our relationship, made all but impossible by my demands and doubts.

I never managed to give you the tenderness I myself sought as a child. The love I knew you needed. I'd read all about it, but still couldn't manage to express it, I just felt it, and what good was that when it never showed?

My beloved Sara. I haven't managed to find her, and I can't help wondering why I'm alone here. Why can't I find your sister, Josefina? I want to put everything right, be gentle and generous, understanding and encouraging.

I was never like that towards her either. I realise that now, even if I thought I treated her better.

Gabriella was the only one I ever treated well.

Why am I alone?

Because that's what I deserve.

Perhaps my punishment is to seek out my dead wife and daughter in this realm?

I remember Sara lying naked beside me. Thin white curtains billowing in the breeze, shading her body.

That was before you, Margaretha.

Before you and your brother and sister, long before her skin turned yellow from the tumour in her liver.

Long before I was left alone with you, your brother, and sister.

Let this stop now.

I'm tired. I want to rest.

But most of all I want to find my wife, my daughter.

Where are you?

I'm here.

And down there on Earth people are going about their business.

32

I see the girl. She's walking with some friends down a street in Ramshäll that's lined with smart villas and lofty trees. They don't see me in the car.

I can wait until she's alone.

I'm patient.

I've learned to be patient.

What am I going to do with her?

She's no more than nine or ten years old. I can find somewhere to keep her hidden, locked away, for years and years. I could take her and kill her. Leave him with lifelong grief.

Look at her walking along.

His daughter.

As if she owned the whole world.

I drive slowly behind the girls, carefully, far enough away for them not to notice me.

She's saying goodbye to her friends now.

And now she's alone on this stuck-up street.

33

Johan Jakobsson is wearing headphones to shut out the noise of the office.

He's listening to Neil Young. *Rust Never Sleeps*: It's better to burn than to fade away, my, my, hey, hey.

Using music to block other sounds is a fairly recent move for him, and he finds he can concentrate better than he used to.

He's looked into Hans Morelia more closely now, so far as he can. There doesn't seem to be anything particularly noteworthy. No criminal record, nothing on any online discussion forums, apart from one thread on Flashback that claims that he set up his company with the help of a criminal network. But as far as Johan can tell the claim seems to have been made by one of the forum's many delusional malcontents.

His company accounts all seem to be in order. His private finances too.

To put it mildly.

With that sort of money I could spend more time with the children, before it's too late.

The only thing that isn't clear is how Morelia got the start-up capital for his business, but he could simply have had good contacts at the bank from the outset.

Johan can feel his lunch churning in his stomach. He belches. Turns the music up.

Rust never sleeps.

Konrad Karlsson. Sleeping now. The big sleep, as Raymond Carver put it.

Let's see what Konrad Karlsson had to say for himself.

The hard-disk of his computer is laid open in front of Johan. He's already looked through a number of folders. Downloaded articles, ebooks, novels, and non-fiction covering a number of subjects.

One folder named 'The ward'.

Johan opens it.

One solitary document of the same name.

He starts reading.

What is her face telling me? Malin wonders.

Margaretha Karlsson is sitting on a bulging red sofa in front of a window that looks out onto a garden full of apple trees. Through the open terrace door comes the irregular tinkle of wind chimes.

Malin and Zeke are sitting on armchairs opposite Margaretha.

She was in her dressing gown when she opened the door, her face puffy and swollen, and Malin recognised herself in those ravaged features, and knows how profound that tiredness can be.

Now Margaretha Karlsson is dressed. Jeans and a pink tennis shirt. Sitting there, she looks like an over-aged boarding-school pupil whose dreams have come to nothing. Only in a house that's far too large, right on the river. A house full of Josef Frank and Bruno Mathsson.

Straight to the point, Malin thinks.

Pile on the pressure.

Lure her into a trap.

'Your business is on the brink of bankruptcy. Your father was rich. His death has come at a convenient time, wouldn't you say?'

Margaretha Karlsson's expression doesn't change.

'I've been going through a bad patch, that's all. You can see that if you look at the accounts. People postpone serious dental work when times are tough.'

Malin nods.

'But as I understand it, you spoke to your brother on one occasion about how much you'd like to get your hands on your father's money.'

Margaretha Karlsson leans forward. 'According to whom? Gabriella? That kid really does think she's something special.'

'Had you ever thought that?' Zeke asks, rubbing a hand over his shaved head. 'That you'd like to get hold of his money?'

'No. That's a ridiculous idea.'

'Did your father ever say that you'd inherit his fortune?'

Margaretha Karlsson purses her lips, gets up and goes over to a sideboard to pour herself a whisky from a carafe, unless it's tequila. Malin can smell the alcohol, and almost loses consciousness from desire and longing.

Dear God.

It never ends.

Never.

'Do you think I'm stupid or something? I can see that you've spoken to that pissed-up solicitor about my father's plans to give his money to charity. And that he was about to sign the papers.'

Shit, Malin thinks. She's underestimated the woman.

'Sure, our finances are a bit rocky. My husband lost his job and is only working part-time, we can't afford the repayments on our loans, and we might have to sell this house, the car and our country cottage. But do you really think I'm stupid enough to kill my own father just as he's about to give his money away? I'd be picked up at once.'

Margaretha Karlsson downs the whisky in one gulp and pours herself another.

Malin catches Zeke's eye and knows he's thinking the same as her: Margaretha Karlsson has contemplated killing her father, has toyed with the idea, but did she actually go through with it? Would she be talking openly with them if she had? Or is she trying to divert their suspicions away from her?

He was your father, Malin thinks.

I don't know how badly he treated you, but he was your father, and I think he did his best. But that isn't always enough. Far from it.

And she sees her own father with a cocktail in his hand. Old and tired, but still radiating some sort of calm. A seriously fucking unfair calmness. And with money.

Is that how you saw your father, Margaretha? As a potential source of money?

'Why didn't you tell us about the donation before?' Malin asks.

Margaretha Karlsson sighs.

'Why do you think?'

'We've been trying to get hold of your brother,' Zeke says. 'Do you have any idea where he might be?'

'How should I know?'

Margaretha Karlsson is angry now. Drinks, then stares at them, seems on the brink of screaming, then she says: 'And what sort of person do you think I am? The sort who'd kill her own father. Who on earth would do a thing like that?'

I'm just as messed up as Margaretha and Yngve Karlsson, Malin thinks. I don't feel capable of taking any emotional responsibility for my father either. Just as little as I do for Stefan, really.

It's tough, so who am I to blame the Karlsson siblings for anything?

Assuming they had nothing to do with the murder.

She and Zeke are sitting in the Conya Pizzeria. The forest-green woven wallpaper is adorned with new pictures, prints of paintings by the city's great *fin de siècle* artist, Johan Krouthén.

Cows in a field.

A red barn bathed in summer light.

Out in the street the cars go to and fro, and the sun seems to burn the pedestrians on to the pavement: no one has the energy to rush about in this heat.

'I wish they'd hurry up,' Malin says, and a moment later their pizzas arrive, and they eat, in silence at first, until Zeke says: 'They wear me out. People like Margaretha Karlsson.'

'Me too.'

'What sort of father do you think Konrad was?'

'Don't know.'

'The drink has taken its toll on her,' Zeke says. 'And the desire for more money. She's grown hard.'

He looks at Malin.

The way you did, he seems to be thinking.

She takes a bite of pizza. Chews, tastes the ham and prawns, feels the melted cheese run down her throat.

'But things can't have been easy for Konrad Karlsson,' she says. 'A single father with three kids. And in those days men didn't really take that much responsibility for their children. You can imagine what people would have said.'

'He was very demanding.'

'Maybe too demanding.'

Malin can see Zeke's shifting emotions reflected in his face.

'I try to be sensible,' he says. 'I take more of an interest in Tess than I ever did with Martin. The only problem is that I'm losing touch with Martin's kids. It's as if he and his wife don't want me to see them. Gunilla's taken over more or less completely. But I get to help raise Tess. There's a huge difference.'

'And what do you want?'

'I want to concentrate on Tess. But that's no good, obviously.'

'You don't really feel you want to see Martin's children?

'Am I allowed to feel that?'

Malin raises her eyebrows in response.

'It would be nice to be able to start over again, don't you think?'

She finds herself thinking of Daniel as she says this. She doesn't know why, but his face comes into her mind, and she feels like calling him. And knows that she won't.

Not now.

He can call me.

Zeke looks away.

'Sometimes. But only sometimes.'

They sit in silence for a while.

'But Margaretha Karlsson seems so cold. It doesn't have to be like that, does it?' Zeke asks.

'People struggle. Try to get things, stuff they think they need. Then they fail and end up bitter, not caring about anyone but themselves.'

'But still . . .'

'Don't think about it, Zeke. There's no point.'

In the car on the way back to the station Malin leans her head against the window.

I know what I've got to do, she thinks. I need to listen to the voices of this investigation.

All those thoughts and ideas that are circulating around me.

Then, once I've caught the bastard who murdered a defenceless old man, I'm going to find someone to love.

I'm going to dare.

I have to dare.

34

A novel, Johan Jakobsson thinks. Or something like a novel. Life at the Cherub, in literary form.

It's all there.

The humiliation of not being able to shower more than every third day. Of having to lie and wait for hours each morning before you can get up. Of being forgotten on a bedpan full of runny excrement, of being left on the toilet out of reach of the alarm.

Staff struggling to get through their duties, stressed to the point of collapse by inadequate staffing levels and an ever-increasing workload.

Management companies, the district council.

The mania for cutting costs.

The hunger for profit. The political madness of introducing the profit-motive into healthcare. The profound immorality of selling off publicly owned care homes.

The doctors' cynicism. The way elderly patients are denied treatment or are made to wait until it's too late. The story of a man with gangrene in one leg, whose doctor thinks the operation can wait for a while, so that he can 'get used to the idea' of only having one leg.

The patient dies on the operating table.

Another dies of an untreated pressure sore that infected her whole body.

Dressings that are used twice, each side, if the pus hasn't

soaked through. Sores that are neglected, stinking with pus, infections eating into bone.

But also glimmers of light.

Unexpected kindnesses.

From anyone.

One chapter is entitled 'the stalwarts', about the people who have devoted their lives to slaving away at the bottom of the heap.

The cleaners.

But mostly the nursing assistants, working day in and day out, night after night, year after year, doing all the heavy lifting, and with absolutely no power to influence their own situation.

And this is where Konrad Karlsson sees the real miracle of humanity.

People like Berit, Siv, and Kent, who retain their good humour and friendliness. Why don't more of them end up incurably cynical?

There seems to be an innate goodness in human beings.

How far can that be stretched before it vanishes?

If the book had been printed, it would surely have sparked a huge debate. The way Maja Ekelöf's documentary novel *Report from a Bucket* did in the 1970s.

Could someone at Merapi have known about Konrad's book?

It concludes with two simple sentences.

Children, the disabled, and old people. How we treat them determines who we ourselves are.

The stench is refusing to leave the flat, and Tove has cycled home during her afternoon break to let in the bloke from Anticimex, who hasn't been able to come before now. She's following the overweight fifty-year-old through the flat, thinking that his synthetic clothes must be unbearably hot.

One of the residents died today at the University Hospital.

Agda Berglund.

She was ninety years old.

She started to get weaker yesterday. Her breathing speeded up and there was no response when you spoke to her. Hilda called an ambulance even though it was obvious that life itself was draining out of Agda in an entirely natural way. But Hilda was paranoid, preferring to be cautious even though the outcome was in little doubt, so Agda wasn't allowed to die in her home of the past seven years.

Things at work have been unsettled. Hardly surprising. But the work has to go on, and she's tried in vain not to think about Konrad Karlsson. His face follows her the whole time she's at the Cherub. She remembers his fragility. His strength.

It feels like the other staff have already forgotten him. No one wants to talk about him.

So this is what death is like.

Hilda said someone from head office had called, demanding that she reprimand the night staff for leaving the front door unlocked. She said she had no intention of doing so, because they were already upset enough. No one would be made a scapegoat.

Then Tove hears the man from Anticimex say: 'Nothing in the kitchen, nothing in the pipes. I can tell you that much.'

Agda.

I knew nothing about her. One of the residents I hadn't got to know at all.

Who was she?

An ordinary person. Just like me, like Mum.

She didn't die alone. Her family, children, and grand-children got there in time.

The man from Anticimex is holding a cable in his hand, with a camera lens on the end. He says: 'I'll film the bathroom as well.'

'The last man who came did that too. He didn't find anything.'

'I'll give it another try.'

'What do you think it could be?'

'No idea. This sort of stench can travel a long way. The worst-case scenario is that it's coming from a different part of the building altogether.'

'Could there be a dead rat under the floor?'

'Not impossible. But we'd have to take the floor up to find out.'

The man is standing in front of her in the hall, seems to be expecting her to say something else. Tove studies him, thinks he looks trustworthy.

'I've got to get back to work,' Tove says. 'Do you mind locking up when you leave?'

The fat man nods, and Tove notices him staring at her breasts. Dirty old sod.

Soon she's on her bicycle, waiting for a bus to go past on Drottninggatan, and feels the wind tug at her hair, and she pedals and pedals, faster and faster, further and further into the summer. Unwilling to think about what's going to happen after that.

Elin Sand is sitting in a room in Merapi's headquarters, towards the top of the skyscraper out in Tornby. Behind her lies Lake Roxen, shimmering sharp and silver in the afternoon light.

Börje and Waldemar are sitting in other rooms. The PR woman, Rebecka Koss, found space for them, and they've been sitting there for hours questioning any employees who stand to gain from the forthcoming sale of the business.

Most of the people Elin has spoken to seem to find the police's reasoning incredible. Would anyone here – me? – have anything to do with the murder of an old man, just to make sure we got our share of the profit? But now Rebecka Koss herself is sitting in front of her, a short woman in her mid-thirties, with a blond bob and snub nose, impeccably dressed in a grey suit, and she says: 'I think it's good that you've talked to us. Now we'll be able to say with confidence that you don't think Merapi had anything to do with this. Nor any of our employees.'

'Because none of them did?'

'I can't imagine that they did,' Rebecka Koss says. 'I stand to make at least ten million if this deal goes through, and I have to admit that the old man's letters and their consequences were problematic. But murder? That feels extremely far-fetched.'

'We have to look into everything,' Elin Sand says. 'Did you know he was writing a book about life at the Cherub?'

Johan called a short while ago to tell them about the manuscript he'd found.

Rebecka Koss shakes her head, but is unable to conceal her surprise. And her curiosity.

'We came clean after his letters,' she says. 'Admitted our shortcomings, and things are much better now. So I'd welcome his book.'

Elin Sand murmurs in response, thinking that the deal will be done long before the book could ever be published, and that's why Rebecka Koss 'welcomes' it.

She tries to find a comfortable position on the minuscule office chair, but it's impossible.

'Was there anything else?' Rebecka Koss asks. 'We've

got a press conference at five o'clock. We're going to issue a statement about the ongoing investigation. Make it very clear how horrified we are that there's a ruthless killer on the loose in Linköping, but that we at Merapi can't be held responsible for what's happened, even if we breached our own regulations by leaving the front door unlocked. I really ought to go and get ready.'

Ten million, Elin Sand thinks.

And feels jealous.

What have you done to deserve that money? What about all the people in the organisation who work a hell of a lot harder than you?

'Aren't you ashamed?'

'Sorry?'

'You heard me.'

'What have I got to be ashamed about? You're the one who ought to be ashamed, seeing as you've completely failed to make society safe.'

35

I let her carry on down the road. I never got the chance to lure her into the car. Didn't dare stop and pull her into the car.

So I'm sitting here alone on my bed. I've got my gun out.

She's his daughter, so she isn't innocent. Or is she?

I can't make sense of my thoughts. Things feel incredibly urgent one minute, only to seem meaningless and empty the next.

I've lived in this city all my life. Even so, I'm almost entirely alone.

Perhaps I should take her just to have some company.

I stand up. Put my jacket on, tuck the pistol into my waistband, and then drive to his house. Stand in his garden and look in through the big windows.

He's not there.

Just his beautiful wife.

His daughter isn't there either.

Where are they?

I know where they might be.

36

Malin is pouring coffee in the kitchen of the police station. There's a chocolate cake on the table.

Must be someone's birthday.

Whose?

Who cares?

They still haven't found Yngve Karlsson. He's not answering his phone, so she and Zeke will have to go out there again.

She goes over to the table. Thinks of all the things she denies herself, and helps herself to a large slice of cake. She eats it quickly standing in the kitchen, rinsing its cloying taste down with large gulps of coffee.

Johan has shown her Konrad Karlsson's manuscript. She'll find the time to read it; it may just contain some useful information.

Should she let Tove read it?

No. For the time being it's evidence.

So far Johan hasn't found anything else of interest on the laptop. There's no obvious suicide note, but he's still looking through Konrad Karlsson's digital correspondence. There was nothing unexpected on his mobile phone. Calls to Gabriella, to Strandkvist, his solicitor.

She's just heard the weather forecast. There's going to be one more fine day, then a storm is supposed to sweep in from the Baltic, a big one, apparently, class three, which

– according to the woman on the radio – is extremely unusual for this time of year.

The last time it happened was in 1934.

The year Konrad Karlsson was born.

Before the weather forecast Malin heard some PR person from Merapi give a statement about the investigation. 'We're doing all we can to assist the police. We're dedicated to playing a positive role in society.'

Done.

She puts the plate in the sink. Aware that someone will get cross because she didn't put it in the dishwasher.

She leaves the kitchen and looks out across the open-plan office. It's already past six o'clock, but several of her colleagues are still there. Johan, Börje, and Waldemar. They look tired, from both the heat and their work.

Zeke is picking Tess up from preschool. He does that a lot.

There's no sign of Sven either. He must be in his room. Probably listening to the voices of the investigation.

Ping. Sven's inbox bleeps, an email from the probation service shouting for his attention.

Who's been released recently? What have they dug out for me?

Sven glances out of the window towards the hospital, towards the protruding green canopy above the entrance, and thinks of the people inside, the healthcare workers, the patients.

Just let me die quickly, he thinks.

No fuss.

Don't let me end up bed-bound.

Then he opens the email. Clicks, reads, thinks: Bloody hell.

*   *   *

Zeke sees Tess come running towards him down the preschool corridor. How delighted she is to see him.

He thinks about what he said to Malin. About wanting to devote his attention to Tess and Karin now.

Is that true? Is that really what I want?

Don't I want to work, just take care of myself? Do I want a family again? What the fuck? Doing the pick-up from preschool several times a week?

Then she jumps up into his arms. The beautiful little miracle from the other side of the world. She smells good, she is soft and warm and love. And Karin is love.

But she's too bossy, she's too smart for me, she wins every discussion, albeit in a sensitive way. Sometimes I almost miss Gunilla's passive aggression.

Tess pulls free of the hug. Looks up at him with her big brown eyes.

'Can we go for drink and cake? Please?'

He doesn't answer immediately.

'Please, Daddy!' Tess says.

Hans Morelia is watching his nine-year-old daughter riding. She is sitting straight-backed on the white Arab, which is almost one hundred and sixty centimetres tall at its withers, and she's controlling the horse perfectly, as if her body were one with the animal. Strands of blond hair stick out from beneath her helmet, fluttering around her face. There's a smile of concentration, and he can see how much his daughter is enjoying all this: the horse, her own skill, and just being alive.

The paddock is in a woodland glade on the Bergfors estate, some thirty kilometres west of Linköping. That's where he has his horses stabled. He doesn't ride, but Lova loves it, and, just because he could, he bought her three horses. The Arab, King, is her favourite.

The riding instructor clicks his tongue and shouts encouragement, and when the lesson is over Hans Morelia and Lova walk slowly back to the car together. The summer evening is mild, but he has to be back in the office soon, there are thousands of pages to be looked over in advance of the deal, due diligence to be conducted on both sides. Nexxus won't find any details missing. His *kaizen*-inspired thinking is going to impress them.

Hans Morelia puts an arm around his daughter and breathes in the smell of her clothes. The sharp, earthy smell of horse combined with the green scent of the forest, and he pulls Lova closer to him, and says: 'How do you think it went today?'

'Well, I think . . .?'

'Did you have fun?'

'I always have fun.'

'What sort of fun?'

'Stop nagging, Daddy.'

And he holds her tightly as they walk towards the car, through the early evening.

He looks over at the edge of the forest. Is that someone standing there among the trees, staring at them?

He looks away, doesn't want to see, and when he looks again the figure is gone.

It was a figure, wasn't it? Someone standing there?

They carry on towards the car.

'Have you noticed anything different lately?' he asks.

'Like what?'

He can't mention the figure he's seen in the garden, because that would frighten her.

'Nothing in particular,' he says. 'So nothing's changed?'

'No.'

As far as Lova is concerned, there's no need for any *kaizen*, Hans Morelia thinks. She's perfect. And he says:

'You know I love you, don't you? That all this business with my work, the money and all that, none of that really means anything. The only thing that matters is you, and our family. And you mustn't worry about what they write about me in the papers. Never. That will never have any effect on you.'

Lova says nothing. Just hugs him back.

Nothing bad must ever happen to you, he thinks.

And he can feel the life rushing through her body, life that in many ways is his own.

Elin Sand went home when they were finished at Merapi. She's taken off her trousers and is now sitting on the sofa in just her briefs and T-shirt.

Waiting.

Waiting until she hears footsteps in the stairwell, the outside door slamming shut, the ring on her own door.

'You're the one who should be ashamed.'

Did she really say that, Rebecka Koss, or did she say 'ones'?

You're the ones who should be ashamed.

Incredibly cheeky, and demonstrating a total lack of empathy.

We.

Do you hear, you stuck-up PR bitch?

WE.

We should all be ashamed, and then she hears Rebecka Koss's parting words, 'make society safe'.

Astonishingly naïve. Society is never safe, no matter how much money you've got. No matter what a man like Hans Morelia might like to think.

Elin Sand closes her eyes.

She feels black inside, and she knows she needs to keep a tight grip on the cynicism that's creeping up on her.

She has to believe in the force of good. Because if she doesn't, why should anyone else?

Malin. She's almost lost her faith entirely.

Waldemar lost his a long time ago. And just look at the pair of them, how often they behave in self-destructive ways. I need to act according to my convictions. That's my only chance.

Why do I care so much about what Malin thinks? Elin wonders.

Partly because she's my idol, in a lot of ways. I want to be as good a detective as she is, as courageous. I want to make the same contribution to investigations. Waldemar would never dare call her 'Poppet' or ridicule her contributions.

Elin knows it's pointless to be angry. Actions alone will raise her status with Malin, Waldemar and the others. Maybe . . .

She hears the outside door close.

Knows who it is.

Her whole body is longing now, and she runs one hand over the scar on her left buttock, the one she got on a call-out when a frightened child stabbed her in the backside with a scalpel.

She is the wonderful woman who sewed her back together.

Steps in the stairwell.

A ring on the doorbell.

Elin Sand stands up. Adjusts her briefs.

Bloody hell, Sven Sjöman thinks again.

A Vincent Edlund was released one year ago after spending the previous twenty years in Karsudden Hospital, and now Sven remembers him. A nursing assistant who gave two residents in an old people's home overdoses of morphine because he felt sorry for them, wanted to put an end to their suffering. That was what he was convicted of, anyway. He claimed he was entirely innocent, that the old people wanted to die, and that he was only helping them to commit suicide. The way he presented it, his actions were a practical political act in favour of euthanasia.

The method used in their current case was different, the murder of Konrad Karlsson was more brutal, but serial killers can get more brutal with time.

And now this Vincent Edlund is free.

We need to check you out, Sven thinks.

But if they let you out, you must be better now?

He smiles wryly.

Then clicks to open a black-and-white picture of a man in his forties. Or is he over fifty?

Vincent Edlund.

Long hair, half his face covered by an unkempt beard. But his eyes are tranquil. Could you have drugged Konrad Karlsson somehow? He could hardly have known you, wouldn't have trusted you.

But could you be our man? Sven wonders.

Did you want to show Konrad Karlsson a bit of mercy?

37

The eyes of Yngve Karlsson's house are lit up in the shimmering evening. The plain stretches out, dark yellow, in all directions, and to the north they can see the tower of Klockrike Church.

As Malin and Zeke slowly drive closer all the lights in the windows go out. They're in a different car this time, a dark blue Audi that, according to Zeke, is 'incredible to drive'.

Why has he turned the lights off? Malin wonders.

Does he want us to think he isn't home? Does he really think we didn't see that the lights were on?

This case seems to be completely devoid of rationality.

They drive towards the house.

No movement in the windows. Outside the shadows of a flock of magpies are chasing each other, to no avail.

Music is blaring inside the car. Zeke wanted it on, it's from his mobile, he said he was feeling tired. And Malin agreed, but only if he drove, so she's having to endure a squadron of Valkyries, Wagner's ominous waves of sound.

Zeke loves it. He says he's been thinking of taking up choral singing again, but don't do it, Zeke. Concentrate on Karin and Tess instead.

They pull up.

Zeke switches off the music, then the engine.

'Do we need to be careful?' he asks, and Malin thinks

back to how she felt when they were here earlier today, the unpleasant sense that someone was watching them.

'Yes, we do,' she says. 'We could be on to something important here, and he could well be desperate.'

'Or else he thinks we're a couple of loan sharks who've come to call in his gambling debts.'

Yngve Karlsson saw the car approach; it could only be coming to see him, and who could be inside it? The car is dark, the detectives were in a white one this morning, and the windows are tinted so he can't see who's inside. Has Dragan sent one of his thugs to beat the shit out of me?

It's going to hurt. A lot. He hit me once, how much more has he got in him? He'll kill me if I don't pay.

That much is very clear.

He sees his hands shaking.

Calm down, Yngve, calm down.

Turn the lights out, get your rifle.

They're not going to get me.

A different car, but it's those cops again. They're walking towards the door, they know I lied to them, they know what Strandkvist the solicitor told me, and I haven't got an alibi. And as the two police officers approach the door Yngve raises the rifle, then lowers it again.

Why would Dad want to give his money away? Yngve wonders. He knew about my debts, the threats I'd received, why couldn't he just have given me the money? And a thought strikes Yngve Karlsson: maybe Dragan and his crew killed Dad so I'd inherit the money and be able to pay my debts.

Can he say that to the detectives?

That could be what happened.

And Yngve Karlsson feels his head raging as his thoughts

collide, and he pulls his finger towards him, wants to send the shot flying through the air towards the two figures as they approach the veranda.

One step.

Two steps.

Slowly, cautiously, because he's in there, Malin thinks.

She goes up the porch steps. Knocks.

No answer.

Calls out: 'Yngve! YNGVE! We just want to talk to you, open up!'

And Malin hears the back door open, and yells: 'Shit, he's running!'

She draws her pistol and runs around the house, the dry grass crunching underfoot, and there's a smell of roses even though she can't see any flowers.

Zeke is right behind her, but she knows he can't keep up with her for long, and Yngve Karlsson is older than her, and didn't seem to be in great shape, and there!

There he is.

With a rifle in his hand.

He's running into a field of rape, and we've got to get him, Malin thinks, we've got to get him. But the rape is taller than it looks, and soon Yngve Karlsson has been swallowed up by the dark yellow, and insects swarm across the field, and Malin rushes on, rushing straight into it.

Zeke shouts: 'Careful, Malin, he's armed!'

Mum, Tove thinks, what are you doing now?

Where are you?

Tove is standing by the open living-room window, trying to ventilate the room and breathe in some fresh air.

The city is buzzing beneath her; the outside terrace of the Pull & Bear pub is packed.

She's been thinking about it for ages, how to tell her mum what she's planning to do in the autumn. She's made up her mind now. That last year at Lundsberg was more than enough for her. Enough to make her thoroughly sick of superficiality, of so many students being mean to each other, almost brutal in the viciousness of their power games.

She made it through.

Because of Tom, whom all the others respected, and probably because she was sending out signals that she wasn't going to take any shit off anyone.

She's given away almost all of her designer clothes now. Apart from the designer scarf Tom gave her to soften the blow when he thought he was the one dumping her. She's given the jacket he bought her to her mum, but only after she'd removed the label: Mum would never wear anything from Dior.

But Tom wasn't the one who dumped her. She ended it. Almost, at any rate, and the scarf was a sick gift that proved how sick the world is.

No fucking Business College.

Never end up like Hans Morelia.

Someone who makes old people's lives a misery. Konrad's.

Her eyes fill with tears again.

Damn.

She feels like doing something completely different. She's heard her dad's stories about Rwanda. Stories from a world where things aren't all about money, and that's why she's applied to do overseas service there. She's been accepted, they called today, they thought her application letter was great.

And they liked the fact that she'd been at Lundsberg.

Mum's going to go mad.

Dad might be proud of her, because he was in Bosnia

during the war there as well. But I don't feel up to calling him, he can find out later.

Like a yellow jungle where death is waiting for you.

Malin's heart is pounding in her chest and she gasps for breath, feeling the rape plants tear at the fabric of her trousers. She can hear Yngve Karlsson some way ahead of her. His footsteps, his breathing.

Or is he behind her?

Have I overtaken him?

And she cries: 'Stop, Yngve! We only want to talk to you.'

But the sounds continue and it feels like they're coming from all directions at once.

Breathing, footsteps, hissing, then all of a sudden she's out in the open. She tumbles into a ditch, rolls over, gets wet, realises she's dropped her pistol and screams: 'FUCK!'

But no sound comes out, because she's underwater and she can feel dirty, tepid water in her mouth, it tastes of soil and minerals, and she throws her head back and that's when she sees him, standing a few metres away, a wild look in his eyes. He's got his rifle aimed at her. His finger is turning white on the trigger, and she thinks: Am I going to die now?

Is this how it ends?

No.

Not yet.

I'm finding my way back; I'm finding a way forward.

Even if I can't see it right now.

38

Why am I thinking about Mum now?

Tove is walking across Stora torget. She sees the people on the pavement terraces. Hears them talking and laughing. The world is tugging at her and she feels like stopping. She looks across the square to see if she can spot anyone she knows, but no familiar faces pop up. Three years at Lundsberg have turned most people into strangers; most of her old friends no doubt think she's too stuck-up for them now.

But this isn't an evening for being stuck-up.

It's been a rough day at work.

Relatives getting in touch, wondering what's been going on, turning up and watching every step they take with suspicion. That makes the residents anxious, and the anxiety produces a peculiar atmosphere that seems to affect the very weakest particularly badly.

They die in threes, as Berit Andersson always says, and today Svea Persson has weakened. As if the heat and events of the summer are sucking the life out of her.

And Werner.

His stomach won't settle, and Tove can still smell it in her nose, wants to get rid of the smell, but how do you do that?

But worst of all is Konrad's absence. The feeling in her stomach is refusing to let go. Anxiety. The awareness that something has gone horribly wrong. That nothing will ever be right again.

She would have liked to spend much more time with him. Talking about Ivar Lo-Johansson's books with him. And about Gatsby.

So she takes a seat at the bar on the terrace outside Stora Hotellet. Orders a beer. She sips the cold liquid, and after just a few mouthfuls her anxiety and the smell in her nose seem to fade and the people around her look friendly. She studies the bottles of whisky behind the bartender. Likes the strong warm feeling she gets from it.

And why not?

Then she thinks about her mum again, and the number of times she must have sat like this. But I'm not my mum, Tove thinks. I'm my own person.

I can handle this.

The whisky appears in front of her.

What's Mum doing now?

What's going on with her, really?

Is he going to fire?

Malin is lying in the ditch, crawling, and he's aiming at her.

Tove, forgive me for everything, and inside Malin a thousand images from Tove's life flit past. The way she used to run through the flat in Traneberg in Stockholm when she was two, her first swimming lesson at the pool in Åkeshov, the way she sits on the sofa in Ågatan and reads and reads and reads.

It can't end like this, on this desolate plain, but Yngve Karlsson is pointing the rifle at her and his hand is shaking. Some way off the bells of Klockrike Church start to ring, and who are they tolling for? Malin imagines the biggest bell in the grey tower swinging back and forth, and what can I say to him, should I try to reach my pistol? It's lying at the edge of the ditch, but I'd never reach it in time. He'd shoot me, is he pulling the trigger now?

Her heart is racing, beads of sweat are breaking out on her forehead, and her stomach clenches. She screws up her eyes, feels a black cloud rise up from her stomach, up towards her lungs.

Gasping for breath.

And she wishes she could find some words, say something that would calm Yngve Karlsson, make him lower his gun and understand that they only want to talk to him.

Who knows what he might have done?

Malin can hear waves in the air, Zeke's voice calling for her, it's as if his voice is from a different dimension, as if Yngve Karlsson has already shot her, perhaps I'm dead, Malin thinks, dead, with my heart shattered by a bullet. But no, I'm still here, and behind me the rape plants are swaying, and the Östgöta sky is lying like a dark blue lid over on the horizon.

The bells ring and ring, and then they stop.

Hurry up, Zeke.

Hurry up.

Zeke is pushing his way through the field.

Where the hell did she go?

Fuck.

He's drawn his pistol. Is holding it out in front of him. The world is yellow and he can hear Malin speak, can hear the fear in her voice: 'Lower the rifle. We only want to talk to you.'

And he walks in the direction her voice came from, calls out: 'Malin?'

The pistol is cold beneath his fingers and the cold makes him calm, but he knows that calm is the last thing he needs to be.

He pushes onward.

And then he hears the shot.

The rifle falls to the ground, falls from Yngve Karlsson's hand. He's just shot into the air, a gesture of desperation. Malin can see the rifle on the ground, her ears are ringing, and Yngve raises his hands above his head, grimaces. Then his face relaxes, as if he's made a decision he's been grappling with for a long time, as if nothing matters any more.

Malin reaches towards the edge of the ditch, towards her pistol, and she hears: 'Lie down!'

But Yngve Karlsson remains standing with his arms in the air, fingers outstretched. Malin can see the church tower between his fingers, and hears Zeke emerge from the rape behind her, hears the splat as he jumps across the ditch and lands on the muddy ground above her.

'I've got him,' Zeke says, relief in his voice.

He goes over to Yngve Karlsson, picks up the rifle and nudges him gently in the back with the butt.

'Now we're going to the house. Nice and calmly. Keep your hands up in the air.'

They walk past Malin, and she follows them through the field, wet and filthy, lost in a dying storm of adrenalin. In the sky the high cirrus clouds over on the horizon are getting thicker and thicker, warning of the sort of storm in which unjust death can be born.

Tove has ordered a third whisky.

What the hell . . .

She thinks about Stefan, and then Konrad again, and others like them.

The lump in her stomach is almost gone now.

Replaced by anger. Resolve.

'I'm Morelia's puppet,' she mutters. 'I hate it,' and she realises that she's talking to herself, but why not?

Mum must have done the same thing thousands of times when she was drunk.

'Hope the bastard dies,' she says quietly. 'Hope he suffers all the sorrows of this world. Hope one day he gets to feel the same torment as Stefan and Konrad.'

39

The dogs are barking in their pen. Howling.

Börje Svärd can hear them throw their bodies against the mesh, the noise like a mechanical bat beating its way through a steel sky.

There must be someone in the garden.

Who?

When one of the city's wild rabbits wanders in this direction by mistake the dogs don't get anywhere near as agitated as this, and Börje gets up from the sofa, switches off the television and goes over to the window.

No sign of anyone.

He feels anxiety spread through his body.

Who would come at this time of day? One of his women? No.

Then he hears the doorbell. The visitor is at the door now, and he leans forward, peers towards the steps, but all he can see is a pair of well-polished shoes and blue trousers.

He makes his way to the door and opens it, and there on the step stands Hans Morelia, smiling, hesitant, uncertain. Then he seems to focus, and asks: 'Have you got a few minutes, could I come in?'

Do I want to let him inside my house? Börje thinks.

Down in the pen the dogs stop barking.

The two men look at each other in the still evening. Börje can see Anna's tormented face before him. He doesn't want to let this man into his home, into Anna's home, because what would you have done with someone like her?

Can a man like you have any redeeming qualities? Is there any sympathy in you at all?

Börje acknowledges Hans Morelia with a curt nod.

'Whatever it is you want, we can deal with it here.'

'I think it would be best if I came in.'

'No.'

And the two men stand in silence, each of them thinking of their love for people who aren't there, a departed and much-missed wife, and a daughter who's sitting playing a video game in a villa just a few kilometres away.

'OK,' Hans Morelia says. 'We'll do it here. I've come because you struck me as a good man when we met at the tennis hall. Trustworthy.'

Börje smiles.

Am I being too harsh?

He had nothing to do with what happened to you, Anna. Unless everything is connected?

'What do you want?'

'I've got something to tell you that I think might be important.'

'What?'

The dogs start barking again, and Börje can almost smell their cloying breath and the air vibrates with the sound of them throwing themselves at the netting.

'Quiet!' he shouts. 'QUIET!'

The animals fall silent, their din replaced by the sound of a large bumblebee repeatedly hitting a window, as if demanding to be allowed passage to the other side of the transparent surface.

Hans Morelia clears his throat.

'I wanted to say that I'm feeling threatened.'

Is that so strange? Börje thinks.

'I received a number of threatening letters, and other things too. But there's one that's connected to the Cherub, so I thought it might be important.'

Why have you come here to tell me this now? Börje wonders. And he realises that he's dealing with a polished businessman, a man who never does anything without reason, who never gives anything away without expecting something in return.

How does your head work, if you see a sick or disabled person as a unit to be dealt with according to a logical system?

'And?'

'Berit Andersson, one of the employees at the home. She's got a son in his thirties – a total failure – he's called me, and sent a few hostile letters.'

'Hostile in what way?'

'He accuses me of being a parasite on society. Of exploiting his mother.'

Isn't that exactly what you do? Börje thinks.

'I've also received an anonymous parcel containing excrement.'

The dogs are still quiet. Maybe they can sense that I'm calm, Börje thinks.

'And sometimes I have a feeling that there's someone watching me,' Hans Morelia goes on.

'How do you mean?'

'It's just a feeling. I think Berit's son might be the one who sent the excrement, and that he's been stalking me.'

'What's the son's name?'

Börje tries to sound neutral, not to let on that he thinks Hans Morelia deserves to be stalked, if only a little.

'Ronny. Ronny Andersson. I think he's unemployed, and he's got it into his head that I'm letting his mother work herself to death. He writes that I've cut the staff, and pay such low wages that his mother is getting more and more ground down. Which is obviously ridiculous. We adhere strictly to the regulations govern—'

'Drop the sales pitch,' Börje says. 'Have you seen him following you?'

'No.'

'And how do you think this might be connected to the murder of Konrad Karlsson?'

'I don't know. But Berit works at the Cherub, and perhaps Ronny wanted to draw attention to whatever he thinks is going wrong there.'

'By murdering an old man? Have you ever met this Ronny, listened to him, explained the way you see his mother's job?'

'No. I haven't had time.'

Bark, dogs. Bark.

'Have you filed a report with the police?'

'We didn't want to file a report at the moment.'

'Why not?'

'We considered that we have the situation, or at least had it, under control.'

But now you've come to me.

Because you're seriously worried? The way anyone would be when a dream is close to coming true? Or because you want to help us solve the murder and think you know something that could be of use? Or to focus our attention in a particular direction? Away from Merapi?

The man in front of him adjusts his blue suit, strokes his lapels, hoists up his trousers.

'Perhaps he's just upset about his mother's situation,' Börje says. 'And his own. Why not try to arrange a meeting with him? Let him get it out of his system.'

'He put a parcel containing excrement through my letter box.'

'You don't know for certain that it was him. There are plenty of people in this city who've taken against you. You must be aware of that?'

'Yes. But it could have been him,' Hans Morelia continues. 'It was just lucky that I was the one who found the package rather than my daughter.'

'You should have reported it. Have you still got it?'

'What? No. I threw it out.'

'And when was this?'

'A couple of months ago, I'd say.'

The two men stand silent in the Linköping evening.

'Well,' Hans Morelia says after a pause.

'Well, what?'

'What are you going to do?'

'You can file a report against this Ronny, and we'll see what happens, but there's not a lot of evidence. And we'll take it into account in our investigation into Konrad's murder.'

'Is that all?'

'Maybe you should get a bodyguard, if you haven't already got one. Just for the time being.'

'Why would I need to do that? What for?'

Börje knows the answer to that.

Your fears are yours alone. No external threat can be real. No one else is properly real to you.

Breathtaking arrogance.

He feels like punching the man standing in front of him until his face is streaming with blood, but he says nothing more, merely turns and closes the door behind him.

A minute or so later he hears the dogs start to bark again.

Their barking echoes across the city, and he knows who they're barking at, and hopes they're never going to stop.

40

It's half past nine by the time Malin and Zeke lead Yngve Karlsson into the interview room in the basement of the police station. The halogen lamps set into the grey, mesh-like internal ceiling lend a soft yet slightly uneasy light to the room. The black walls disappear into themselves, and Malin has a sense of being in an infinite space, like out in the field when she began to wonder if Yngve Karlsson had already fired his rifle.

Am I dying now?

Am I dead?

Do old people ever feel like that, as they lie there for hours waiting for help, for a little empathy?

They sit down at the table.

Malin and Zeke on one side, Yngve Karlsson on the other, facing the one-way mirror that gives anyone in the observation room a full view.

Sven is in there. Karim too. He drove to the station when he heard what had happened, wanted himself and Zeke to conduct the interview seeing as Malin seemed far too upset after what had happened out in Klockrike. But Malin doesn't feel upset. She told Sven that she and Zeke were going to question Yngve Karlsson: no one else.

Yngve is leaning forward over the black table, and his face is calm and still, no bitterness.

Zeke switches on the tape recorder.

'Why did you run?' Malin asks. 'With a weapon, and

everything? You must see how suspicious that looks. Particularly when you don't have an alibi for the night of the murder.'

She really wants to ask about the rifle, and why he aimed it directly at her, but it would be a mistake to start at the wrong end, in case she gets aggressive.

Yngve Karlsson sucks his lips, doesn't answer.

'Just tell us,' Zeke says, 'Did you kill your father to get hold of his money? It'll feel better if you confess.'

Yngve Karlsson leans even further across the table, and Malin can smell his sour breath.

'I didn't kill my father.'

Malin sees how exhausted he is, as if he's finally breathing out, and only sleep can put a stop to it.

'So why did you run?'

'I ran because I thought you were some people to whom I owe an awful lot of money.'

The exhalation seems to come to an end.

'I gamble a lot. And I've borrowed money I can't pay back. I flipped out. I just wanted to be left in peace, not have to worry any more.'

'And you expect us to believe that?' Zeke says.

'Yes. I owe Dragan Zyber money, I'm sure you know who he is. I might end up in the lake just for mentioning his name, but what have I got to lose now? Nothing.'

Dragan Zyber. A nasty piece of work over in Motala.

I can understand why you're afraid, and Malin recalls her own fear out in the field. She reaches across the table and taps Yngve Karlsson's nose.

'Was that why you took aim at me? Because you were frightened?'

'I don't know. I got confused.'

Malin is inclined to believe him: mad with fear, he turned his desperation against her, them.

'I don't know,' Yngve Karlsson repeats. 'It's like someone else took over and was controlling me. I wanted to fire. I wanted to earlier on today, the first time you came. Shoot all my problems away, even though I know that's impossible.'

'Earlier today?' Zeke asks

'I was watching from a distance when you arrived.'

And Yngve Karlsson breathes out with a deep sigh, and before Malin and Zeke can say anything he goes on: 'Maybe I aimed the rifle at you and threatened you so I could get some sort of punishment. So I could sort everything out. I've lost my job as well.'

'Why didn't you tell us about your debts?' Malin asks.

'I didn't want you to think I needed money.'

A simple explanation, Malin thinks. A plausible explanation.

'So you wanted to sort everything out by murdering your father? To get your hands on the inheritance?' Zeke says.

'No, I didn't murder him. You have to believe me. Anyway, sorting out an estate like that can take years. Dragan would have lost patience by then.'

'Have you got GPS in your car?' Malin asks.

'Yes.'

'Then we'll be able to check if you went anywhere that night.'

'Great, go ahead. You'll see that my car was parked outside the house the whole time.'

Yngve Karlsson leans back in his chair and rubs his eyes.

'You can think what you like, but I feel much calmer now. I'm glad I didn't shoot you.'

'I did love my father, in spite of everything,' Yngve Karlsson says, and the words whirl around inside Malin. She wants to get out of the interview room now, stifled by the stale atmosphere in here.

Do I love my dad? she wonders. Can I ever love him again, in the straightforward, simple way I did when I was little?

And she can discern the desire in Yngve Karlsson's eyes, the hunger, the lure of gambling, and recognises that she shares that look. She feels thirsty, her throat feels dry, her heart muffled, and she longs for someone else's skin, a heart beating inside someone else's ribcage.

I'm alone, Malin thinks.

I feel your loneliness as my own.

And she sees the rifle again, its barrel pointing at her, the trembling finger on the trigger, she sees Daniel Högfeldt's face, Tove's, unknown men's faces, and she breathes, breathes deeper than she's done for a long time.

A shot was fired.

But it wasn't aimed at me.

'I forgive you for what happened out in the field,' Malin says.

How can she forgive him? Karim Akbar wonders. I'd have great difficulty forgiving someone who pointed a gun at me. She's got to take over after Sven. Then I can leave with a clear conscience.

Christ, she's brilliant.

Malin comes out of the interview room. Looks at him, says: 'Nice suit, Karim. Are you going to a party tonight?'

'Just being here is like being at a party, it's such a spectacle,' he calls after her, thinking that he might miss this after all, and then wishing he was at home with Vivianne. And the child that's growing inside her.

Lights. Sounds.

The world has no directions, her body is the needle of a compass, spinning around, around, and Tove feels sick, wants to get rid of the whisky and beer, and she stumbles along Ågatan, and oops, I just walked into a chair, and what's happening, what's going on? The ground vanishes and she falls slowly, yet strangely quickly to the right left right, hits something hard, no, soft, and feels something sharp against her cheek. My face stings, but I need to keep going, crawling now, and my stomach contracts and there's a bitter taste in my mouth, and now I'm on all fours, throwing up, in the midst of all these people, completely alone, and what's going on? I'm only a hundred metres from home, but how am I going to make it that far?

The world is like a thousand-piece jigsaw.

Every piece the whole world.

I'm a piece, all the pieces, and Tove tries to stand up but stumbles again, tunnel vision, widescreen, tunnel vision, widescreen.

Mum.

Where are you?

Help me home.

You always found your way home when you were like this.

41

Friday, 13 August, Saturday, 14 August

Malin is standing outside the station, having turned down offers of lifts from Zeke and Sven. She needs a walk, needs something else, needs to confirm something to herself.

It's dark now. The cones of light from the street lamps embrace her, the hot air of the day is mild now, and she slowly fills her lungs.

Thinks about Stefan.

How he is right now.

She meant to call the care home today, keep up the pressure. But she hasn't had time, and she wonders about calling now, and takes her mobile out, leafing through the numbers in her contacts, but then she stops.

No one at the home will answer at this time of night.

The car park is deserted. As if everyone has fled the world.

Daniel.

His face the other evening.

He's single again.

As lonely as me?

And as Malin sets off towards the city centre she calls Daniel's number. She has no idea where he is, what he's doing, where he is in his life, but perhaps they could cheer each other up.

'Malin?'

He answers on the third ring, as she's marching quickly down the path that runs through the patch of woodland towards the hospital car park. She can't see any shadows in the dark.

'Hi,' Malin says. 'What are you up to? We didn't get much time the last time we met. I just wanted to say it was good to see you again.'

'It was good to see you too. But I've just gone to bed. Like most people at this time of night.'

'I'm on my way home from work.'

Silence.

The sort that follows a pointless remark.

'Anything new in the Konrad Karlsson case?' Daniel eventually asks.

Now he's being a journalist again, Malin thinks, laughs and says: 'I thought you were in bed? You're not supposed to be working.'

'I didn't mean it like that.'

She realises that his remark was intended as an attempt to keep the conversation going.

'Sorry.'

'What for?'

'I don't know.'

'Is everything OK, Malin?'

She laughs again.

'Sure, everything's just the same as usual.'

Everything and nothing, she thinks.

'How about you? Same as usual?'

Silence at the other end of the line, and Malin has reached the hospital car park now, is walking through the rows of parked cars.

'Helen and I broke up. I don't know why, but we broke up.'

'We should meet,' Malin says.

'Maybe we should,' Daniel says. 'Any suggestions as to when?'

'How about now? Soon. This evening. Tonight.'

Daniel considers this.

'Not tonight, Malin. But coffee would be good. How about Espresso House on Trädgårdstorget in half an hour? They're open late.'

Coffee.

No.

'No work talk,' he says.

Right.

Not at all what I wanted, but: 'OK.'

Daniel is wearing a freshly ironed shirt, and looks like he's had a shower, and he makes Malin feel grubby.

But he's looking at her fondly.

They're sitting in the back room of the café, the one with a big skylight in the roof, surrounded by young people who are more lying than sitting on the big red sofas. She doesn't recognise a single one of them. None of Tove's old friends. They're younger than her.

He half closes his eyes. Takes a sip of his latte and smiles, and she wonders why he's smiling, she hasn't said anything funny.

'It's nice, sitting here with you like this,' he says.

What am I supposed to say to that?

This wasn't a good idea. But it was me who called him.

'I'm happy to be back at the paper,' he says. 'I missed journalism.'

She takes a sip of her tea.

Nods.

His brown eyes don't look tired, and he's kept himself in good shape. She can tell.

'But the paper's haemorrhaging money. Don't know how long it's got left.'

'No job talk, we said,' Malin says.

Daniel raises his eyebrows.

'Sorry.'

'So you broke up with Helen?'

Daniel looks at her, and she regrets asking when she sees how sad he looks.

'We didn't work well together. How about you?'

'Me?'

'Been seeing anyone?'

'I was seeing a doctor for a while.'

'But you didn't work well together?'

'I didn't work well for him.'

Now it's Daniel's turn to regret his question. Maybe he can see sadness in my eyes?

'Don't worry,' Malin says, and then asks: 'Are you running much these days?'

They get lost in a conversation about apps, intervals, shoes, training programmes, and then they talk about some television show Daniel likes. They talk about the world, places they'd like to visit but will probably never get to, and Daniel asks about Tove, and Malin replies that Tove's doing well. And without them noticing, an hour passes, and they're left sitting alone in the big, brightly lit room.

'We're closing now,' a woman's voice calls from over by the entrance.

A couple of minutes later they're standing facing each other in Trädgårdstorget, about to go in different directions, and she sees the way his body moves beneath his shirt, sees him looking at her, and asks: 'Shall we go back to yours?'

Daniel smiles. Shakes his head.

'No?' Malin says. 'What do you mean, no?'

'I mean no,' Daniel says. 'But I'd like to see you again.'

She feels a shiver run through her body, then something inside her collapses with disappointment.

Give me what I need, for fuck's sake.

He reaches forward, strokes her cheek.

She feels like batting his hand away. Wants a longer, more intense touch.

Then he removes his hand. Looks at her.

'See you,' he says.

'I don't know about that,' Malin says.

'Don't be silly,' Daniel says, then leaves her in the deepening Linköping night.

42

I move through the garden towards the house. Creep down the basement steps, try the door.

It's open. The girl must have forgotten to lock it.

Fear and doubt are quivering inside me, but I open the door nonetheless, go into the blackness and feel my way through the dark cellar, towards the sound I can hear.

I see light.

A recreation room. With big, dark paintings on the walls.

I go up the stairs, slowly, and the sound of the television drowns out any creaking. Such rooms! The opposite of mine. Shiny and expensive. Metal and gold, leather, oil paintings.

I head towards the room with the television. The big glass doors.

In my hand is a pistol.

I'm shaking. I can do this, and there, around the corner, there they sit, his wife and daughter. They've no idea that I'm here. That I even exist.

She's lying on her mother's arm, asleep.

I can do this. I can take their daughter away from them.

I hear something else now.

A car stopping on the drive, a door slamming shut.

I have to get out.

And my courage deserts me and I go down the stairs far too quickly, my pistol lowered, and I feel my way through the darkness, towards the basement door, I make sure I shut it behind me, then up the steps and through the garden, away to my car.

I drive away.

Cursing my own cowardice.

43

There's something lying next to the front door. Something far too big.

A body.

A threat?

Me?

The self-preservation instinct kicks in before concern.

A fraction of an instant of shame.

Malin knows what it is that she's looking at now, doesn't want to see, she's tired and she can see the vomit surrounding Tove's body.

But you are breathing, aren't you, darling Tove?

What have you done, what have I done, what is this world doing to us? For fuck's sake, Tove.

You're asleep, aren't you? You're just asleep, and Malin races the last few steps towards Tove. Yes, she's breathing. Malin crouches down beside her, putting one foot in the vomit, feels it squish beneath the sole of her sandal.

She puts one hand on Tove's back.

Her chest is moving, up and down, up and down, and then she notices that she's lying in the recovery position. Did she put herself in that position, or has one of the neighbours been a Good Samaritan? Not that it really matters, and Malin nudges Tove to one side, hears her body drag on the ground. She opens the door and tries to pick Tove up, her limp, sleeping body. Any tiredness is gone now, and Malin is grateful to all those brain-dead hours in the gym and the fifty-metre pool at Tinnerbäck for the fact that she can actually lift her daughter and carry her into the flat, can lay her on the bed in what was once a little girl's room but is now something else.

What? Malin wonders.

A cocoon, a chrysalis, a waiting room. You shouldn't be here, Tove. Not lying here like this.

I shouldn't have to help you like this.

She undresses Tove. Tove doesn't wake up; she's far away in a strange, dreamless land. Malin throws the stinking clothes in the laundry basket, then puts Tove back in the recovery position, and her daughter has no awareness of what's going on. She could be anywhere at all, and anyone could be doing absolutely anything to her.

Malin pulls the covers over Tove's body.

Goes to the cleaning cupboard. Gets out a bucket, a mop, and a rag, fills the bucket with warm water and disinfectant, then goes out to clean the front step, feels the cold stone beneath her bare knees.

She scrubs.

Removes all traces.

And when she's finished she goes to bed, thinking about Daniel Högfeldt's 'no'. Then she falls asleep, before she even has time to think about falling asleep.

Johan Jakobsson is awake, sitting at his computer at home in Linghem.

His family are asleep, and in their sleep they become mysteries that can never be solved.

That's why I love being a police officer, Johan thinks.

Because the mysteries get solved. Because there's always another mystery waiting to be solved.

He's been looking for information about mercy-killer Vincent Edlund, who has recently been released after serving his sentence for murdering two elderly patients. Sven wanted him checked out, and Johan Jakobsson can't help wondering: Why has he been released at all?

He's never shown any remorse or expressed the slightest regret, according to documents Johan has received from Karsudden Hospital.

Vincent Edlund was sentenced to secure psychiatric care for the murders of two men in the Stintan old people's home in Hallsberg. The case attracted a lot of publicity, but was quickly forgotten, the way crimes against the elderly tend to be.

And now he's out.

Released just a week before the case that resembles theirs, in which an old man hanged himself with the cord of his alarm button.

And now another alarm button.

Too many of them for coincidence?

Johan feels his way through cyberspace. For the first six months after his release Vincent Edlund lived in Brotjärn, one hundred kilometres from the care home in Hälsingland. But Johan has looked into what happened there, and there seems little doubt that it was suicide.

Where does Vincent Edlund live now? Where is he registered?

Nowhere.

Johan checks the vehicle registration database.

One hit.

A campervan registered to Vincent Edlund.

Where could he have bought that? Johan looks up the registration number in the database of vehicle sales.

Stavén's Cars in Linköping, out in Tornby.

Well, well, well.

Johan knows they have a reputation for good service. He dials the number of Stavén's Cars, even though it's the middle of the night. The answerphone clicks in, referring callers to a mobile number.

He calls the mobile.

Even though it's the middle of the night.

A man answers after the sixth ring.

'Stavén's Cars. I mean, Peter Stavén.'

The man sounds so sleepy that his statement sounds like a question.

Johan gives the man a few seconds to wake up before apologising for phoning so late and explaining why he's called.

'Do you know where Vincent Edlund took the camper-van?'

'I do, as it happens,' Peter Stavén says, apparently unsurprised by the question. 'He's got it parked up at the campsite out in Glyttinge. He came back a few days ago, wanted to get the fuel line replaced. He mentioned it then.'

'So he's in Linköping?'

The man who killed old people.

Our man?

'As far as I know,' Peter Stavén replies.

'What sort of impression did you get of him?'

'He seemed a bit eccentric. Paid cash for the vehicle. Said it had taken him a long time to save up for it.'

'Anything else?'

'Look, it's the middle of the night. I should be asleep, and so should you.'

A head in a noose.

Someone gasping for air.

A final breath that becomes a mystery.

Have we got you now? Johan thinks, clicking to end the call.

PART 3
Despairing love

[The wind]

Where is the wind now, the whetted-knife exhalation?

It's still sweeping across Linköping. Making the city's flags and weathervanes tremble anxiously in the night. The lights of the buildings go on and off; the city's inhabitants are getting ready for a new day.

Hurry up, Malin. You're close now, so close.

No one wants to see themselves in a cracked mirror. After one mystery comes another.

Grief comes to everyone. Death, followed by more death.

A stranglehold, a bullet from a pistol.

They're working themselves to death, someone cries.

That money's mine, someone else shouts.

A third whispers: they're so alone that they'd rather die.

What's the price? whispers the wind.

What's the price you have to pay for treating those who've gone before you as garbage?

Weakness, whispers the wind.

I shall tear its throat out, in your name.

44

Tove, at the kitchen table. Awake, with watery eyes and green-tinged skin, a mug of black coffee. She grimaces, and Malin knows only too well how bad she's feeling, knows all about the jack-hammer throbbing inside her head.

Her towelling dressing gown is both rough and soft against her body. The kitchen window is wide open, in spite of the chill in the air outside.

Tove raises her head, a resigned look in her eyes, but not quite as tired as Malin had been expecting.

'I don't feel up to going to work today.'

Malin smiles, says: 'Queen of the night, queen of the day. Isn't that right?'

'You don't even believe that yourself, do you?'

Malin remembers the few times she pulled a sickie because she was hungover. That's just how Tove feels now, and maybe she could do with a day off; it's been a tough week for her, what with Konrad Karlsson's death and the trip to see Stefan.

'I can call for you, if you like,' Malin says, and the next minute she's speaking to Hilda Jansson.

'This is Malin Fors, Tove's mum. I'm not calling on police business this time. I'm afraid Tove isn't well, she's got a stomach bug.'

'OK, thanks for letting us know. When do you think she'll be back?'

Malin takes a gulp of coffee and looks at Tove again.

'Tomorrow, with a bit of luck. How are you getting on?'

Hilda Jansson sighs.

'It's been hot, and the atmosphere has been tense. Not the best conditions for our residents, but we're struggling on.'

As she's talking to Hilda Jansson, Malin is simultaneously reading an article in the *Correspondent* in which they try to make a big deal out of the fact that the door to the Cherub was left unlocked at night. Rebecka Koss has fallen back on 'ongoing restructuring', as well as health and safety legislation: in case of fire, the doors need to be easy to open.

As slippery as eels, Malin thinks. An answer for everything. Bad answers, though.

She sips her coffee and ends the call to Hilda Jansson.

She's already spoken to Sven, who updated her about Hans Morelia's visit to see Börje, what he said about Berit Andersson's son, and what Johan has found out about Vincent Edlund. At last, the investigation is starting to move forward, they can see potential ways to proceed now, possibly rather too many.

Konrad Karlsson's call log and emails haven't produced anything of interest, nor has the security camera in the Horticultural Society Park. The one outside the park, on Trädgårdsgatan, was evidently broken on the night in question. And there have been no tip-offs from the public. And Yngve Karlsson's GPS has shown that his car was parked outside his house in Klockrike all night.

Malin realises that she should have asked Hilda about Berit's son, but perhaps it's better to wait until they've spoken to the son.

If they're actually going to talk to him.

Why wait, though?

She calls Hilda back.

'Fors here again. There was one other thing. This time I'm calling as a police officer.'

Malin outlines what Morelia had said about Berit's son, and concludes by asking how much Hilda knows about the matter.

'I don't know anything about it,' Hilda says. 'But a lot of people here are having trouble, of course, and the wages are barely enough to live on. And if you're like Berit, and have got a mortgage on a ramshackle summer house, then I can understand that things must feel very difficult.'

Malin takes another sip of coffee.

'Her son, Ronny, have you ever met him?'

'No.'

'And Berit's never mentioned these letters he's supposed to have written?'

'She talks about him from time to time. But nothing about any letters. So, do you think we can count on Tove being back tomorrow?'

A strikingly green face on the other side of the table.

'You can count on it,' Malin says, and hangs up.

Malin's on the point of being late. Zeke's picking her up in a few minutes, they're taking his car today, and she shrugs off the dressing gown and pulls on some briefs and a flowery blue dress.

Colder outside today.

Thick grey clouds have swept in, and the paper is saying that the summer storm that's on its way across the country from the Baltic is going to collide with another storm from the south.

That there is a possibility of some really bad weather.

Almost a tree-felling storm.

So Malin puts on the jacket Tove gave her, and calls out goodbye from the hall, and Tove replies: 'Come here, Mum, I want to ask you something.'

Malin hesitates, and at that moment hears a car horn out in the street. Must be Zeke. Not bothered about waking up any of the neighbours.

'Haven't got time.'

'Yes, you have.'

Something in Tove's voice makes Malin go into the kitchen anyway.

Tove fixes her with a firm stare.

Malin looks at the digital numbers on the clock without actually registering the time.

'Have you done anything else about Stefan? We really do need to move him from there. You said you were going to check. You've got to. You're got power of attorney.'

'I don't know if you've noticed, but I've got my hands full with a murder investigation.'

'Sometimes you have to be able to multitask.'

Malin brushes her fringe aside and bites her lip, trying to hold back, but fails.

'That's rich, coming from you, pulling a sickie because you got totally hammered. For fuck's sake, Tove, pull yourself together!' Malin catches her breath. 'And what are you going to do in the autumn? Have you got any idea?' Tove looks away. The flicker of stubbornness she showed just now vanishes and she slumps on the chair, and says: 'As soon as you get time, OK?'

Stefan.

Alone.

The stench in his room.

Maybe we could try to move him here, to Linköping? Impossible.

'I promise,' Malin says. 'But it's summer, lots of places are closed, it's hard to get hold of them on the phone.'

Tove wants to protest, Malin can see that, so tell me, Tove, tell me what you want, what you're thinking. But Tove slips away again, and the look in her eyes is impossible to read.

The car horn again.

'Zeke,' Malin says. 'I've got to run.'

She straps on her holster in the hall.

'Off you go, then,' Tove calls from the kitchen. 'Make sure you catch the bastard who murdered Konrad.'

Zeke is clutching the wheel with both hands. He's driving too fast, as if he can't get to the campsite where Vincent Edlund is supposed to keep his campervan quickly enough.

He looks worn out, Malin thinks. Having a four-year-old in the house must take its toll when you're almost fifty.

'How's Tess?' Malin asks.

'Fine,' Zeke says, and she can tell he's shut off inside himself.

'She's a great kid,' Malin says, thinking about how the investigation into Tess's adoption, and whether there was anything improper about it, had been abandoned.

Zeke nods.

Then switches the radio on.

The local news, and they're leading with their murder, although they have nothing about either Vincent Edlund or the drama out on the plain at Klockrike yesterday. Instead the reporter says that the police are floundering, and that Police Chief Karim Akbar, who usually takes a keen interest in the media, is steering clear of journalists and keeping things under wraps.

Then they go on to talk about the storm.

The speed at which the two storms are approaching

each other remains uncertain, but it does appear to be a very unusual weather system.

They're driving up towards Ryd, past the villas of Valla, and on the other side of the forest Malin can make out the orange-panelled buildings of the university. They drive past the blocks of social housing, and between the buildings Malin can see women wearing the niqab, and she wonders what their bodies and faces look like under the black fabric.

Their children playing.

The girls unaware that they may one day be forced to wear the same outfit as their mothers.

They drive past green-painted houses from the sixties and seventies, then turn off towards the swimming pool at Glyttinge, and the small campsite alongside it.

Vincent Edlund.

Are you the man we're looking for?

Malin can see the caravans in the distance now. The smart mobile caravans belonging to visiting tourists are lined up neatly in front of the pine forest, close to the entrance to the swimming pool. Slightly off to the side, closer to the motorway, there are a few grey, run-down, static mobile homes, lived in full-time by people on the fringes of society.

By their own choice, or not.

The clouds are weighing the day down, the sky. A few people are moving about over by the tourist caravans, but otherwise this is a lonely place.

Caravans are made for freedom, Malin thinks. But here they're tethered to the ground with heavy, invisible chains.

Is there a murderer here, inside one of these caravans? Malin wonders to herself. She feels her pulse quicken, and her heart seems to demand more space than she's got in her ribcage.

45

Waldemar Ekenberg is breathing heavily. The shabby stairwell in the block of flats on Ladugatan seems to be squeezing all the air from his lungs.

It's started to rain outside, a serious downpour, but Waldemar is sceptical about the weather forecast. Are they really likely to get that sort of storm in late summer?

On the other side of the road is a bingo hall. They saw a few teenagers go inside, and Waldemar can't help wondering if they couldn't find something more productive to do with their lives.

Börje Svärd is standing by his side in front of the door, which bears a sign with the name Andersson. The letter box is crooked, and when Börje rings the bell there's no sound at all. So Waldemar steps forward and knocks gently on the door, so as not to alarm anyone inside.

They hear footsteps and muttering. The lock clicks, the door opens, and in front of them stands a tall, rangy man dressed in blue tracksuit bottoms and a white T-shirt with the Coca-Cola logo. Waldemar estimates that he's in his mid-thirties, but he looks older: his face is drawn and his stubble patchy. His hair is long, dark, and greasy, and he looks at them wearily and says: 'Who are you? What do you want?'

They introduce themselves, and Waldemar says: 'We'd like a word. Can we come in?'

Ronny Andersson hesitates.

Does he look guilty? Waldemar wonders. Is he capable of harassing anyone?

Suddenly the look in his eyes changes, becomes full of anger, and Waldemar wonders briefly if Ronny Andersson is going to attack them in a moment of madness, like a pistol shot out of nowhere, but then the anger in his eyes vanishes again and he gestures to them.

'Sure, come in. I should warn you, though, it looks a right tip. Pretend you haven't noticed.'

'We've seen most things before,' Börje says, and they follow Ronny Andersson into the flat's single room, through the tiny kitchen alcove whose sink is overflowing with pizza boxes, dirty plates, and empty beer bottles. The cupboards, in contrast, look clean and tidy, as though they actually housed something valuable.

The room contains a large, unmade bed, the grey textured wallpaper is full of holes where pictures must once have hung, and in front of the single window is a large, flat-screen television. There's a full ashtray on the floor, empty beer cans, and the room reeks of smoke and sweat, of hopelessness. Ronny Andersson sits down on the bed.

Waldemar and Börje remain standing: there are no chairs in the room. Ronny looks up at them.

'Hans Morelia sent you, didn't he? You're doing his dirty work for him as well, aren't you?'

'We're not doing anyone's dirty work,' Waldemar says, feeling his irritation growing. Who the hell does this grubby little semi-alcoholic think he is?

'You've sent him letters, and you've been following him,' Börje says. 'That's what he says, anyway.'

'Does he, now? Sure, I've written to him, tried to see him. I've called a few times. But following him? No, definitely not.'

'He also claims that you put a package containing excrement through his letter box.'

'He's mad.'

'As you know, someone was murdered at the care home where your mother works, a home which happens to be owned by Merapi. So we're wondering what you know about that.'

Good, Waldemar thinks. Give Ronny Andersson free rein to talk, and maybe he'll say something they can work with.

The look in Ronny Andersson's eyes changes again, and he says: 'I don't know anything about that. Why would I?'

He pauses before going on in a matter-of-fact tone that contrasts sharply with the content of his words.

'But it's good that people are focusing on Merapi and Hans Morelia's methods. They're all bastards, the lot of them. My mum's working herself to death on an insane rota of nightshifts that's exhausting her. And for what? A salary that barely covers her rent and food.' Waldemar can see the anger in Ronny Andersson's eyes as he goes on: 'And Morelia earns billions while people like my mum, good people, honest people, who work without complaining, work themselves to death without ever having enough money to save for a rainy day, or go on holiday, or buy a tiny house for themselves. Christ, it's got to stop, and if Konrad Karlsson's death helps bring that about, then so much the better.'

And yet you don't actually work, Waldemar thinks.

'I could never work for someone like Morelia,' Ronny Andersson says, as if he'd read Waldemar's mind.

Then Ronny Andersson grinds to a halt. He starts drumming his fingers on his knees, evidently waiting for their next question.

'Did you post excrement through Hans Morelia's letter box?' Börje asks, and the question makes Ronny Andersson raise his eyebrows slightly, and he doesn't answer.

Merely shakes his head.

'I don't suppose,' Waldemar says calmly, 'that you had anything to do with Konrad Karlsson's murder? That you staged it specifically to focus attention on the injustices at your mum's workplace?'

Ronny Andersson shakes his head again.

'Did you think that was a way of making things better for your mum?'

'She deserves an easier life,' Ronny Andersson says. 'She's struggled her whole life, always taking care of other people, and what has she got for that? A fucked-up back and the privilege of being shat on by men like Hans Morelia. He ought to be put in the stocks in Stora torget.'

'What were you doing on the night between Monday and Tuesday?'

Ronny Andersson looks up at them.

Waldemar tucks his fingers in, and the sound of his knuckles cracking echoes around the room.

'I was drinking beer,' Ronny Andersson said. 'As many as I could afford. I drank them here, with Bambam Martinsson.'

'Can we have this Bambam's number?'

'What for?'

Not a bad morning, Waldemar thinks, then goes on to ponder the excrement that was pushed through Hans Morelia's letter box. He looks at Ronny Andersson, resigned, yet with a glimpse of desperation in his eyes, and wonders: What might you be capable of, if your cosy little world got shaken up?

46

It's raining now. The sky can no longer keep hold of all that water, and Malin wishes she'd had the foresight to wear her raincoat.

She and Zeke are heading towards the campervan that must belong to Vincent Edlund.

Is he there?

The few people visible in the small campsite soon vanish as the rain gets harder, and Malin and Zeke huddle beneath the little awning above the door to the vehicle.

They knock.

Malin feels her pistol beneath her jacket. Over the years she's learned to suppress her fears, and the previous day's events out on the plain are forgotten.

The metal cold and hard against her body.

Daniel yesterday. The feel of his hand against her cheek.

She can still feel it, as a gentle heat.

He said no.

He's more sensible than me. But I want to, I want to see him. At least I can admit that to myself.

The gun is cold and heavy. The wet docility of this place could soon switch to wild panic, if Vincent is inside his tin-can of a home and has anything to do with their murder.

Then the door opens.

A man in his fifties looks out.

A bushy grey beard covers half his face. A broad nose

sticks out like a double-barrelled shotgun between long curtains of hair, and his black eyes are tranquil, as if they've seen everything.

'There's no need to tell me who you are,' Vincent Edlund says. 'I've been expecting you.'

'Can we come in?' Malin asks. She huddles up, as if to demonstrate how unpleasant the rain is, and a sudden gust of wind tugs her jacket open and reveals her gun.

'You won't be needing that here,' Vincent Edlund says as he lets them in.

The interior of the campervan is meticulously tidy, there's nothing there that doesn't seem to have a purpose.

There's a neat pile of newspapers on one worktop, a few tins of food in a sculptural arrangement designed to occupy as little room as possible; this is a man used to living in a confined space.

Vincent Edlund sits down opposite them on the fixed red bench that surrounds a metre-high plastic table.

'I've been expecting you,' he repeats. 'Since I read about the murder in the old people's home. It was only a matter of time before you found me.'

Malin feels her heart beat faster.

What's he saying?

Is he confessing?

She can hear the rain on the roof of the campervan.

Then Vincent Edlund goes on: 'I had nothing to do with it. Just so you know. You've got nothing on me, have you? Apart from what happened twenty years ago.'

I'm not answering that, Malin thinks, and says instead: 'If you knew we'd be coming, and you're innocent, why didn't you get in touch with us?'

'I've paid my debt to society,' Vincent Edlund says, scratching his beard. 'Now I just want to be left in peace.'

'How do you make a living?' Zeke asks.

'Early retirement, but you already know that. I'm pretty much regarded as unemployable, and I've also got an auto-immune disease.'

Zeke nods.

'Do you have anything against old people?'

'When I was younger I couldn't stand to watch them suffer. So I took things into my own hands. And the old men wanted it, no matter what their relatives say. I didn't think it was wrong at the time, and I don't think it's wrong now. But I realise that society, and people generally, think it's wrong. And I've got no desire to go back to prison. They'll just have to suffer.' Vincent Edlund pauses. 'I don't want to end up in Karsudden again. This campervan is like a cell, and that feels reassuring, but at least I can open the door whenever I want to.'

What about the relatives? Malin thinks. The fear the people you killed must have felt? Did none of that get through to you? Years of treatment, and nothing got through?

Or did the old people want to die? And asked for your help? But you were still found guilty of murder.

'It's a merciful release if people who are suffering are allowed to die,' Vincent Edlund says. 'They wanted to die, and I helped them. Shouldn't we all be allowed to make decisions about our own lives?'

'Are you talking about Konrad Karlsson now?' Malin asks, contemplating the peculiar tranquillity inside the campervan, as the increasingly heavy rain on the roof actually has a soothing effect.

Vincent Edlund laughs, his beard shaking with laughter.

'No, no. I'm talking about Evert Grusom and Albin Ingvarsson, the men I was convicted of murdering.'

Malin looks at Vincent Edlund.

His eyes.

How calm they are.

Maybe he's telling the truth?

'There was a suspicious death at a home in Hälsingland six months ago, when you were living in the area. And now there's a similar case after you've shown up in Linköping.'

Vincent Edlund looks Malin in the eye.

'I'm not a murderer. But I'd be willing to help anyone else who wanted to die.'

'Have you got an apprentice?'

'No,' Vincent Edlund laughs.

'Do you get a thrill out of killing old people?' Zeke asks, and Malin can hear the distaste in his voice. 'A sexual thrill, I mean.'

'I'm not even going to dignify that with an answer. I've got an alibi for the night of the murder. I was with my girlfriend, here in the caravan,' and just as he finishes the sentence the door opens. A young blond woman walks in, probably thirty years younger than Vincent Edlund, not much older than Tove.

Malin looks at Zeke. The expression on his face is as surprised as her own must be.

You poor little thing, Malin thinks. How did you end up here?

The young woman sees the look on their faces and says: 'Vincent and I were pen pals when he was at Karsudden. We're soulmates. We think exactly the same things.'

'OK,' Malin says.

'OK, what?' the woman retorts, quick as a flash.

Malin feels her cheeks blush.

'Alexandra, tell them what you and I were doing on the night between Monday and Tuesday. Tell the detectives in detail what we were doing here in the caravan that night. I'm sure they want to hear absolutely everything, down to the last drop of sweat.'

47

The warm water of the shower encloses Tove, making the blood in her veins rush to her skin, and her whole body turns red, not lobster red, but a pale, watercolour red, as if she were made of discoloured liquid.

Drinking.

It tastes so good, and it's wonderful to feel the world drift away. Sorrows lift, Konrad's face vanished yesterday. Even Stefan's situation didn't seem too bad.

It's wonderful to feel how everything becomes a white cloud slowly spreading across the sky, drifting towards the horizon and dissolving of its own accord.

Mum must love that feeling.

And I love it too, Tove thinks, but not as much as Mum. I'm not like her, I'm only nineteen, I'm in control. And Tove turns off the shower, and the shabby bathroom slowly gets cooler as the steam disperses.

It's just a temporary thing. While I'm feeling sad.

She gets out of the shower, grabs the towel from the hook, and dries herself.

Her body.

I'm taller than Mum. I've got her small, firm breasts, but she's in much better shape than me.

The headache pills have worked. She's managed to keep down coffee, a pasty, and a Coke, and enough time has elapsed now. The alcohol must be out of her system by now.

She gets dressed, jeans and a T-shirt, drinks some water straight from the tap in the kitchen. Then she pulls on her raincoat and takes her mum's car keys from the dresser in the hall.

Just minutes later she's sitting behind the wheel, steering the car through the rain, out of Linköping, north, putting her foot down and driving towards what has to be the right thing.

I have to do something, or I'll go mad, she thinks.

What can we do? Malin wonders, pushing the weights up away from her.

Three times twelve, fifty kilos; she can't manage more than that unless she's got someone to spot her. She's on her own in the stinking gym, where the air seems to have stood still for decades. No Elin Sand today.

Nice.

I'm being ridiculous, Malin thinks. What does it matter who can bench press more? Her T-shirt is wet with sweat, but good sweat, and she feel like yelling out loud, but what?

Bloody Tove.

Bloody drink.

I just tried calling her, but her mobile was busy and she didn't pick up at home. Out somewhere. Maybe with some friend, although she doesn't really see much of her old friends.

FUCK.

FUCK FUCK FUCK.

Malin pushes the bar up for the thirty-sixth time as she yells.

Clunk.

And the bar is back in its cradle and she curses her own weakness. Or strength. Same difference, really.

No matter what happens, it will be fine. Won't it? And she wants Daniel again. Wants to feel everything that this, the gym, the station, her job, isn't.

They had a team meeting a short while ago.

The suspicions against Yngve and Margaretha Karlsson are considered weak. Nothing new has arisen there, nothing that could tie either of them to their father's death. The pair of them will inherit his fortune seeing as he never signed the papers donating his money to charity. Gabriella will also inherit some money, but any suspicions against her are similarly weak.

But Malin isn't ready to let the brother and sister go altogether, wants to keep all their options open, and Yngve Karlsson is still in custody. Aiming a loaded weapon at a police officer is a serious offence. He's likely to stand trial for that, or at least for threatening a public official, possibly even attempted murder.

They also discussed the connection to Dragan Zyber. Elin Sand thought they ought to take a look at him, but the others all thought that was too much of a long shot.

Waldemar dismissed the idea by saying: 'Her imagination's running away with her again.'

Malin felt like telling him to shut up. Wanted to come to Elin's defence, but let it go.

There are some battles you have to fight for yourself, and she could see Elin Sand clench her teeth, a peculiarly resolute look in her eyes.

Then they talked about Vincent Edlund.

What a man.

They considered bringing him in, wanted to bring him in, but on what grounds? There's nothing concrete to bind him to their murder, or the death of any other elderly person, since he was released from Karsudden. They talked about whether he could have got into the home without being seen, how anyone could have done that, but of course the security procedures were utterly hopeless. With a modicum of luck and skill it would be perfectly possible to get in unseen. Just like Malin herself had done the other night. Although she didn't mention that.

Börje described their interview with Ronny Andersson, and how desperate he had seemed.

With good reason, according to Börje.

And Malin thinks of all the people who never seem to end up in the right place in their lives, who never manage to sort out their souls, their desires, never reach the place where reality and dreams meet.

She sees herself in the mirror in the gym, her bulging biceps, and looks away, doesn't want to look at that red-cheeked woman.

Elin Sand had talked to the employees at the Cherub once again, both day and night staff, to see if they had anything more to say, anything at all, now that they had a bit of distance from what happened. None of them had seen anything, and there was nothing to suggest that they were involved in the murder. None of them has any sort of criminal record.

The interviews at Merapi's head office had also been fruitless.

And someone called Bambam had confirmed Ronny Andersson's alibi.

Yet Malin can't help feeling that something is on the point of happening in the investigation, and knows that Sven shares her conviction. The voices are audible now, and soon something is going to crack and open up, as long as she keeps her ears and mind open.

Tove made the calls from the car. Over and over again, trying to reach the Social Services department of Ljusdal

Council. She battled her way past receptionists who kept pointing out that it was Saturday, and finally managed to talk to the duty officer for care homes in the district.

She tried to sound older than she is. Made her voice deeper, explained why she was calling, that her brother Stefan Malmå wasn't at all happy at the care home in Sjöplogen, that the standard of care had deteriorated dramatically since Merapi took over and the old staff left, that she was on her way to Sjöplogen for a meeting, and was there any chance she could look at alternative accommodation while she was in the area?

She said her name was Malin Fors, that she was Malin Fors, Stefan's half-sister and guardian, and the woman at the other end said: 'Have I understood correctly? You want to look at other homes today? Without any notice? I'm afraid that can't be arranged, it's quite impossible.'

'I have a letter ready to send to the paper,' Tove said, and outlined the contents of the imaginary text, including how she had found Stefan lying in his own excrement.

'I don't really want to have to send it to the local paper.'

And the woman fell silent.

Considered the threat.

Tapped at her computer.

Presumably looking up the name Malin Fors on the Internet and finding articles about Tove's mother, all of which would suggest that she was a woman who meant what she said.

'I'll put you through to one of my colleagues,' she said, and after ten rings another woman's voice came on the line: 'There are places in two homes. I'll call back in ten minutes to confirm that they can see you.'

And now Tove is walking slowly behind a nurse who is showing her around one of the homes. There's a tranquillity to the building, a modified villa beside the river in

Ljusdal. It doesn't smell like a hospital, it smells of humanity and warmth, and the light is gentle. Four people in wheelchairs are sitting in a day room with leaded windows looking out on to a lush garden.

She looks at them from behind as they sit there in silence.

Calm.

As if they're happy here, have found the right place.

Can deal with a life without words.

The nurse turns to Tove and says: 'Do you think your brother would be happy here, Malin?'

48

Running along beside the water, feeling the heavens throw cold raindrops in your face, clamouring for attention, running away from yourself, sweating, feeling your heart pound in your chest, running away from all the desires that lurk as a wonderful, terrible danger.

I want something, Malin thinks. I do, don't I?

Am I cured of my bout of not-wanting?

Vibrations against one thigh, the mobile in the pocket of her raincoat, and Malin knows she has to answer, knows it could be about the case, something could have happened, a breakthrough. She slows down and takes shelter beneath a tree, and presses to take the call without checking to see who it is. With the phone pressed tight to her ear, she says breathlessly: 'Fors.'

She's standing still now, beneath the big oaks by the sluice gates on the edge of Tannerfors, and she catches sight of an almost dry park bench under one particularly leafy oak, but resists the temptation to sit down.

'Mum, it's me.'

Tove.

Malin feels like clicking the call away, ashamed at her disappointed reaction, but asks: 'Are you feeling better now?'

'Much better.'

And now she's jealous of Tove's youth, remembers how she could shake off terrible hangovers by midday when she herself was young. The last time she fell off the wagon it lingered for several days.

'I felt better by lunchtime.'

There's something hesitant about Tove's voice, and Malin gets suspicious, what's happened now?

'Where are you?'

'I'm with Stefan.'

'What?'

'I'm with Stefan.'

'How did you get there?'

'I took your car.'

'Are you mad, Tove? Driving the day after . . .'

'I felt fine.'

Fine?

Nothing's fine, Malin thinks, and walks over to the bench, sits down, and feels her backside get wet, despite the fact that the bench had looked dry.

'I felt I had to come. And see if everything was the way it should be.'

Malin fills her lungs with air, and she can't be angry with Tove for worrying about Stefan. Can't, won't.

'And how is it?'

'Nothing disastrous. But it's not like it used to be. It feels cold here, Mum.'

Tove pauses, then says: 'I want him to move.'

'We've already talked about that. It would be impossible to find another home at short notice. You know what a shortage of beds there is everywhere.'

'But there isn't. I've sorted it out.'

Tove.

How could you have done that?

'I called the council. Said I was you. Threatened to send a letter to the paper describing the state we found Stefan in, and now I've been to look at two homes with spare places. He can move if we make our minds up within a week.'

'You pretended to be me?'

'Yes, because you're his legal guardian.'

And she wants to shout at Tove, make her realise what she's done, but at the same time she realises the significance of her daughter's actions, the depth of love that they demonstrate, and the extent of her own failure to show the same love in a simple, practical way.

'You're crazy, Tove, you know that, don't you?'

'Yes,' her daughter replies, and in her mind's eye Malin can see Tove as prime minister, head of the Red Cross, or something similarly grand.

'The first home was best. It's in Ljusdal itself, by the river. Only seven residents. Stefan would be number eight.'

'Then that's where we move him.'

Tove doesn't respond, and a middle-aged couple in waterproof jogging outfits run past, and Malin feels the cold against her buttocks.

'I'll be heading home soon,' Tove says. 'I promise to drive safely.'

'How is he?'

'He seems OK. I think he smiled just now. He seems to like me being here.'

Vincent Edlund.

Zeke Martinsson is sitting at the kitchen table in the flat he shares with Karin Johannison. He can hear the sound of a DVD from the living room; Tess is watching one of those animated Japanese films that she and Karin are so fond of. He doesn't mind them himself.

He's been thinking about taking up choral singing again.

He's had an email from the head of the choir, asking him to come back. And people like Vincent Edlund make him feel like going back to singing, to the simple, honest camaraderie of other people's company.

Johan spent the day looking into Edlund's old murders, and found nothing that could link them to their current case. But it's still not impossible that the wretched little man they met today had something to do with Konrad Karlsson's death, that he's actually rediscovered his former penchant for killing old people. How could we put pressure on him? Zeke wonders, as he listens to a cheerful Japanese song and Tess's delighted laughter.

Should I go out to the campervan again?

Not me.

Waldemar, perhaps. He wonders what Waldemar is doing now. Then he goes out into the hall, sees Karin lying down in the bedroom reading a book, and he picks up the phone.

He hesitates for a long time.

Aware of what he's about to do.

Then he calls Waldemar's number.

'Maybe we should look into Vincent Edlund a bit more closely,' he says when Waldemar answers.

'You mean I should pay him a visit?'

'I don't mean anything,' Zeke says, regretting that he called.

'I know what you mean,' Waldemar says, and hangs up.

I'll do this on my own, Waldemar Ekenberg thinks as he walks through his garden in Mjölby. Holding his hands up to shield his face from the rain.

The storm is approaching now.

The bushes are bent almost to the ground, and the windscreen wipers are going to have to work overtime on the drive to Linköping.

Vincent Edlund.

Reading the report into the preliminary investigation

left little room for doubt. He was guilty of two brutal murders. Nothing less.

Waldemar has no problem with what he's about to do, even if he has recently started to find violence less satisfying.

He steels himself against the gusts of wind out in the street. Can feel the anticipation in his body as tiny doses of adrenalin make their way into his blood.

Apply some pressure.

Show who's in charge.

Once a murderer, always a murderer.

That's what he'll teach Vincent Edlund.

My way, Waldemar thinks. In my very own special way.

49

The chorizo sausages from Maxi are sizzling on the grill.

Johan Jakobsson sees it as an act of defiance to have a barbecue even if the weather has decided to build up to a storm.

Down in the garden, under an apple tree that's shaking in the wind, the children are playing a game, but it's impossible to tell what. Perhaps they're hunting insects?

The rain doesn't bother the children, and their yellow raincoats offer good protection against the weather. He himself is almost completely covered by the roof jutting out over the terrace.

I'm hopeless at barbecues, Johan thinks as he looks at the burned sausages, and then he feels something warm, moist, on the back of his neck, not rain, but soft lips.

'Are you getting on all right, darling?' His wife walks around him with a bottle of wine in one hand, an umbrella in the other. 'I opened this one. The bottle you gave me.'

'Expensive.'

'Bound to be good,' his wife says, then disappears indoors again.

Johan looks down towards where the children are playing.

Thinks: This is a good evening. One of those evenings when nothing bad happens.

Vincent Edlund hears a car pull up outside the campervan, but can't be bothered to get up, he's too engrossed in a completely unrealistic episode of *CSI*. Probably one of the campsite's temporary visitors who's gone the wrong way. Then the car stops, a door opens and closes, and he begins to suspect that someone has come to see him.

Alexandra's gone into the city. Was going to have a few beers with an old friend. He's not happy about it, but knows he shouldn't try to stop her. He needs to loosen the leash sometimes, otherwise she'll get fed up with him, because what is he really but a dodgy old bloke?

Ha.

He laughs silently to himself.

He's not an old man yet. I've still got plenty of energy, he thinks. He still hates weakness. The day he feels weak he knows what he's going to do. He's planning to jump in front of a train.

Or put his head in a noose.

It will be a relief.

He knows that.

Like morphine.

Now there's a knock at the door, hard, continuous, and he gets to his feet, but leaves the television on. Gary Sinise is doing his best to look tough on some New York street, and almost succeeds.

Vincent Edlund composes his features.

Opens the door.

On the other side, just a metre away in the rain, stands a man dressed in crumpled, scruffy clothes. He stinks of smoke and looks tired, but Vincent Edlund recognises his strength, and feels instinctively that this isn't a man to be trifled with, underestimated.

'Waldemar Ekenberg,' the man says. 'Linköping Police.'

Elin Sand is leaning back in the cinema seat. Huge faces with massive mouths in front of her.

She's on her own.

She likes going to the cinema alone. Imagining other stories, different to the ones playing out before her eyes. But tonight the stories don't grab her.

She's angry.

Fed up with not being taken seriously.

Now she's looking at an alpine landscape.

An aeroplane.

She can smell popcorn, and thinks: I'll show you what I'm capable of. Just you wait.

Malin is standing by the kitchen worktop, eating heated-up meat stew from the freezer.

Trying not to notice the stench.

Anticimex are going to come again. When was it? Tomorrow? Thank goodness they work weekends.

She picks at the food, not hungry in spite of the weight-training and running, but she knows she's got to eat, keep her strength up.

There's no buzz of voices outside the window. No one's going anywhere tonight, not even to get away from something. It occurs to her that she's got stuck in no-man's-land, somewhere between towards and away from, but that there's no movement in her life at all. She can't even look for that in her relationship with Tove. Her daughter is already gone, only home temporarily for the summer, and then she'll rush away, off to whatever her life is going to be.

Daniel.

I'm really only after a body, after physical contact. Not some fucking hand on my cheek.

Unless I felt something else? And am still feeling it?

And she sees a calm sea within her, knows that she isn't that sea at all. She's waves lashing against a breakwater, over and over again, before finally moving on towards uncharted territory.

She wants a drink.

She always wants a drink, will always want one, and there's something indescribably wearisome in that, in the predictability of desire. What have I really got to look forward to? I'm not even forty yet, but I'm stuck on my own in my squalid, stinking flat, picking at a tragic little dish of meat stew.

Bloody hell.

Then she thinks about work.

Maybe I should move back to Stockholm? There's nothing tying me to this dump any more.

Sees herself in Sven's chair, in his office. Malin Fors, the boss. But that isn't her. She never wants to sit in that chair, bear that kind of responsibility.

I've got enough of that already.

Konrad Karlsson.

No one's life should end the way yours did. No one can claim to have the right to strangle another person.

Tove, Stefan, and me. We're responsible for each other.

That has to be it.

How else could I bear it?

Waldemar is standing still inside the campervan, struck by how tidy it is: there are worse places to live.

He says nothing, and sees the man in there with him get nervous, disgustingly scared, as scared as the old men he murdered must have been. Vincent Edlund can't seem to decide whether to sit or stand, and Waldemar measures his physical strength with his eyes, his strength, agility, and the weaknesses in the other man's body probably outweigh its strengths. He takes two steps towards the man and takes a swing at him, and before Vincent Edlund, killer of old men, has time to react, Waldemar's fist connects with his cheekbone and he collapses on the floor of the van, lying at Waldemar's feet, spitting, hissing and groaning. Then he turns his bearded face towards Waldemar and whispers: 'What the hell was that all about? Are you mad?'

And Waldemar kicks him in the stomach, then kicks again, in his ribs, but not too hard. Vincent Edlund gasps for breath, and Waldemar lets him recover, kneels down beside the prone body, breathes, lets his smoke-poisoned breath hit the man in the face, then sticks two fingers in Vincent Edlund's nostrils and pulls him towards the bench.

'You need to get one thing seriously fucking clear in your head,' he hisses. 'I'm the one who asks the questions here, OK?'

Cowering, Vincent Edlund nods.

He looks drained, Waldemar thinks. Just as he should.

'Your alibi for the night of Konrad Karlsson's murder is fake. Isn't it? You weren't with that Alexandra at all. What the fuck would she be doing with an old man like you?'

'I was with her. Ask her again.'

Waldemar hits Vincent Edlund again. A slap across the cheek this time.

'You're lying. Tell me about the old man in Hälsingland. You strangled him, didn't you? Then you came down here and strangled Konrad Karlsson. It turns you on, doesn't it? Watching them die. Their weakness makes you feel strong, doesn't it?'

Waldemar feels like smashing his fist into the face on the bench. The tough guy is sobbing now, shaking his head, saying: 'No, no, no.'

'What do you mean, no?'

'I had nothing to do with that.'

'Don't lie to me, you sack of shit.'

And he hears a car stop outside the campervan, a door slamming.

'Alexandra,' Vincent Edlund whispers.

'You're not fooling anyone,' Waldemar says.

He's applied pressure, and just about everyone would have talked by now. He knows he can put the fear of God into people, and he turns away and leaves the sobbing figure.

On his way out of the van he meets a young and surprisingly beautiful woman.

He stares at her.

'You need to sort out that sack of shit on the bench in there.'

He walks towards his car.

Stops.

Runs back into the campervan, where Alexandra is now sitting next to Vincent Edlund. Waldemar stands right in front of them, and looks darkly at them.

'Get out,' the woman yells. 'Get out!'

'Shhh,' Waldemar whispers.

She calms down.

'You're not lying to me, are you?'

She tries to spit in his face, and Waldemar dodges to one side. He leaves the van, thinking: Have I gone too far this time? Can you ever go too far in the search for the truth?

Then he gets into his car and drives home to his wife in Mjölby.

50

Sunday, 15 August

Karim Akbar lowers three eggs into the boiling water. One of them cracks, and he swears:

'Shit!'

'It's only an egg,' he hears Vivianne say behind him.

'Yes, but still,' he says, without turning around.

'He's kicking now. Come and feel.'

Karim turns around. There she sits. In a luxurious dressing gown, and she looks impossibly beautiful this morning. Someone he wants to get to know, not just look at. Someone he wants to listen to. Touch.

He goes over to her, opens the dressing gown, puts his hand on her warm belly, and feels the kicks.

The miracle.

Maybe he wants to stay here after all, in this moment, in this city, in this life, for ever. Maybe there's nothing better anywhere else.

The stench in the flat.

Malin and Tove don't notice it as they sit and share an early breakfast together. One good thing about smells is that you tend not to notice them after a while, although the memory of them lingers.

Someone else from Anticimex is coming today. An

emergency call-out. With a camera that's supposed to be able to see into the smallest cracks.

Half past three.

Malin will have to remember to be home to let him in.

The window facing St Lars Church is open. The oncoming storm is now predicted to be even stronger, but for the moment the rain has stopped, as if forces are gathering for a frontal attack.

Tove leans across the table.

'I've been thinking, Mum.'

'What about? Have you changed your mind about the care homes in Ljusdal? Was the other one better, the one by the river, or was it the other way around?'

She sees Tove's weary eyes darken.

'You really don't care about Stefan at all.'

She says it as a statement, and Malin wants to protest, refute the accusation, but knows that Tove is right, at least in part.

Then Tove repeats: 'I've been thinking.'

A pregnant pause, and Malin feels like getting up, heading off to the station, to work.

'He really ought to be with us. In a home here, in Linköping. So we can visit him more often. So it doesn't have to be such a big deal every time.'

Malin picks up her sandwich, takes a bite, chews, is about to swallow before saying anything, but she can't stop herself: 'And how the hell do you think that would work? Do you imagine social services here would welcome Stefan with open arms? They'd refuse to find him a place.'

Crumbs flying.

Tove bites her bottom lip.

'People still have the right to move, even if they do have special needs, Mum. You know that.'

'Do you really think it's that simple? That you can just do what you like?'

'You don't want him here,' Tove snaps. 'It suits you much better to keep him as a distant idea that you can project your pathetic theories of loneliness on to. Take some responsibility, Mum. He's your brother.'

'Don't lecture me about responsibility.'

Tove leans back and laughs.

'You panic whenever there's a glimpse of responsibility that isn't connected to your work. Because that involves emotions, and you're terrified of any sort of emotion. And you know that perfectly bloody well.'

What can I say to that? Malin thinks.

My daughter is sitting in front of me, analysing my emotional life.

Well, fuck her.

'Be quiet, Tove. You don't talk to your mother like that. You keep saying he ought to be near us. Near us? You're home for the summer, then you'll be off again, God knows where, to Lund, Stockholm, wherever. You're hardly likely to go to university in Linköping, so we're basically talking about me here, not us.'

'We're talking about Stefan. Your brother.'

'But I don't want him here.'

There, it's said.

I confess.

I want to keep my disabled brother at a distance. I want him to have a good life, but not here.

I need to live my life in peace. Why is that so fucking hard to understand?

Tove goes to stand up.

'You're pathetically selfish. Just like Grandma and Granddad.'

'Don't mention me in the same breath as them. And never

take the car again without asking for permission. Never. And certainly not when you've got a hangover.'

'I wasn't hungover.'

Malin turns her head away. Snorts.

'And how could you tell them you were me? That's against the law, Tove.'

'What was I supposed to do? You don't give a damn about Stefan, after all. So what are you going to do about it? Report me?'

'It's not right.'

Tove gets to her feet. Glances out of the window.

'Right? Really, Mum. Are you nineteen again, or what?'

And Malin looks at her daughter. For her it seems so obvious that the boundary between right and wrong is fluid, something you decide as and when situations arise. Principles mean nothing, actions everything.

Tove walks out of the kitchen. Shouts from the hall: 'I hope I never end up like you, Mum.'

Malin walks through a Linköping that's tormented by rain once again. It's gushing from the skies now, and the wind is getting stronger and stronger. She has to lean into the headwind, and the wind tears at her raincoat, trying to get at her skin.

The gale can't disguise the stench from the bins on Trädgårdstorget, where the market traders dumped the last of their produce yesterday.

Damn.

Tove. She's right, even though she's wrong, and Malin isn't about to back down on this one, she needs to trust her instincts, and she knows how she feels.

Why don't I want to have Stefan here?

Because he's a reminder of Mum and Dad's betrayal?

Why did Yngve and Margaretha Karlsson hardly ever visit their father in his care home?

Because he reminded them of loss, of betrayal, and the opposite applied to Gabriella, who did use to visit him. For her he was a link to her dead mother, and Malin can't help finding the idea rather touching. And she thinks about Berit and Ronny Andersson, their disappointments, and how a man like Ronny could find any number of strange ways to vent his frustrations.

She walks past the tobacconist's on Trädgårdsgatan with its advertisements for lottery scratch cards – now, apparently, with an increased chance of winning. Four cards for one hundred kronor.

Lottery tickets.

My only hope of getting rich, Malin thinks. Scratch cards, live on TV4! So many people in the same situation, tragically.

But she never buys lottery tickets. Doesn't believe that unrealistic dreams can actually come true.

I don't believe in luck, she thinks, and feels a warm gust of air as a bus drives past, and the world suddenly feels like a good place.

I have no idea what I do actually believe in.

Waldemar Ekenberg pulls up outside Börje Svärd's house. Blows the horn, and hears the dogs start barking in the garden.

Then he sees the gate open, and there's Börje, out in the rain. His smile seems wider without the moustache to drag his cheeks down.

Waldemar decided not to smoke as he drove over, and aired the car as best he could in such awful weather, doesn't want Börje to have to endure the stench of stale smoke. He does this several times a week, picking Börje up in Valla on his way to the station.

'All right?' Waldemar asks.

Börje smiles.

'I had that red-head here last night.'

Another lover, Waldemar thinks, with a pang of envy.

'So you're happy, then!'

He starts the car and they head out on to the main road in silence.

'I paid a visit to Vincent Edlund last night.' Waldemar clutches the steering wheel, and notices Börje looking at his swollen knuckles.

'OK.'

'Zeke's idea.'

'Really?'

A tiny, fleeting change in Börje's expression. As if he were briefly entertaining doubts about the morality of what might have happened inside the campervan.

Then his face resumes its usual calm expression.

'How did it go?' he asks.

Waldemar shakes his head.

'No?'

He shakes his head again, as they drive past the main cemetery, with all its long-dead and forgotten occupants.

'I get fed up with myself sometimes,' Waldemar says. 'Fed up of what I can't stop enjoying.'

'So learn to enjoy something else instead.'

'You don't think it's too late?'

'I don't know,' Börje says.

51

Malin walks into the station, says hello to the other members of the team.

Sunday working for everyone today.

Only Börje and Waldemar are missing.

Johan Jakobsson is crouched over his computer. He's rubbing his elbow, and Malin knows it's been troubling him. In the end he'll have to have an operation. He's had four cortisone injections, each one stronger than the last, but they haven't stopped the inflammation.

But his eyes look brighter. Who knows what he might be able to unearth for them?

Something else about the American purchase of Merapi? Something that could be linked to Konrad Karlsson? It wouldn't be the first time that the big, bad business world attacked its smaller, more human counterpart.

But Malin has a feeling that this could all be about that smaller, yet paradoxically larger, world.

Is this about Vincent Edlund's dreams? His longings, desires?

She doesn't know.

Zeke waves at her, and she waves back. He waves again, beckoning her over, and she walks across to him.

'Waldemar went to see Edlund last night.'

'I know. He sent me a text.'

'Maybe it was a stupid idea for him to go.'

'Maybe,' Malin says. 'But sometimes we need him.'

Elin Sand is sitting at her desk. Her long legs are tucked under her desk, and her hand almost covers the mouse. She's got her back to Malin, and is scrolling through something. Perhaps Johan has discovered something new about Yngve and Margaretha Karlsson's finances that he wants her to look through. Or something about Konrad Karlsson's own finances. Unless he's found something in Konrad's manuscript, something Malin hasn't noticed.

What a piece of work.

She read it last night, before falling asleep.

Who'd want to get old?

'No meeting today,' Zeke says. 'Sven's at the hospital, having his prostate X-rayed. Just a check-up. And we all know what we're supposed to be doing.'

Do we? Malin thinks. Having an X-ray on a Sunday? Has Sven suffered a relapse?

Her stomach clenches. Not again.

Sven. His prostate operation.

He couldn't piss normally for six months.

Who'd want to get old?

Not me, Malin thinks as she walks out to the kitchen.

On the way she passes Zeke. He's talking on the phone, snapping: 'No, I've got to work today. You'll have to do it. Not up for discussion.'

Malin gets herself a cup of coffee, then has a sudden idea. She calls across the open-plan office: 'Elin, have you got a few minutes?'

She wants to test Elin's already proven ability to tease out hints of the truth from people who may not even be aware that they possess them.

Elin stands up, a little too quickly. A little too readily. A bit like an eager puppy.

She wants to take Elin down into the basement, to the

cell in which Yngve Karlsson is languishing. Just to see what happens.

'Don't worry,' Malin tells Elin. 'I just want your help with something.'

Hans Morelia is sitting in his Maserati. He's put the roof up, and is waiting for the garage door to open. From the low-slung driver's seat all he can see is the increasingly dark sky and the roof of the neighbour's house.

The deal will soon be complete.

The gang from Stege Solicitors, led by the desperately unfashionable Robert Wernegren in his green jacket, have made their way down to Linköping from Stockholm on a Sunday, and he's about to meet them in a conference room that's been booked at the Hotel Ekoxen. They're going to spend the day going through the documents to do with the transaction. Line by line, letter by letter. They could have done that in the office out in Tornby, but he prefers neutral territory.

It's not far to the Ekoxen, but the weather's so awful that he'd rather take the car.

Besides, people will be impressed when he shows up in the Maserati. The black leather seats, the dashboard in black Tibetan mahogany, and the shimmering paint with real silver in the pigment is practically made for a day like this.

He starts the engine.

Listens to it purr.

It sounds like a perfect piece of human engineering, and he loves that sound, forgets how much when he's not driving the car, the way the sound waves seem to cut the air like a knife.

In just a few days' time he'll be a billionaire. His family's finances secure for generations to come.

For all of Lova's life.

He puts the car in gear and drives out of the garage. Turns left, down towards the city.

Briefly notices the old black car parked some way down the street, but not the fact that it pulls out and follows him.

Yngve Karlsson is asleep when the custody officer, a young man with tattoos of snakes on his lower arms, knocks on the cell door and opens it.

What am I hoping he might say? Malin wonders, but Elin seems to be in no doubt.

Even so, she asked a few moments ago, in her inimitable, dark voice: 'What do you want from this, Malin? Just tell me, and I'll do my best.'

Malin could hardly say that she didn't know, so replied instead with Sven's mantra.

'We need to listen to the voices of the investigation. In a few years' time you'll understand what I mean. But for now, just do as I say.'

Elin Sand nodded. Didn't seem to be annoyed.

'We need to hear what Yngve Karlsson's voice can add to the investigation,' Malin added. 'Trust me. I know what I'm doing.'

Now he's sitting, not quite awake, on the bunk in front of them, looking like he doesn't understand why he's been woken up. But then he looks at Malin and Elin and his face hardens.

'Good morning,' Elin says, and introduces herself.

Yngve Karlsson doesn't answer.

'I need to ask you a few more questions,' Elin Sand says.

Yngve Karlsson nods, and Malin can't help thinking that he must miss the whining winds of the Östgöta Plain, that a big storm must be truly dramatic out there. But now he's locked up in this cramped cell, and she wonders once again why he ran from them, why he threatened her with the rifle. Perhaps some people are simply always running, all their lives, until one day they get fed up of running, to find themselves standing in an isolated field, pointing a loaded gun at a police officer.

'Ask away,' Yngve Karlsson says.

'Have you thought of anything else we ought to know about your dad?'

'No.'

'Nothing at all?'

'Christ, how many more times do I have to tell you?'

Then Elin Sand asks if they've made any decisions about the funeral. Says that she knows they won't have access to their father's body until the investigation is finished, but perhaps they've already given the matter some thought?

And Malin feels like stopping her.

Too personal.

Straying from the point.

But Yngve Karlsson lights up, says: 'I spoke to Gabriella the other day. She's the one in charge. She had a suggestion about a coffin, a very plain one, which strikes me as a very good idea. Just a bit of simple carving by Gunnar Kanevad.'

Kanevad.

Linköping's favourite. A woodcarver.

What does his work cost?

I'd have to win the bloody lottery to be able to afford something like that, Malin thinks.

And she looks at Yngve Karlsson. Who had no contact with his father, yet wants to spend money on woodcarvings for his coffin. Even though he might not even be allowed to attend the funeral.

She thinks of his house, and how it will deteriorate still further if he's sent to prison for what he's done. She thinks how weary he looks, done in, somehow, and he says: 'I still can't believe that Dad was going to give his money away. That he didn't realise what it would mean to me. Will mean. I'll be able to repair the house. Go travelling. See more of the world than that bloody plain.

'And I'll be able to pay off my debts, and all the interest. That's the first thing I'm going to do.'

When you get out, Malin thinks.

Elin Sand follows Malin up the stairs to the office. Feels like asking what the interview was all about. If she did her job well.

The voices of the investigation.

What a load of bollocks.

I'm sick of being treated like someone who's a bit backward, she thinks. Or am I just being over-sensitive?

At least Malin wanted me with her when she went to see Yngve Karlsson.

That must mean something.

Does she understand anything about me?

52

Gabriella Karlsson has just spoken to Gunnar Kanevad over the phone.

He's happy to help carve the coffin, he'd read Konrad's letters and seen him on television, thought he'd made a significant contribution, had been courageous, 'so awful, what's happened', and 'sorry for your loss'.

She looks around her living room.

The books.

The few items of furniture.

The surfeit of loneliness.

He agreed to do the work cheaply. She only haggled to prove to herself that she could, to show Granddad that she wasn't wasting his money.

But Granddad is gone now.

Gone.

At last, she thinks, it's time for me to move on. As long as they find a murderer, I can move on.

Do they suspect me?

When they find a perpetrator I shall be free.

At long last.

The world belongs to me now, Hans Morelia thinks as he parks his Maserati outside the Hotel Ekoxen. He enjoys playing with that thought. The stupidity of the megalomania, the self-satisfaction he considers he can allow himself.

The world is his, and he knows what he's going to do with it.

They're going to travel.

The Taj Mahal.

The pyramids.

Tokyo.

Borobudur.

Machu Picchu.

The Grand Canyon and New York and the Eiffel Tower and the whole fucking world.

I shall show Lova the world, everything that belongs to her.

He looks at the time.

Just past eleven, he's fashionably late, and he gets out of the car, happy that the suits from Stege are having to wait, and what's that? Isn't that the car that was parked along the street just now, the black, nondescript old banger? Has it followed me here? He curses himself for not taking the advice of the security consultants.

It is the black car, and there's someone sitting in the front seat.

Hans Morelia feels his stomach clench. He wants to get inside the hotel, but something happens, the car's headlights, they're flashing, barely visible in the rain, but they definitely flashed. Now they're doing it again, three long, three short, three long.

SOS.

He tries to read the number plate, but the car's registration has been taped over.

He can't see the person sitting inside. The windows are obscured by the rain.

For a moment Hans Morelia considers going over to the car, but he doesn't dare. Instead he flees into the hotel, crouching in the rain, feels like going up to the reception desk to say that he's being followed, but is he really? Does he know for certain? He'd like to ask them to call the police.

But something makes him walk past the reception desk to the lift, then up to the conference room on the third floor where they're waiting for him, his head of finance, Kim, the departmental bosses, Gerd and Roger, and then the army of made-to-measure suits that make up the Stege team, their incredibly expensive advisors, but he can afford it.

Am I still scared? he wonders as he greets the visitors, looking forward to when all this is over. It will take until late into the evening to go through all the paperwork, and before he sits down he goes over to one of the windows and looks out.

The black car is still parked out there in the street. A hand with a cigarette between its fingers is hanging out of the window in spite of the rain.

When they break for lunch a couple of hours later he goes over to the window again.

The car is still there.

It's raining more heavily now.

Hans Morelia hurries to the bathroom, locks the door and fumbles with his phone.

Digs out the number of the police. Börje Svärd, that was the officer's name. He seemed to listen to me last time, to respect me.

Börje Svärd stands up in the office. Calls to Malin: 'I've got a call. You'll have to take this one, I don't want it.'

'Don't want it?'

'No, you'll have to take it.'

Börje must have forwarded the call to her mobile, because a moment later Malin feels her phone vibrate in her jacket pocket. Might as well answer. She's been staring at her computer for several fruitless hours.

There's a pattern in this case.

She can sense it, just can't see it.

She clicks to take the call.

Someone breathing.

A voice that sounds like it's coming from a small, enclosed space.

Panicky words blurted out.

'I think I'm being followed. By a man in a black car with concealed number plates. I think it might be Ronny Andersson.'

Malin recognises the voice now.

Hans Morelia.

And she feels like hanging up on him, leaving him to his fate. Maybe it isn't poor Ronny Andersson at all, but some murderer who's after him, so why not let him get shot, then? But she doesn't hang up, perfectly aware that this may be important to their case, so she says calmly: 'Where are you, Hans? And who's following you? Are you sure it's Ronny Andersson? Are you in immediate danger?'

Silence at the other end of the line.

Hans Morelia seems to catch his breath, then takes an age considering something. Malin can't help wondering what.

'Not immediate, no, I don't think so. I'm at the Hotel Ekoxen. There's a man sitting in a black car outside. I haven't been able to see exactly who it is, but he signalled to me with his headlights, and he's been there for ages, he was parked outside my house when I set off this morning.'

'The Ekoxen?'

'Yes.'

'We're on our way,' Malin says.

'Good. But you'll have to be discreet. I'm in the middle of a very important business meeting.'

* * *

Elin Sand has stopped at a fast-food kiosk in Borensberg. She's on her way to Motala, but suddenly felt hungry.

Her pistol is tucked by her side, underneath her open raincoat.

She takes a bite of her hamburger as the rain hammers on the roof above her, and there seems to be a reasonable chance that one of the maples growing near the kiosk will fall on top of her.

If Yngve Karlsson owes money to Dragan Zyber, then Dragan could have murdered Konrad, or ordered his murder, in order to secure the inheritance. The others aren't taking that possibility seriously enough.

Stranger things have happened.

Through her contacts she knows that Dragan Zyber hangs out at a pizzeria down by the river, not far from the centre of Motala. It's more a front than a serious business, but that's where he runs his pathetic little empire from.

Maybe she shouldn't have set out alone.

But she's not frightened of anyone. She's no rookie, not by a long shot.

She wants to gain Malin Fors's respect, once and for all.

A bastard like Dragan shouldn't be allowed to frighten anyone. And certainly shouldn't attack an old man. And if there's even a microscopic chance that he did that, he ought to be checked out.

She just needs to finish her hamburger first. And maybe have a hotdog as well.

53

You'll have to be discreet.

Who the fuck does Hans Morelia think he is?

King of the whole world.

He's as arrogant as the rest of his breed. Or is he genuinely unaware of the way he treats other people?

Malin lets Zeke drive.

They head past the hospital.

Zeke is driving calmly, sensibly, and Malin has space for her thoughts.

Hans Morelia's arrogance is the arrogance of money. Money itself is enough, takes precedence over everything else.

He exploits weakness and illness and our shared assets in order to enrich himself. How shameless would you have to be to do something like that? Perhaps you actually have to love the shame of it, Malin thinks, take pleasure from it.

Morelia loves money. The power it gives him, the image of himself. The possibilities. He won't stay in Linköping once those billions have landed in his account.

He's no philosopher, no great thinker; his arrogance is the arrogance of action. He sees an opportunity and he grabs it, without the slightest thought of the consequences it might have for other people.

Twelve hours in a shitty sanitary pad.

Bed sores oozing with pus.

Depression that leads to suffering and premature death.

Someone like Hans Morelia has a lot of lives on his conscience.

Who knows how many people get sucked under in a harsh society where people like him make the rules?

Malin feels sick as they head down the slope to the Hotel Ekoxen, and tries to stay calm by staring at the rain streaming down the windscreen. The tall white brick building seems to scrape the undersides of the clouds. Beside it sits the green expanse of the Horticultural Society Park. The oaks rise up towards the sky like huge balls of chlorophyll, ready to be torn to shreds by the storm.

Not a soul on the streets.

They've all taken cover.

A man like Hans Morelia would never think that way, about the fact that he has caused people's deaths, and will go on doing so. Malin knows he doesn't think like that, he'd find the very notion absurd.

Money is always right.

The movement of the markets is the template for the universe.

They turn the corner and, sure enough, find a black car with taped-over number plates, and Malin wonders whose car it is: who's following Hans Morelia, if indeed anyone is? Ronny Andersson? He seemed harmless enough, according to Börje.

A silhouette behind the tinted windscreen.

One man stalking another?

The whole thing could also be a mistake, the paranoia of an insecure and cowardly man.

They tug the collars of their raincoats up, and the rain is hard, hungry now.

A woman in a red dress cycles past, utterly soaked, as they walk up to the car.

There are cigarette butts in a puddle of water on the

driver's side, and Zeke taps on the window. It opens slowly and Malin sees who's sitting inside, recognises him from the description Börje gave them, and Malin thinks that it makes sense, it works, the way everything somehow fits together. The car is a mess, the glove compartment closed, but the lock looks broken.

'Ronny Andersson,' Malin says. 'Can you get out of the car?'

She makes her voice sound friendly, and inside the car she sees Ronny Andersson's eyes shimmer and turn almost black.

He opens the door. Gets out.

Doesn't seem bothered by the rain.

'We've had a report about this car,' Zeke says. 'About the fact that it appears to be following someone. Would you know anything about that?'

Ronny Andersson leans against the car, tall and rangy, and his acne-scarred skin looks pale in the terrible weather.

He takes a deep breath.

'I like sitting here,' Ronny Andersson says, and Malin sighs before saying: 'Give over. We know you followed Hans Morelia here. Why did you do that?'

'It's a free world. He's imagining it.'

'You don't like the fact that he's about to make an awful lot of money,' Zeke says. 'You know what he's doing in there today, the papers he's about to sign, and you don't like it.'

Ronny Andersson stretches his back, somehow manages to light a cigarette, spits on the wet tarmac, and says: 'He's a bastard. And my mum has to pay the price for that. Do you know, she's got a shabby little summer house outside Hackefors that she inherited from her dad. It's falling apart. She wouldn't need much, small change to someone like Morelia, to repair and maintain it. But now she's losing it. Granddad's house. Where's the justice in that? Mum works for Merapi. But does she get a share of the profits?'

Malin says nothing.

'Stalking someone is against the law,' Zeke says.

And Ronny Andersson starts to laugh.

He laughs loudly in the rain, and the gusting wind distorts the sound of his laughter. It becomes the sound of a madman, and Malin catches herself smiling, and forces herself to stop.

When he stops laughing Ronny Andersson says: 'I just wanted him to know that I existed. Throw a bit of grit into the machinery, maybe have a word with him. Since when has it been a crime to talk to someone?'

'Don't do it again,' Malin says.

'Because if you do, we'll take you in,' Zeke adds.

'Now get out of here,' Malin says. 'And take that tape off your number plates.'

Ronny Andersson does as he's told. Drenched by the rain, he gets into his car and drives off, down towards Hamngatan.

Are we doing the right thing? Malin wonders. Letting him go?

Is he as harmless as we think he is?

A classic malcontent.

Could he have anything to do with the murder? To focus attention on Hans Morelia and his own mother, albeit in a very warped way? The thought won't go away.

But he's got an alibi.

He isn't the type to kill.

But who is? I've never found a particular type. Just people with problems, people who've ended up in impossible situations, people who've fallen in love with money and power.

He's harmless, Malin thinks. Then she hears a familiar voice behind her.

Hans Morelia is standing beneath one of the hotel's white umbrellas, and he's angry.

'You should have arrested him. He's a lunatic.'

Malin can see the fear in Hans Morelia's eyes.

She finds herself feeling oddly warm inside at the sight of how frightened he is, and neither she nor Zeke says anything.

'I'm in the middle of an extremely important business meeting inside the hotel. It can't be right that an unemployed layabout can stalk me and ruin my concentration. It can't be right.'

'What he's done so far isn't enough to warrant an intervention,' Zeke says. 'In our considered opinion he hasn't actually committed any offence against you. It isn't even possible to say for certain that he did actually follow you here. And you haven't documented any of the previous occasions.'

Hans Morelia swallows. Searches for words, but remains silent.

'Everything has its price,' Malin says. 'You should know that. See if you can do anything about his mother's situation. I'm sure that would get rid of him. He's just frustrated that people like you make billions while his mother struggles to put food on the table.'

Don't try any of that socialist crap on me, she expects him to say. But instead he says: 'I'll see what I can do.'

'That sounds good.'

'If you're worried,' Zeke says, 'I'd suggest that you to talk to your security advisors. They may suggest a bodyguard. You'd be able to afford one, after all.'

'They have suggested that.'

Then Malin and Zeke get back in the car. Drive away.

And in the rear-view mirror Malin watches as Hans Morelia walks back into the hotel. His umbrella gets caught by the wind and turns inside out, turning into a white mushroom showering rain on the man it's supposed to protect.

Back to his money.

His beloved money.

54

Bloody rain.

It's ruined the summer, Elin Sand thinks as she runs at a crouch towards the pizzeria where Dragan Zyber is supposed to hang out.

The pizzeria is in a detached wooden building by the river, on the edge of the centre of Motala. The little building is surrounded by tall birch trees, and in the gravel car park stands a single, shiny BMW. She parks alongside it.

Lucky Pizza.

She takes hold of the handle of the crooked door and pulls it towards her, then pushes, but nothing happens. The door is locked and the room inside is dark, but Dragan Zyber must be here, the BMW in the car park can hardly belong to anyone else.

She peers in through a window. Battered cane furniture, a dormant pizza oven.

A back door in the rear of the building.

Unlocked. A messy storeroom, a rumbling freezer. Male voices beyond another door.

She steps inside, feels the weight of her pistol, the pulse of adrenalin through her body. She opens the second door, and finds herself looking into a smoke-filled room. Four dark-haired men, their lower arms covered in tattoos. They're playing cards, and their conversation stops abruptly at the stranger's arrival.

They look up at Elin, who sees the surprise on their faces.

Then the man she recognises as Dragan Zyber smiles. His lips are thin, and his black eyes flash with amused intelligence.

'And who the fuck are you?' he says, standing up.

Zeke stops at a red light by the entrance to the hospital, and Malin reads a banner that's been hung up outside the medical school.

We're creating the future.

How can anyone create a future?

Men like Hans Morelia are the ones who are creating the world to come. A world in which the only certainty is the law of the jungle: be in no doubt that I'll eat you alive if you show the slightest sign of weakness, if you leave your throat unguarded.

They've checked Ronny Andersson's registration number. The car belongs to him, nothing odd about it, and they decided back at the hotel to ignore the fact that he'd covered his plates.

A tacit agreement between two experienced detectives.

'So what happens now?' Zeke asks. His voice is unexpectedly soft, and Malin is bemused by the number of different tones of voice Zeke has, hundreds of different voices and emotions in one and the same larynx.

We're creating the future, and the light switches to green. Malin sees room number seven at the Cherub in her mind's eye, and thinks that nothing but the past was created there. Then she realises that she's wrong, the future is being created there.

Hans Morelia's future.

Anyone else's?

And she thinks about Ronny Andersson. The despair beneath his cockiness, the anger that is barely concealed behind a tragic façade of coolness, and she says: 'I need to check an address. There's someone we need to go and see.'

The clock on the dashboard says half past two, and it can't be too early, can it, if she was working last night? Malin wonders.

Elin Sand is still standing in the doorway to the inner room of the pizzeria, and she can feel Dragan Zyber's breath in front of her. He's a big man, taller than she is, and even more muscular.

She presses one arm against the pistol beneath her raincoat.

She's asked Dragan what he was doing on the night between Monday and Tuesday. The other men around the table gave him an alibi, and he asked: 'Am I supposed to know something about the murder of an old man? Women, children, and the elderly are off limits. You've got a very vivid imagination.'

She took a chance and threw her theory in Dragan Zyber's face, unwilling to show any fear or weakness to these men, and Dragan Zyber just laughed, as if the whole idea were absurd.

'Yngve Karlsson owes me forty thousand. Would I have someone killed for that sort of money? I've never had anyone killed, and you lot know that.'

And now Dragan Zyber is laughing scornfully again.

'Do your colleagues know you're here? Are you trying to play the hero?'

Elin Sand answers, and realises immediately that her answer comes too quickly: 'They know I'm here,' and she realises that Dragan Zyber knows she's lying. He snaps his fingers and in a matter of seconds the men have grabbed her and pushed her down on the card table, and she's strong, but together they're much stronger.

Dragan Zyber fumbles for her pistol. Gets hold of it,

and one of the men holds her in a headlock. She feels the barrel of the pistol in her nostril.

'You should be happy you're not getting this in your cunt,' he hisses.

And just as suddenly as the men grabbed her, they let her go.

Dragan Zyber takes the bullets out of the gun, then tosses it towards Elin as she gets to her feet.

'There's pizza through there,' he says, pointing towards another door. 'On the house. But perhaps you're not hungry?'

Malin and Zeke use the police code to get into the building where Berit Andersson lives.

Her flat in Johannelund is on the ground floor, and outside what must be her bedroom is a flowerbed that no one has shown any love for many years. It looks even more pathetic now that it's utterly waterlogged.

Rubbish and cigarette butts and a dead shrub floating in muddy water.

They walk over to the door with the name Andersson on it. Graffiti on the walls of the stairwell.

Malin rings the bell, hears the angry sound on the other side of the door.

She rings four times, and realises that they're waking Berit Andersson up, that she's still sleeping after her shift last night.

Slow footsteps.

The door opens.

And there stands Berit Andersson in a green towelling dressing gown, much like Malin's. Her face is puffy with sleep, and when she sees Malin it assumes a peculiar expression, surprise and fear, but also shame.

Shame, Malin thinks. Shame at the way your life has turned out.

Is that the way you feel, every day?

'Police, again,' Berit Andersson says. 'What do you want?'

'Sorry if we woke you,' Zeke says. 'But we need to ask a few questions. Can we come in?'

Berit Andersson nods wearily.

'I'll put some coffee on.'

They sit in the kitchen.

Three ladder-backed chairs around a pine table.

Red cupboards.

The coffee is good and strong, and Berit Andersson looks more alert now, smoking a cigarette after first asking if they minded.

'I know Ronny's angry,' she says. 'Angry about most things, really. Angry because he thinks I'm wearing myself out for nothing. He's got a bit obsessed about that, but what good does that do me?'

'Do you know if he's been stalking Hans Morelia?'

Berit Andersson shakes her head.

'No. But I can imagine he's got a few things he'd like to say to him.'

'Has your son ever shown any sign of a violent temperament?' Zeke asks.

'No, never. He's a good boy. Always very considerate. He's just lost. Hasn't found his way in life yet.'

He hasn't got a criminal record, Malin thinks.

'Have you found your way in life?' Malin asks, and is taken aback by her own question, how personal and almost poetic it sounds, and how badly it suits this run-down kitchen.

'I look after other people,' Berit Andersson replies, and stubs out her cigarette. 'I enjoy it, caring for others. I like the old people. I really do. A lot. They have so much to give, even though they're ill and exhausted. I used to like staying a bit longer with Konrad Karlsson. Listening to his thoughts about different things. I always tried to be nice to him.'

Malin looks at Berit Andersson as she says this.

Are you telling the truth? she wonders.

I'm sure you are. But have you got the energy to live up to your own truth, night after night, injustice after injustice, one meagre wage packet after the other?

'Your son told us about your summer house. That you've got to sell it.'

Berit Andersson raises her eyebrows before taking a sip of coffee.

'He told you that? Well, it certainly needs to be repaired, and it costs me money pretty much every month. But things aren't so bad yet that I've got to sell it.'

'Good to hear,' Zeke says.

'I go out to the cottage as often as I can. I was thinking of going today. I can cycle there in half an hour. But in this weather it will have to be the bus.'

Then she lights another cigarette.

'That place means a great deal to me.'

Malin stands up.

'If your son happens to mention Hans Morelia in a way that strikes you as odd, could you let us know?'

Berit nods.

But the look in her eyes says something different.

'Shit,' Malin yells when they get out into the rain.

Zeke stops.

'What is it?'

'Shit. What time is it? What the fuck's the time?'

Zeke looks at Malin.

Thinks quietly to himself that she's never going to feel at home in the world.

55

Mum rang, in a panic. She'd forgotten about Anticimex, and wasn't going to be able to get back to the flat in time to let them in. Unless she didn't actually want to. Tove persuaded Hilda Jansson to let her have half an hour off, things were relatively quiet at the Cherub today, as if the storm were making the residents unusually tired.

'Half an hour, no more,' and now Tove is standing in the kitchen, watching a tall, skinny man in his fifties slither about on the floor, sticking a tiny, snake-like camera into any holes he can find under the kitchen cupboards.

'I can actually film with this,' he said before he started, proudly holding up the snake in front of Tove.

The stench is worse now, in the damp air of the flat, and Tove hopes he finds something, a dead rat, a mouse, anything, as long as it means they get rid of the smell.

'I'll go down into the pipes as well,' the man says, getting to his feet. He leans over the sink and pushes the snake into the plughole, it seems to be almost infinitely extendable, then he does the same thing in the bathroom.

He sniffs his way through the flat.

Tove looks at the time.

Half an hour has passed now.

Mum didn't mention their row this morning when she called, didn't mention Stefan. And she knows her mum is right about one thing: she won't be staying in Linköping when autumn arrives.

Rwanda. Voluntary work. Maybe? Yes.

You need training to be able to do any real good. But there's time for that. One thing she does know is that she doesn't want to hit fifty and find herself sniffing around a flat to try to work out where a really disgusting smell is coming from.

She applied to study literature in Lund. Just because. And she wrote a few short stories and sent them to the creative writing course in Gothenburg.

But being an author . . . It's impossible to make a living that way, and slowly, slowly, the scent of that as a career is fading from her mind. She looks out of the window at St Lars Church, shrouded in rain, and all of a sudden Linköping feels even more claustrophobic than usual, more insular, and she knows she has to get away.

The lump in her stomach is smaller now.

Konrad is probably fine, wherever he is now.

And what right have I got to dump Stefan on Mum? I understand her, Tove thinks. Even if I don't want to. We, none of us, want to surrender any of our precious freedoms. It's better to keep Stefan at a distance, so we don't have to take responsibility for him.

The way a lot of people seem to feel about their parents.

He can move into the better of the two homes in Ljusdal, the one by the river, Tove thinks. He'll be fine there. The staff seemed good.

Mum and I both love him. Of course we do.

But he'll be better off there than with us.

Elin Sand keeps both hands on the wheel.

They're shaking.

She's trying to concentrate, keep her eyes on the road, on the forest, in case any unnerved animals decide to dash out on to the road.

Cascades of rain on the windscreen. A thunder of noise inside the car.

How the hell could I be so stupid? she thinks. Risking my life like that?

What was I hoping for?

I wanted to be a hero. No. To be like Malin Fors, Waldemar Ekenberg. Gain their respect, stop them patronising me.

They're just going to think I'm mad. She just couldn't stop herself; she felt she had to go to Motala.

To surprise herself, to make something happen, see where the ball ended up.

Mad.

And then she feels laughter bubbling up in her stomach, and soon the car is filled with the sound of her giggling. At least we know that Dragan Zyber didn't have anything to do with this, she thinks. I'm certain of that now.

'He didn't find anything,' Tove says. 'He filmed it all with a fancy camera, but he didn't find a thing. Just said the smell was a total mystery.'

Malin looks at Tove, sitting opposite her at a table in one of the medieval-themed wooden booths in the Hamlet restaurant.

Ceasefire.

When she got home from the station Malin apologised for being insensitive, and Tove said sorry in turn. As they embraced in the hall Malin became aware of the stink in the flat, and said: 'Let's go and have steak at the Hamlet. To celebrate the truce,' and now mother and daughter are sitting there, they've talked about Stefan, and, without actually saying why they don't think he should be moved to Linköping, they've agreed that he should move to the care home by the river.

Tove is sipping a cold beer.

Just one tonight, Tove, no more, Malin thinks, but is unwilling to say so out loud. The beer looks insanely tempting, the condensation on the glass, but then she remembers all the times she's been disgustingly drunk in the bar of the Hamlet, when she used to be one of the alcoholics they can hear laughing and shouting in there now, like they always are.

The steak is good, the Béarnaise sauce too, and they eat in silence until Tove asks: 'Are you getting anywhere with Konrad's murder?'

Malin would like to say yes, but are they making any real progress?

'We're doing our best.'

There's less sadness in Tove's eyes tonight. She isn't drinking as fast.

The investigation.

In principle, they've written off Konrad's children and grandchild as suspects. There's nothing to suggest that anyone at Merapi tried to silence an elderly troublemaker in advance of the sale of the business, and Vincent Edlund appears to be innocent, in spite of his record for murdering old men. Even so, Malin can't help feeling that they have made progress, and that she's being carried towards the truth.

She's felt like this before, and it's simultaneously frustrating and satisfying.

Could the answer lie in something said by Yngve Karlsson in his holding cell earlier today, when he was talking to Elin Sand?

Was one of the investigations' voices audible there, a voice that I can't yet interpret?

Elin Sand has evidently questioned Dragan Zyber, how on earth did that come about? He has an alibi. And Ronny Andersson is just an upset son.

'We're making progress,' Malin says. 'But we don't have a suspect yet. Everyone we've looked into so far has an alibi.'

Tove takes a small sip of her beer.

'I still can't understand it,' she says. 'Who would want to murder him?'

'He never said anything to you? Anything at all? Nothing that ever seemed odd, unusual?'

'No,' Tove replies, and Malin remembers something that Berit Andersson said, something that struck her as odd when she first heard it.

I always tried to be nice to him.

Tried. That was what she said.

'Do you know if Berit Andersson got on well with Konrad?'

Tove nods.

'He liked her, I know that much. A lot. Why?'

Malin shakes her head.

'Nothing, really,' and she thinks that she's just being over-sensitive about the meaning of words when it can't always be easy to be nice at five o'clock in the morning, when you're exhausted and full of pent-up bitterness.

They've finished eating.

A sense of calm settles around the table.

And mother and daughter look at each other, smile shyly, before Malin reaches across the table and takes hold of Tove's hand.

They hold on to each other; in the warmth of the restaurant, then in the rain and darkness and wind, they hold tightly on to each other to stop themselves falling.

When they get home to the flat Malin calls Daniel. Listens to the phone ring. Hoping that he'll pick up.

56

Daniel sounds sleepy.

'It's me.'

'What do you want?'

'I thought you were going to call.'

'I've been run off my feet at work.'

He's awake now. And Malin is talking in a quiet voice so Tove can't hear, and shuts herself in the bathroom.

'If you'd like to meet up, I'd like to meet up,' she says.

He says nothing for a few moments.

'Not now, Malin. I'll call you tomorrow.'

'Can't I come over now?'

'In this weather?'

'I don't care about the weather.'

'I've got to sleep.'

Why are we playing this game? she thinks. You want to, just as much as me. You need it just as much as I do.

'We've got to take it calmer this time,' he goes on.

'How do you mean?'

'Not to use each other as an escape, but to see each other because we really want to. And we need to know why.'

The yellow walls of the bathroom.

The stench.

'You've turned into a proper philosopher.'

'No, I've just got older.'

'Wiser?'

'With a bit of luck.'

She remembers his body. That's what she needs right now, not words.

'I want you,' she says.

'Well, you can't have me. Not the way you want. Not this time, Malin. If we're going to embark on something together, we need to start off on the right foot.'

Fuck you, she thinks, and hangs up.

57

Monday, 16 August

Malin is standing in the kitchen, reading the *Correspondent* on her laptop. Tove has already gone off to work, and the coffee tastes bitter and good, hot on her tongue in a way that makes her whole body wake up and snap to it.

Their case is no longer the lead story.

It's been replaced by Morelia's deal. Beneath a photograph of the Hotel Ekoxen, the article explains that it was the site of last-minute adjustments to a deal worth billions. The text is vaguely critical, suggesting that Morelia bought most of the institutions that make up his empire for a price that was way below their market value. And that he's making an astonishing profit from what was a politically motivated sale of shared social assets.

Just reading it makes Malin feel sick.

It's like me buying up a police district, slashing the funding with efficiency savings to the point where the staff can no longer do their jobs, then selling the whole lot to an American security company so that they can run the police service as a profit-making business.

The politicians responsible for creating this mess ought to be made to answer for it.

Someone ought to stop Morelia.

Malin knows it's a naïve hope. What we're witnessing now is part of a never-ending cycle. The way the rich and powerful team up to steal from everyone else. Shamelessly, consciously. It's always the same.

Malin closes the laptop.

Only a short item about their case, saying that the police are investigating a man with previous convictions for murdering elderly men. Vincent Edlund's name isn't mentioned. The article was written by Daniel Högfeldt, and Malin can't help thinking that he's lost his edge.

But she knows she's just annoyed with him for rejecting her again.

She can see him in her mind's eye, his handsome face, and she hasn't really got any sort of comeback if he wants to play hard to get.

Then she does something that she never usually does, and she doesn't know why she does it this particular morning, with the storm raging at full force, broken branches scattering the ground in St Lars Park, pigeons cowering under the eaves of the church.

She goes into the living room and switches the television on, and finds herself staring at Steffo Törnqvist as he tucks into seared goose liver and apple sauce and sips happily from a glass of champagne.

Malin settles on to the sofa.

The news, followed by the weather. Nothing much has happened.

Nothing about Merapi, and nothing about the murder either.

After the news Steffo Törnqvist accompanies an elderly woman to a corner of the studio, where she picks a scratch card at random.

What would she do with the money?

That depends how much she wins. Go on a cruise, maybe. And make some improvements to her little place in the country.

And the woman scrapes. First one square, then the next, and by the time she's finished she's won three hundred thousand kronor, and the mixture of happiness and disappointment is clearly visible on her face.

Then the woman is gone, already on her way back to normal life in Karlstad, Borås or Gävle. But Malin can't stop thinking about the woman, and she realises what it is that she hasn't noticed, what she's been missing, and the case opens up, a tiny opening, improbable, perhaps, but still a possibility, the way openings in investigations often are.

She stands up.

Thinks: Shall I call, or do it face to face?

Thinks: Face to face.

I'll go and see her. Who knows what might have happened.

Is all of this going to reach its conclusion today?

Malin looks out of the living-room window. The storm is gathering the rain into steel cables that stretch through the air. Part of a roof flies past. And she hears Steffo Törnqvist's voice, advising people to stay indoors today. It could end up being even worse than the big January storm of 2005.

Be careful, Malin, she thinks.

Take it nice and gently.

Hans Morelia hasn't slept all night. He got up several times to stare down into the storm-ravaged garden. He thought he saw Ronny Andersson's car drive past, but it didn't come back, and could have been a hallucination brought on by tiredness.

Lova came to their bed at four o'clock in the morning. Crept in between them, and she was warm, and put her arm around his neck the way she always does. She did it in her sleep. An unambiguous sign of love.

He's going to see the security consultants today. It would be just as well to get some bodyguards.

He pulls Lova closer to him.

Are the police going to be able to solve the old man's murder?

Point nine of his letter to the paper. Hans Morelia can still remember it:

Treat others the way you yourself would like to be treated.

The old boy certainly wasn't stupid. Far from it.

But now he's silent.

For ever.

And my money's on its way.

58

Gabriella Karlsson lives on Vasagatan, close to the Abisko roundabout, on the third floor of a yellow-plastered building that looks like it was built in the thirties.

Malin is standing in the pale pink stairwell, she's shaken off the rain, after dodging another piece of roofing out in the street. It was slicing through the air like a ninja star, seemed to be aiming at her throat.

Malin has rung the doorbell, but can't hear any footsteps behind the door. She's hoping to surprise Gabriella in case she really has got something to do with this, if there's any truth to Malin's theory.

No one home.

She tries calling Gabriella instead. No answer.

So she calls Zeke, says she's on her way in, has an idea she wants to run past him.

She heads back down the stairs.

Perhaps Gabriella is at the university?

Might try to find her there, Malin thinks, but first the station, must talk to Zeke first. Perhaps I'm being too hasty?

She goes out on to Vasagatan and hurries through the rain towards her car, parked just outside the door, but stops on the pavement. She can feel the storm tugging at her, the rain drumming angrily on the hood of her raincoat.

She sees a blue Volvo drive past.

Elin Sand is sitting in the passenger seat. It is her, isn't it?

A woman in the driver's seat. I've seen her before, Malin thinks, and searches her memory, but can't remember who the beautiful woman is.

The gutters are rattling above her as a figure approaches along the pavement, huddled up, trying to make itself smaller, and Malin can't help thinking that the person could be snatched off the ground at any moment.

It's Gabriella Karlsson, her red hair sticking out from her hood, and she makes a dash for the door to her building with an anxious look in her eyes. When she reaches Malin she grimaces and bends over to catch her breath before straightening up again.

'Hello. Have you found out something about Granddad? Or are you still treading water?' She's evidently been out for a run, seeing as she's wearing black jogging bottoms beneath a tight rainproof jacket.

If Gabriella Karlsson had previously looked uncertain, she is now clipped and correct. The water, rain mixed with sweat, is running down her forehead, and Malin finds herself thinking that there is unexpected power in that body.

'Or do you suspect me now?'

'I don't suspect you,' Malin says. 'You seem to have been the only person who really cared for Konrad.'

Gabriella nods.

Lets out a deep breath.

'Can we go inside?' Malin asks, and a few moments later the world is free from howling wind and rain.

'He's going to be buried soon. A simple coffin, but with some carving by Kanevad.' Gabriella's words echo in the stairwell, and Malin realises that this sudden practicality is a way of keeping her grief under control.

'The carving sounds nice,' Malin says, before asking the question she came here to ask: 'How many scratch cards did you take when you went to see your grandfather the evening before the murder?'

Gabriella looks surprised.

As if it were the stupidest question in the world.

'Four,' she says. 'You can buy four scratch cards for a hundred kronor. They're supposed to cost thirty kronor each these days, but there's an offer on at the moment at the old price, twenty-five each, so I bought four. There's also another offer on right now, giving you an extra chance if you actually win something. Granddad loved scratch cards. He liked the fact that it was all down to chance, nothing else.'

'So you're sure – four cards?'

'Quite sure.'

Gabriella wipes the water from her face.

'Why? Is there something funny about that?'

Malin considers what to say, looks at Gabriella, then replies: 'We only found three scratch cards in your grandfather's room. All of them losing cards. There should have been a fourth one.'

'We only did three of them. He wanted to save the last one until later that night. In case he was up late. He thought he might want a bit of entertainment later on.'

Why didn't you say so before? Malin thinks. You probably didn't even think about it.

'Thanks,' she says, instead of reprimanding her. 'Where did you buy the cards?'

'From the tobacconist's on Djurgårdsgatan.' Gabriella pauses before going on: 'If the fourth one was a winning card, there are plenty of people who could do with the money.'

Zeke is sitting opposite Malin in the open-plan office at the police station.

He's leaning forward, and Malin can see that he's listening intently to what she's saying. She goes on, calmly and methodically:

'So imagine,' she says, 'that this fourth card turned out to be a big win, two hundred and fifty thousand, half a million, a million, and someone saw the card after Konrad Karlsson had uncovered the win, took it, and murdered him to keep him quiet.

'You mean someone killed him for a lottery win?'

Malin nods slowly.

'It's a bit far-fetched, but it feels like the only good lead we've got right now.'

Zeke's turn to nod.

'If the winning scratch card is the motive, then one of the night staff could be our perpetrator after all,' Malin goes on. 'Or Margaretha or Yngve, who could have gone to see him later that evening, after Gabriella.'

'But what are the chances of that fourth scratch card actually getting a big win? Vanishingly small, surely?'

Malin frowns, but isn't sure why.

'It's about as likely as an old man being murdered. We'll have to check with the Swedish Lottery to see if a winning card has been sold in Linköping recently. If any prize has been claimed.'

'Gabriella could have scratched all the cards for Konrad, then went back later to get the fourth card – which would mean that she did it.'

'I don't think so,' Malin says. 'She loved him, and she seems to be the only one connected to this whole business whose finances aren't a complete mess.'

She thinks for a while.

'Berit Andersson,' she says eventually. 'She could have done with the money.'

'Always assuming the missing card was actually a win.'

'We'll have to investigate,' Malin says. 'See if anyone who might have been in Konrad's room, no matter what their alibi, has had any money paid into their bank account recently, the sort of sum that matches a lottery win.'

'Are we telling Sven about this?'

'I'll do that,' Malin says. 'You and Johan can start digging.'

Sven sits up on his desk chair, and through the window behind him Malin can see the white panelled façade of the hospital, the green canopy above its entrance.

People visiting the sick in spite of the storm, hurrying in through the revolving door, they can't get in fast enough.

'It's an interesting theory,' he says. 'A little far-fetched.'

'I know. But it's worth a try.'

'Don't talk to anyone until you've spoken to the Swedish Lottery company. If this checks out, you may be able to get a confession if you've already got all the facts.'

'We'll hold back,' Malin says, even though she'd rather start questioning people at once.

Sven looks at her intently.

'You've been listening to the voices of the investigation.'

Malin smiles.

Says nothing.

'You know I'm leaving at Christmas,' Sven Sjöman goes on. 'Have you given any more thought to taking over when I'm gone?'

'I've done some more thinking.'

'And the answer's still no?'

'I don't know, Sven. It feels like I need to shake up my whole life. And that includes the possibility of taking over from you. But I don't know if it would suit me. At the moment.'

'You know what I think,' Sven says.

He leaves another long pause.

'It's time for you to grow,' he says. 'You're too good to carry on playing solo. And you seem to be keeping everything under control.'

Malin closes her eyes.

I'm no good at anything really.

Just look at Tove. She couldn't have had a worse mother.

And now this desire for Daniel again. Not only to feel him inside her, but just to have his body close to hers.

'Don't be so hard on yourself the whole time, Malin.'

She opens her eyes and looks into Sven's face, the reassuring, warm smile that has always been able to calm her down, drive her on.

'Now go and catch our killer,' he says.

He shakes his head.

'A sodding scratch card. Bloody hell. There's not a lot you don't see in this job.'

59

Johan Jakobsson clutches the phone in his hand. He is being put through to someone at the Swedish Lottery who's responsible for winning tickets.

In his mind's eye he can see a wind-tormented Gotland, with bewildered Stockholmers cycling around in the driving rain, wondering what happened to their holiday.

They've talked about going on a cycling holiday to Gotland, the whole family. Renting tandem bikes. But a few weeks ago they found a cheap last-minute trip to Bulgaria. Cheap because the weather at home has been so good up to now. He's looking forward to playing with the children on a foreign beach. They're going to be setting off in just a few days, the last week of the children's summer holiday.

But first they need to clear up this case.

He and Elin Sand have checked out the banks. She's very good at that sort of thing. Waldemar is being way too hard on her, and Malin ought to show her more respect as well. She probably sees Elin as competition.

None of the people connected to the case has had a large sum of money paid into their account recently. That may not necessarily mean anything, because you can get a lottery win paid out in cash.

The line crackles.

Then a soft-voiced woman comes on the line.

She introduces herself as Cornelia, and Johan gives her a brief explanation of why he's calling.

The woman taps at her keyboard, then says that there have been no scratch card wins worth more than ten thousand kronor claimed in Linköping in the past month.

'Could a high-value scratch card have been sold here?' Johan asks.

'I've got no way of knowing that. If we knew in advance which outlets held the winning cards, and what amount they were for, there's too high a risk of the system being corrupted.'

'So there's no way of checking if a high-value scratch card could have been sold in Linköping?'

'I'm afraid not.'

The woman sounds genuinely apologetic.

'Are you working on a particularly nasty case?'

'You've probably read about it,' Johan says. 'The elderly man who was found murdered in a care home.'

Silence on the line.

'That's awful,' the woman finally says. 'Bloody awful.'

Johan hears her tap at her keyboard again.

'A winning scratch card has been redeemed in Norrköping, at Tellus Tobacco, Holmengatan 31. Two hundred and fifty thousand. Two days ago.'

Malin is holding the bundle of printouts of passport photographs in her hand. Grainy but sufficiently clear pictures of the people whose names have arisen in their investigation into the murder of Konrad Karlsson.

The car is vibrating gently as Zeke drives it along the E4. He's having to parry gusts of wind, and the world in front of the windscreen is obscured. Malin looks at the dark yellow fields of rape and the dense forest beyond them. The storm makes the fields move like miniature seas, the rape discoloured water you could drown in.

Zeke has turned the stereo on, and the sound of an

unusually melancholy piece by Wagner fills the car. The gloomy notes seem to match the day.

Malin leafs through the pictures.

Hans Morelia.

Billionaire. If he had been in Konrad Karlsson's room in the care home, would he have bothered to take a scratch card worth a pathetic two hundred and fifty thousand kronor? If he hired someone to do it, their photograph isn't in the pile.

Perhaps the scratch card that was redeemed wasn't actually Konrad's fourth card. This whole line of inquiry is a gamble, but even so it seems to make sense, and there's a logic in the fact that the card was redeemed in Norrköping. Travelling to another city to claim the prize could be a way of concealing the crime.

Hans Morelia's thin face. Proud, but his eyes have a degree of warmth in them, as though he is actually capable of love, in spite of everything. Could he have wanted to talk to Konrad Karlsson, persuade him not to write any more letters for a while, then things got out of control and, when he saw the scratch card, he just took it with him?

Unlikely, Malin thinks.

Pictures of Konrad's children, Margaretha and Yngve.

It can't have been Yngve, he was in custody when the scratch card was redeemed, but Elin Sand has printed out his photograph anyway.

Margaretha. A neutral look on her face. She could have done with the money.

Gabriella Karlsson.

Just because.

And Vincent Edlund.

The crazy guy, the one Waldemar gave a hard time to. Could it have been him?

Ronny Andersson.

Desperate about his mother's situation. She could certainly use two hundred and fifty thousand.

And then pictures of the staff.

Hilda Jansson, Lisbeth Stark, Siv Kramer, Stina Bersén, Kent Sjöberg, Maj Gröndahl, Berit Andersson, and, last among the pictures, Tove. And Malin starts when she sees Tove's photograph, at the notion that she could even be a suspect. But of course she was first inside the room after the killer. She could have taken the scratch card if it was in the room, if there was a winning card there at all.

But she couldn't have killed anyone. She knows the difference between right and wrong.

Even if the boundary can be fairly fluid at times.

Then it occurs to Malin that Tove was out of town with the car two days ago – what if she stopped in Norrköping on her way up to Hälsingland?

Malin dismisses the thought and brushes her fringe aside.

Your own daughter.

Just stop it.

There has to be some end to all the suspicion, and Zeke lowers the music, says: 'Don't worry. Elin only included that one for the sake of it. She asked me, said she felt awkward about it, but I told her you'd be angry if she didn't include it. That's right, isn't it?'

Then Malin's phone rings. Daniel Högfeldt. What does the vulture want now? More information about the case?

'Not him again,' she mutters under her breath.

'Who?' Zeke asks.

'Daniel Högfeldt.'

Malin takes a deep breath.

Unless he's calling for personal reasons. Maybe he wants to fuck.

Make love.

Meet up.

But he rejected me, and I can't handle this. Not again.

And she rejects the call, even though she doesn't want to, even though she wants to hear his voice.

Zeke sighs.

'Give it a chance, Malin. He's OK.'

Keep out of this, she feels like saying, but says nothing.

Holmengatan 31 is a four-storey modernist building not far from the old factory that's now a smart university and cultural centre. The tobacconist's is squeezed in between a dry cleaner's and a shop selling computer games. Behind the grimy window there's a sign for Yellow Blend cigarettes.

The owner, a Mustafa Sillén, has been forewarned, and when they walk into the shop a dark-haired man with sharp features is sitting behind an old-fashioned counter, its glass trays full of merchandise. He didn't want to say over the phone if the scratch card had been redeemed by a man or a woman, even if he remembered the win very well. He said he was concerned for his customers' privacy, and had had bad experiences with the police in Iraq.

He spoke perfect Swedish over the phone, just a trace of an accent, and Malin guesses that his surname indicates that he's married to a Swedish woman.

'Welcome,' Mustafa Sillén says. 'You must be from the police. Can I offer you some chocolate?' He holds out a basket full of chunks of plain chocolate. 'Not many customers today.'

'I don't suppose even the urge to smoke can make people leave their homes on a day like today,' Zeke says.

Another man comes out through a plastic curtain, with tinted blond hair and a moustache, a round face with a receding chin.

'My husband,' Mustafa says. 'Peter.'

And Malin thinks momentarily of her Peter, who betrayed her, but forces his face from her mind, and this new Peter says: 'I was here too. It was the first time anyone's claimed such a big win here. We called the Swedish Lottery to make sure it checked out, then I ran to the bank and got the money out while the customer waited here. It was all rather exciting.'

Malin puts the photographs on the counter.

'Would you mind taking a look at these?' she says. 'Was it one of these people who redeemed the scratch card?'

Tove's picture on top.

'Not this pretty little thing,' Peter says, and Mustafa shakes his head and moves the photograph aside.

They work their way through the pile, evidently pleased to be playing a part in one of life's dramas.

'No.'

'Nope.'

'Not you either.'

And then they come to the last but one picture.

'Bingo,' Peter says.

'Hardly the right game, under the circumstances,' Mustafa chides.

And Malin can't help smiling. Even if the whole scenario is somehow deeply depressing, she can see how everything fits together now, or almost, anyway.

Justice?

Is that what we're going to dispense now?

The smile freezes on her face, and she feels angry.

Her whole being is full of rage against the world.

We're close to the truth now, she thinks, as the shop door opens with the ring of the bell.

So this is the truth.

I didn't need the money, but it was mine. I wanted to distribute it as I saw fit.

Anger.

Poverty.

Injustice.

An entire lifetime of hard work and humiliation, frustration, and sorrow channelled into hands around my neck.

No words.

Just silence, and I heard myself gurgle, waiving the air with my one good hand, but what good did that do?

The wind, the cold wind, had come to me. It was time for me to move on, and I looked into those eyes, tried to tell them: I understand you.

Stop now.

But there was nothing but action in those eyes. The conviction that this had to be done.

Just like what you're about to do now, Malin Fors. That has to be done too.

Perhaps you were hoping that the truth would be different.

I have a feeling that this doesn't stop here and now. For me it all came to an end in an old people's home next to the Horticultural Society Park in Linköping.

If there was any emotion in that final room, in that moment, it was loneliness.

But I'm not alone now. I reached the light, in spite of everything.

*Because all the things I did wrong were still done out of
love.*

Love that meant well.

My beloved wife is with me, and Josefina is here too.

*Perhaps all it took was clarity, both my own and that of
the living, for us to see each other again?*

We are souls of air now.

Sara and Josefina.

My perception of love.

Father has been here.

*Told me he hanged himself out of shame, because he was
going to lose the farm. That Mother drove him to it.*

But everything is peace and love now.

And we are waiting for you, for all those we love, Gabriella.

There's no rush.

Don't hurry.

60

Malin looks at the time as she shakes the rain from her hood.

Quarter past two, and she feels hunger grab hold of her stomach, but they need to do this now, no time for food. The air in the stairwell in Johannelund is stagnant, as if nothing has happened here for decades.

A flickering bulb.

Malin wonders if the woman inside the flat is asleep, if she can sleep, and what her dreams are like.

Is she dreaming of a house? A cottage?

A renovated cottage that the bank can't take away from her?

Or is she dreaming about an aching back, a working week made up of thirty-five heavy hours?

Perhaps she dreams about love?

For herself. For her son.

Malin turns towards Zeke. He looks impossibly tired, and the wrinkles on his forehead and around his eyes are deep.

Sadness.

He runs one hand over his bald head, nods at her, and Malin rings the doorbell, once, twice, three times, four, but no one comes to the door.

'Shall we go in?' Malin asks.

Zeke nods, and she takes out her key ring, the lock pick. Then they're inside Berit Andersson's flat, and Malin starts to worry, what if she's hanging somewhere inside, in a noose, like Konrad Karlsson?

But the flat feels abandoned. Some children are playing in the playground outside the window. Defying the storm, but it's starting to die down now, isn't it? There's a fallen tree behind them, an ash that gave up the ghost.

The kitchen is empty. The bathroom too. Zeke says: 'Maybe she's at her cottage, out near Hackefors. Have we got the address?'

Malin shakes her head.

She gets her phone out and calls Johan, and within thirty seconds he's told them how to get there.

'Be careful,' he says. 'Do you want me to send backup?'

'No,' Malin says. 'We'll take this nice and gently.'

The forest seems to be closing in on itself. Barely visible through the side windows of the car.

They're heading away from the Landeryd road, before the turning to the golf club, and the gravel road is full of potholes. The car is lurching, as the windscreen wipers struggle to keep the screen clear.

Visibility is practically zero, and Zeke drives slowly.

Malin leans forward.

Tries to see.

But the world is shrouded in rain, and suddenly Zeke yells: 'Shit!'

He slams the brakes on, but the collision is unavoidable. The car hits a tree trunk blocking the road, an obstacle that was invisible until the very last moment.

Malin is thrown towards the dashboard, then back in her seat.

A shriek of metal.

Then everything falls silent, apart from the rain hitting the car.

They're both panting for breath.

'Are you OK?' Zeke asks.

'Fine,' Malin says. 'No blood, nothing broken. You?'

'No worries. But this car isn't going anywhere.'

'We'll get a patrol,' Malin says, and they get out of the car and realise just how hard the collision between car and oak tree was, brought together by the storm. The car's wheels have been pushed into the chassis.

But the rain seems to be diminishing in strength slightly.

And they walk towards Berit Andersson's cottage, getting wetter and wetter.

The house stands on an isolated site, on a slope leading up to a patch of woodland. A white fence surrounds a garden with neatly trimmed grass and flowerbeds with tall roses, red and white geraniums bursting out of the dark, fertile soil.

Everything seems peaceful beneath the grey sky.

The little wooden house is painted yellow, but Malin can see how badly the paint is peeling. Beside it stands a large oak tree whose branches are resting on the felted roof.

A small veranda.

Water gushing from cracked drainpipes.

There's a sunlounger tucked out of the rain on the veranda. A table with a rose-patterned wax cloth.

Berit Andersson is sitting on the sunlounger, asleep. Once again, Malin wonders what she's dreaming. But she dismisses the thought, walks closer, and hears the whistling of the wind merge with Berit Andersson's snoring. She's sleeping with her mouth open, sleeping deeply, possibly beyond dreams, but she's going to have to wake up now, wake up to an afternoon unlike any other.

*   *   *

Zeke pats her on one cheek.

Says: 'Wake up. Wake up, Berit.'

And slowly the woman on the sunlounger comes round. She shakes her head, seems to remember where she is, seems to see the figures standing there, unexpected yet expected, on the sheltered veranda of the summer house she inherited from her father, where she must have played as a child. The house that the bank was going to take from her.

'You two,' she says, trying to sit up. Malin helps her raise the back of the chair, and Berit Andersson pulls herself together and gives her a look that seems to say: I know why you're here.

'I need coffee. Sit yourselves down,' Berit Andersson says, then stands up and walks into the house, her back bent. Through the window they see her make coffee, and Malin wonders if they ought to be keeping a closer eye on her, what if she comes out with a knife? Tries to run, maybe? But Malin has a feeling that Berit Andersson isn't going to do anything like that. And she comes out with a tray in her hands, three coffee cups, a coffee pot, sugar bowl, and a small jug of milk.

From the veranda they have a view across the fields down towards the Åtvidaberg road.

It's a beautiful place, Malin thinks, as Berit Andersson pours coffee and sits down opposite her and Zeke, with her back to the view.

She looks at them for a long time without saying anything.

Then she says: 'It's nice here, don't you think?'

Malin and Zeke agree.

They let Berit Andersson take her time, find her own words, the words that Malin knows are coming.

'And they wanted to take this away from me.'

They let the sounds of the storm be the only noise for a while, filling the silence, until Malin breaks it.

'We know you redeemed the fourth scratch card in Norrköping.'

Berit Andersson nods.

Gathers her breath, and her face tenses into a thousand wrinkles. She puts her hand in her pocket, fumbles with a packet of cigarettes, lights one. Takes several deep drags.

'I told him about the cottage. About the bank. Asked if I could borrow some money from him. The scratch card was worth two hundred and fifty thousand. But he refused.'

And everything falls silent.

Malin can hear the three of them breathing, at this particular point on the planet.

'I thought: I'll steal the scratch card. And then of course I had to kill him. Or sedate him. But if I didn't kill him, he'd figure out that it was me who took the card. It would be easier to kill him if he was asleep. So I tricked him into taking the sedative. I got it from the nurses' office. Hilda isn't great at keeping track of things, although she'd never admit it.'

Malin closes her eyes, then opens them again.

'And when he was drifting off to sleep, I asked him again, "Can I borrow some money?" I figured that I'd been kind to him all those years, and he had money, he was in a position to help me, but he wouldn't. You know, he just shook his head. Kept on shaking his head, no, no, no.

'I thought about the bank. I got so angry I almost passed out.

'Then I put my hands around his neck, and I couldn't see anything, everything was black. I could hardly breathe, and I squeezed and squeezed and squeezed, and the bed broke and then that was that.'

Malin and Zeke remain silent. Waiting for Berit Andersson to go on.

'I tried to make it look like he'd hanged himself. That sort of thing does happen. Old folks hanging themselves from the cables of their alarm buttons.'

Berit Andersson takes one last deep drag on her cigarette before stubbing it out in her empty coffee cup.

'I've got the money under the bed in there. In plastic bags. I haven't touched any of it.'

Malin takes a sip of her coffee.

Hears the wind again.

Feels a slight gust against her neck, and it's warm and cold at the same time, and she knows she never wants to feel that wind again.

'Ronny's going to be so upset,' Berit Andersson says, looking out across the garden before lowering her eyes.

Berit in the back seat of the patrol car. Her hands cuffed.

Malin looks at her, then at the house she is leaving for ever.

Sees the drowned world disperse in all directions.

And Malin wants to scream.

Scream, scream, scream.

But she remains silent. Knows that no scream can be heard in a storm like this one.

61

Tuesday, 17 August

Malin stares at her computer screen. Rubs her eyes, takes deep, deep breaths.

No rain today, the storm has moved on, leaving just a thin layer of cloud covering the sky.

Hans Morelia is staring out at her from the *Correspondent*'s website. In a live broadcast from Merapi's head office he announces that the deal with the American company Nexxus has been concluded, 'a milestone in the provision of care in Sweden, possibly internationally, and proof that diligent and conscientious work pays off'.

What's he saying?

He's mad, Malin thinks. Her neck feels sore after the collision with the tree yesterday. She recalls how frightened Hans Morelia had been outside the Hotel Ekoxen the other day, but that fear seems to have blown away now.

Grey suit, red silk tie.

Neatly combed hair.

Self-confidence personified.

The press conference is approaching its conclusion when Malin hears Daniel's voice off-camera.

'The murder of Konrad Karlsson, how do you explain that, the fact that one of your employees killed him while she was working for you?'

For a moment Hans Morelia seems to lose his grip, but mere seconds later Rebecka Koss takes the microphone.

'We're here to talk about the conclusion of the deal. There'll be a press release about that other business later on today.'

'What do you have to say about the fact that your care workers' wages are so low that they can hardly survive on them?'

'That's all for now,' Hans Morelia says, adjusting his hair and tie before stepping down from the podium.

Börje and Waldemar are questioning Berit Andersson, for the third time, in the gloom of interview room one.

The money was indeed under the bed, and she is cooperating fully, without showing any real remorse. Malin closes her browser, thinking that Berit Andersson is a woman who has been pushed to the limit. And when that happens, there's no regret.

They've tried to get hold of Ronny Andersson, but have been unable to reach him by phone, or at home.

Malin looks out across the open-plan office.

Case concluded.

The summer can move towards its end in peace now.

The city's inhabitants can sleep soundly, as if this occurrence were merely an aberration. And out on the streets today there are twenty new multi-millionaires, looking just like everyone else.

Malin gets up from her chair. It's already four o'clock, and she wonders about going down to the gym, but changes her mind.

The sun is shining outside.

I'm going to walk home, she thinks, slowly, and enjoy the late-summer air, the breeze against my skin. I shall take possession of the world, and then I shall sleep, properly, for a very long time.

* * *

There's a black car parked to one side of the car park in front of the police station, and Malin knows immediately whose it is. The driver's door opens and a tall, gangly figure gets out. Has he got something in his hand? No. He walks straight towards her, and she squints in the oddly harsh light, tries to see his eyes, see if there's anger or sadness in them, and to start with he seems to speed up, but then he stops. Malin can see the sorrow in Ronny Andersson's eyes now, and he seems to slump, and she goes over to him, suppressing an urge to put her arm around him. He looks up at her blankly, about to say something, but can't seem to find the words.

'I'm sorry,' Malin says. 'I'm sorry it turned out this way.'

'That bastard,' Ronny Andersson says. 'He's made a billion, and my mum's locked up in there. He's the one you should be arresting, he was the one who drove Mum to this.'

The sorrow in Ronny Andersson's eyes switches to anger, and he talks more loudly, almost shouting now: 'You should lock that bastard up for good. Throw away the key. He should be shot,' and Malin knows he needs to scream, knows she has to soak up that scream herself, so she just stands there, lets him yell right in her face.

'My mum!' he shouts, pointing towards the cells in the basement. 'He's taken her life away! She'll die in there, and he's responsible for that. How the fuck could you let that happen? Is he just going to get away with it? You have no idea what I'm capable of right now, no idea! Do you hear me?'

And then the anger is gone, replaced by mute grief,

and Ronny Andersson's knees give way, and he curls up on the tarmac, sobbing.

'Go away, leave me alone.'

But Malin doesn't move.

'Go,' Ronny Andersson whispers, and she leaves him, walks away from the police station and all the broken people, walks through the city, and when she gets home to her flat on Ågatan the strange smell has gone, vanished, as if it had never existed.

Tove is lying on Malin's arm. She's fallen asleep beside her on Malin's bed. Outside the window the stars are shining in the clear night sky, and Malin finds herself thinking that beyond that quivering black sky there are unquiet souls, people she once knew and who have now left this earthly life. Somewhere beyond that beautiful, terrifying sky is angel dust, drifting through unknown space.

Tove is tired after working an extra evening shift, and Malin feels her daughter's weight on her arm, filling her with life.

She strokes Tove's hair with her free hand. Thanks to her, Malin can put up with anything.

Thirst.

Shame.

Fear of love.

Hatred, violence.

And loneliness. This wretched loneliness.

Then she thinks about Stefan. Things have happened quickly today. In just a few hours he was moved to his new home. They're going to see him there in a week or so, and Malin strokes Tove's cheek, knows how upset she is by the truth behind Konrad Karlsson's murder.

But not surprised.

Tove's smart. Mature and sensitive enough to understand how violence arises.

We're going to be all right, Tove. No one can take our love away from us.

She hasn't felt up to talking to Sven about his job. She doesn't know what she wants. But her desire for something, anything, has returned.

Daniel.

We're older now.

Alone. We can't hurt each other, can we?

Malin looks out of the window again. Tries to calm her thoughts. Imagines she can see birds of prey circling distant stars, and perhaps there are unknown creatures flying through space, hungry beasts surviving on all the evil that human beings do to one another.

Stefan.

He ought to be here, in Linköping, near me, maybe near you, Tove, but near me at any rate. You were right to start with.

We're the only people he's got.

But I can't do it. Don't hate me for that.

She pulls free of Tove.

Heads out into the Linköping night.

62

Daniel can see how tired and sad she is as she stands at the threshold of his flat, looking at him in silence. There's no fear or panic in her sadness, and he sees himself reflected in her, in the emotions that shape her.

Give in, he says to himself, and he gestures to her to come into the flat, closes the door behind her, and she stands in the hall, waiting.

He's about to say something, but she puts a finger to her lips and hushes him.

No more words, she seems to be saying, we're done with that. You're right, she seems to be saying, we mustn't escape into each other, we've done enough of that.

We're here now.

Older.

Stupider. Wiser.

I'm here now, you, we are here.

His body is warmer and harder than she remembers, but also softer, his hands more gentle, as he sweats above and below her. She runs her fingernails down his back, the way she remembers that he likes, and the moonlight breaks through the clouds as they drift off across the sky. Was this what you used to feel like, Daniel? Softer than Peter, more considerate, or am I the one who's changed, getting harder while you've got softer?

I put my hand around you, my mouth, you don't taste of anything, and we've both been longing for this.

We'll be kinder this time.

Not ruin it.

Just love each other.

Love all the goodness of the world into existence.

63

Hans Morelia looks out across the city from his terrace.

Sun, storm, sun.

All in the space of a week.

He waves away a sluggish hornet, his head slightly muzzy after the champagne in the office yesterday, but he feels happy. He thinks of everything that lies ahead for him and his family.

He hasn't yet said anything to his colleagues about his plan to take some time off and travel the world, to spend as much time as possible with Lova and do things she thinks are fun.

Kaizen.

Every detail of life, improved. The tiniest aspects made more beautiful.

At first he expected the Americans to oppose his wish for time off, but they said they could understand why he needed it.

'The value of this company stretches beyond you. You've done a great job.'

The city.

The same as it was a month ago, a week ago.

The same greenery in the Horticultural Society Park, the only sign of the storm is a single large tree lying on the grass. According to breakfast television news, the damage wasn't as bad as predicted. A thousand acres of forest destroyed in Småland. Roofs torn off a few barns. Homes flooded. But nothing insurmountable.

No longer any waves on the water at the Tinnerbäck pool.

The swimmers are back.

Yet the city is different. A city he knows he's going to leave.

He hears someone come out on to the terrace behind him, Lova, judging by the lightness of the footsteps. Presumably wondering if they're going to be leaving soon, they're planning to go down into the city, to Rocklund's horse-riding shop to buy some new boots, at long last.

Lova has been nagging.

I could buy the whole shop for you, Hans Morelia thinks. I could buy it a thousand times over for you.

The bodyguards aren't due to start work until the afternoon, but that can't be helped.

Lova puts her hand on his back, small and soft, and he wishes he could stay like that, feeling her touch, knows it's worth more than all the money he could ever earn.

'When are we going, Daddy?'

'How about now?'

'OK.'

Riding boots. What do they cost?

A thousand kronor. Or seven and a half thousand?

The ones Hans Morelia buys his daughter cost the latter, and he pays with his debit card, and then they go out into the summer sun and head toward Bosse's ice-cream parlour.

Not many people about. He looks around.

That Ronny Andersson hasn't shown up again since the business at the Hotel Ekoxen, but he must have his hands full at the moment, now that what his mother did has been uncovered.

Hans Morelia takes Lova's hand, looks at her blond hair shimmering in the sun. She's wearing a white dress that's a little too tight, he doesn't know where it's from. When she was younger he often used to buy clothes for her, but he's stopped that now. The last few times he tried he got it completely wrong.

I shall learn what sort of taste you have, he thinks. And then I shall spoil you.

I only have one daughter, and she's only going to grow up once.

He squeezes Lova's hand and she squeezes back.

They reach Stora torget, where people are quietly drinking coffee on the pavement terraces.

'What flavours do you want?' he asks when they reach the ice-cream parlour.

'Blueberry and After Eight,' Lova replies. 'What about you?'

'I'm going to have caramel,' he says.

As they walk back across the square in the opposite direction, he can't help thinking that the people walking towards them are looking at him, that they recognise him.

Is that derision he can see in their eyes?

No.

More like admiration.

He has done what everyone dreams about. Has made himself properly rich, and he feels the sun on his face.

They reach the old savings bank building, and even its grey bricks look beautiful today, and then he sees a man, a tall, rangy man emerge from a doorway, out of the darkness, into the blinding light.

★   ★   ★

I'm going to do it now, Ronny Andersson thinks, taking a firmer grip on the pistol in his hand.

The pistol.

Bought long ago from an old friend who could get hold of such things.

A lovely, unregistered gun.

The gun that he's fired so many mornings, alone at the shooting range. The gun that's left powder stains on his fingernails. The gun he's kept carefully greased, hidden away under the kitchen sink.

He lay awake all last night, thoughts racing through his head.

Realised that the only way to stop those thoughts was to take matters into his own hands and get some sort of justice that way.

And as he walks up to Morelia it feels like he's in a perfectly clear jet-stream, an immaculate, radiant now, no one shouting at him, all he can do is this, this, this.

And he raises the pistol towards Morelia, looks into his eyes.

You're going to die now.

How did you die, Hans Morelia?

A shadow, a movement in front of him.

He fires.

Hang on.

No.

Something's wrong, this isn't what was supposed to happen.

Lova Morelia sees the man coming towards them, realises something's wrong, so she takes a step forward and swings the bag containing the riding boots at him. The movement makes her lose her balance and she tries to stay upright, but she stumbles in front of her father, and then she hears a sharp, loud noise, feels an intense pain in her chest, or does the pain come first, then the noise?

And she drifts into blackness, then out of it, into whiteness.

And now she is floating, sees her dad clutching her body, pressing his face against her cheek, and she hears him scream, and a few metres in front of them the unknown man puts the pistol in his mouth and fires.

She hears her dad scream.

Sees him shake and tug at what used to be her body.

Lova Morelia wishes she could whisper something in her dad's ear, but knows he will never be able to hear her.

That she will never be able to comfort him.

That he will never, ever stop screaming.

Epilogue

There's another old man in room number seven of the Cherub old people's home.

He's breathing. The air that comes out of his nostrils becomes a wind that makes its way through the city, becoming Malin Fors's breath, and this new air manages to change her dreams, making them gentle as cotton wool, night after night, hour after hour, second after second.

Malin Fors is able to rest in the gentleness of people's love for each other. And in a room close to running water in Hälsingland, Stefan is breathing. He is far away yet still close, as deep inside her dreams as anyone alive can get.

Responsibilities, Mum, Tove whispers to her in her dreams.

Don't worry about us.

About me.

I always survive.

We are love, Mum.

And, carried on a different wind, Tove looks out of the window of an aeroplane, and the jungle beneath her is speckled green, the camp's white tents are clouds on the Earth's own chlorophyll sky.

There's no horizon, Tove thinks. Only new stories.

Don't miss the other titles in the *Malin Fors* series

MIDWINTER SACRIFICE, SUMMERTIME
DEATH, AUTUMN KILLING, SAVAGE
SPRING, THE FIFTH SEASON and
WATER ANGELS

Out now in paperback

**Also available as eBooks
and as Digital Audio Downloads**